With ev[...]

Marjorie J. Macbay.

(Hope you enjoy it!)

POMPEII TO THE EAGLES

After the eruption of Vesuvius in 79 A.D., Emperor Titus granted compensation to the homeless from Pompeii and her sister towns, yet the orphaned Lucius Varres of Herculaneum and his freedman, Abroticus, wish only to make for the frontier of Agricola and the Eagles of the Ninth Legion.

In the hectic daily life of Rome crowds of homeless and bereaved attracted a horde of predators eager to turn the disaster of others to their own purposes and it takes the efforts and skills of gladiators, Christians and kindhearted women to protect Varres and Rotus from two of these.

At last the young men reach the Eagles just as the Great Thane Calgaich plans assault on Agricola's forts. Native loyalties, loves, old doubts, new faith set each of the friends on his own course, until a Roman standard found in a Caledon village sets Calgaich's priests and advisers a problem that nearly wrecks their influence.

Pompeii to the Eagles

MARJORIE GORDON MACKAY

ROBERT HALE · LONDON

© *Marjorie Gordon Mackay 1978*
First published in Great Britain 1978

ISBN 0 7091 6713 X

Robert Hale Limited
Clerkenwell House
Clerkenwell Green
London EC1R 0HT

Photoset by Kelly and Wright
Bradford-on-Avon, Wiltshire
and printed in Great Britain by
A. Wheaton & Co., Exeter, Devon

ONE

Abroticus the slave eyed Servilia covertly. As the old cook bent to put curling irons on the fire, she winced and gritted toothless gums on a searing stab of pain.

"Is it bad today, old one? Let me tell the Domina, that she may send for a doctor."

"And spoil this outing for the boy—for you all? No indeed, I shall rest when you have gone, *without* the hindrance of a medicus and his potions. Meanwhile fill these provisions into your basket, then rouse the boy and leave my kitchen to me. I have a task to perform that no mere male can take part in."

Gently she slapped the tall young Briton out of her way as she heaped two roasted pigeons and more apples, olives and cherries to the pile of food she had indicated, and was adding eggs when he stopped her.

"You are feeding two people for three days, Servilia, not an army for the duration of the Saturnalia. We shall never use all this."

"You will. Now go. The mistress will come presently for me to dress her hair and we shall not require your presence."

Abroticus laughed. "Nor does the lady Lucia need her hair to be curled. It is much more beautiful the way she usually wears it, smooth and braided and soft."

He caught the look she shot at him and laughed again.

"Do not fear. My preference is for copper tresses . . . or

5

grey." and he tweaked her wispy locks.

"Oh, go waken the boy, rascal, and tell him what is afoot today, then for the love of the gods be gone and let me rest."

In the atrium, cool and dim in the early light, Abroticus met his young master's mother and noticed again how defenceless she seemed in her widowhood, yet strong in a serenity of her own. She answered his greeting kindly with her accustomed gentle authority, and added smiling mischievously, "It seems I must become a lady of fashion before I visit my sister this morning. Servilia insists that the kinswoman of the wealthy Vetellius Vettius do credit to his material success. Eheu, the vagaries of fashion are not for me, but I must not disappoint poor Servilia. Tell me, does her leg pain her today? I feared so in this heat, but I fear also that she will again refuse to let me send for a doctor."

"On that she is quite positive, mistress. She has already pressed the point to me."

"Then let us be gone with all speed that the poor creature may rest." Loudly she ended, "Go Roticus, call my son. Servilia, are my hair irons hot?"

Varres was lazing. Well he knew it was time to get up but today there was nothing to urge him from his hard narrow cot, for today he was no longer a schoolboy. For months he had been bored by the instructions of his old grammaticus; rhetoric, the stupid playing at lawsuits and pleading pro and con ridiculous cases, seemed to him the occupation of fools, impecunious schoolmasters and young boys. He wanted to fight, not argue, to build, to make, to be part of the growing world of Rome and of his nation's life. Not to his liking were the endless doses of potted history predigested and regurgitated by a wizened old Greek wearied in the service of rich men's sons. Not for Varres was learning by rote of masses of poetry or "Memorable Sayings and Doings" written by old Valerius Maximus of his grandmother's day. Life for a fourteen year old boy should be lived in deeds, not words; lessons should be learned in experience not by precept.

6

Varres agreed with his own arguments completely.

All this he had tried to explain to his mother many times lately, but when Lucia's face took on its wistful, slightly worried look, he had stopped explaining and had talked to Rotus instead. Abroticus being a man would know what a boy wanted to do.

Indeed he had and had listened with masculine sympathy but for long he had put off his young master with the same remarks as other boys had from their uncles or grandfathers "You need education to get you anywhere these days". To which Varres had retorted tartly, "See where education got you — thousands of miles from home, a slave in a Roman household."

Yet Rotus as usual had the last word. "If I had had an education such as yours I might have become a general, and conquered your country's legions. Then your father might have become *my* slave." And as usual, too, Rotus tempered reproof with a chuckle.

"You must remember, little stripling, most of the education I had was on my father's land under the weight of his heavy hand — and it was a very heavy hand".

Varres rose with a bound. Rotus had, like his father, a very heavy hand when necessary.

"Come, young one — you say that you are ready to leave the discipline of the school, yet you cannot discipline yourself even this once. Up! Dress and be speedy, for today we go driving through the three towns and tonight we sleep like men, under the stars, on the island."

Morning ablution was the usual perfunctory affair. Why waste time in washing himself when he would swim in the public baths before the evening meal? But today, he remembered in time, was no ordinary day. Perhaps he ought to wash again?

He did wash again and rubbed his skin dry till it shone smooth as an apple from the fruit table, as the slave noticed as he handed fruit and honey to his mistress. The young face was smoother than an egg, he grunted inwardly, although

7

the legs were thick with black down and indeed the forearms showed a dark fuzz too. When would the lad's beard show, when grow long and thick enough to be shaved and consecrated to the gods?

But at fourteen had he himself, the lad from the hills been any older, stronger, tougher, more bearded? As he remembered the youth that he had been, Rotus recalled his own limbs, slim and smooth, until of a sudden, in his sixteenth summer, he had sprung to dark manhood with beard, chest hairs and all. It had been that very summer when he had first met Rufina, of the glorious locks and slender limbs and eyes that wooed the very soul from him. Rufina. . . .

Enough. Ten winters had passed since then and this was the tenth summer. Winters he could bear, except for that terrible one long gone, but these sultry summers were a trial to his north bred temper; and this summer was unusually sultry. But Abroticus of the far hill lands had the patience and perseverance of his race to make him endure what he could not cure and even to enjoy each day as it came.

Today was a day to enjoy.

"You have hand baggage to take, Domina?"

"Yes, Rotus. Servilia has prepared that too. Oh Varres, do not look so despondent. I do not intend to come sailing with you. I shall merely drive with you to the house of your Aunt Marcia in Pompeii, where I shall remain until you come for me again. Soon Aunt Marcia will. . . ."

"Yes Mother, I know. She's going to have a baby."

In relief at knowing that his mother would not be at hand for the next few days to restrain him, he burbled on. "She's going to have a cousin for me—a sentimental thought; but I am not impressed. If it turns out to be like Uncle Verellius it will be a mean, ugly, pompous little stick. In any case I shall be a man before it becomes interesting."

"Oh Varres. How disrespectfully you talk. You know that your Uncle Verellius Vettius is a very successful business man, and if you wished, he would teach you his business."

Rotus grimaced into the fruit dish he was carrying away. How innocent his mistress was, how trusting. She thought the best of everyone, just as her husband had done, but Tribune Varres had had a soldier's experience by which to cast his final judgments. Varres the elder had been a fine man.

"Learn Uncle's business? Indeed no, mother, I wish for a man's life." Was the boy then not so unworldly as he seemed? "Anyway, everyone is a successful business man in Pompeii, unless he is a slave or a woman."

"Oh Varres," Lucia said again and smiled fondly at her son. He was such a child still. What a pity to see him grow up. Yet, grow he must, she thought, as later she stepped on to the narrow pavement with the boy in front and the slave behind and walked towards the South Gate where hirers would have a carriage waiting for them.

Even thus early the paving stones were hot to the feet and the air sultry and heavy. Early shoppers jostled and sweated in the market. Lucia turned to see how her house slave handled the luggage and smiled gently on his lean face. Poor Rotus, it must have been very hard to have been snatched from his hope of a future and sent so far from home, a captive of the Romans, when all that he had been doing that Autumn day was buying new headstock from his southern neighbours; but, of course, as soon as Varres became a man then she would be bound by her late husband's word to offer Abroticus manumission. He would be freed to go as he wished, doubtless back to that land of opal mists to look for the beautiful Rufina.

Lucia never quite knew how far into Britain her husband had penetrated with Cerealis and his legions, but Rotus had spoken of his own country as well beyond the Roman frontier. He told of a beautiful land, if somewhat cool in climate. Lucia drew her travel cloak about her at the thought, then loosened it again as a shaft of morning sun struck full upon her shoulders. The day was hot and would be hotter.

The carriage awaited them. An oily obsequious hatchet-faced Eastern bowed the lady Lucia to the traveller's seat and bent to put the hand baggage beside her, but the Briton forestalled him. Deftly he placed the two packages with his left hand, tossed a coin and took the reins with his right, and steadied young Varres with his knee as he stirred the ill-fed horse to action.

As the equipage plodded sombrely through the town gate and along the straight road to the South, Lucia relaxed, Varres clicked his knuckles with impatience and the slave smiled to himself. This funereal pace could test his charge's endurance for another half thousand paces, and then perhaps it might be time to test the mother's tranquility.

At last Rotus ventured his persuasion.

"So slow is this dead old lump if horse flesh and so cheerful is the morning that I would ask to be relieved of the task of driving. May I give the reins to the young man beside me?"

At her nod the lad sprang forward and grinned widely, but, as always, Rotus was attentive to his duties. "This nag will not survive till we change hands again if he is not fed at once. We must give him something on which to keep his knees up." He took an apple from the hamper of food and a handful of oats from his girdle pouch and strode to the horse's head. Then he crooned soft words in the tired beast's ear and was rewarded by a nudge of its mouth in search of more fodder. "Now, perhaps, Pegasus, you may try to fly?"

Varres laughed as he flicked the reins. "More like he'll drop like Icarus if this heat continues, but at least we'll let him try."

Plod turned to amble and amble broke into trot, and before she knew it Lucia was gripping her seat and reminding herself not to direct the driver.

Rotus was pleased. The boy was ecstatic and the Domina too seemed gently happy. Somehow it was important to the slave that this day be one of content. The sun shone, the day was hot and under the wheels of their carriage the road bowled smoothly on.

Too soon the high flats of the first town appeared on the skyline, harsh and obtrusive in the sun. There was a block of tenements back there in their town of Hercules too, but it was mellow and welcoming to those who needed cheaper houses, not garish, brash and over-crowded as the several insulae of Pompeii. Lucia's sister, as befitting the wife of a successful business man, occupied a beautiful and gracious home away from these slums, but many of her husband's underlings were glad to live in the flimsy wooden buildings that loomed higher as the travellers approached.

Perhaps it was these that dulled the day's brightness as they left the carriage at the town's gate, or perhaps it was the heaving mass of people in busy streets. At last however, they were actually on the threshold of Marcia's palatial dwelling and a weary old doorman was about to usher them to the presence of his mistress.

"No need," Lucia said, "I know the way," but a strident voice complained from within. "Why do you hesitate, Caecilius? Usher the guests to my presence as is your duty."

So this was Marcia's mood today, petulant and imperious, her sister thought. Ah well, haste on tomorrow evening but one.

"Come, Varres, greet your aunt and then you may be gone. Take my travel bag and let Rotus rest awhile."

In the briefest possible time Varres was out again, impatient to be off, and his mother and aunt accompanied him. Varres was in high spirits.

"Goodbye, Aunt. Thank you for the denarius. I hope your baby is a red-haired girl — Rotus thinks copper haired females are wonderful."

To forestall a retort, Lucia claimed her slave's attention and put out her hand. "Rotus, trusted friend, take good care of my son."

"Indeed I shall, my Domina." He took the outstretched hand and pressed it to his forehead. "Indeed I shall. With my life."

11

TWO

The moment passed but the intensity of it remained to surprise at least the woman. She had spoken when she did to cover the young man's embarrassment in the presence of her sister and because of her son's thoughtless farewell to his aunt.

"I must speak to my son about this compassion for other people's feelings," Lucia thought. "What was it that Citizen Paulus had called sensitivity for others? 'Caritas' was it not?" Rufus or Phebe could explain to the lad what his mother found difficult to put into words, but as yet the boy was too young to mingle with the brethren. There was still too much risk in that for an immature lad. When he was older she would take him to one of the brothers.

"Red-haired females" indeed—surely the boy could feel something of other people's reactions: his slave's periodic longing for home and his own people, his aunt's disapproval of everything to do with poor Rotus, or at least the need so patent in the Vettii that they should have a son: a bag of sesterces already lay upon the child's cot, and in due course there would be a hired freedman for his tutor, and later schooling abroad in Greece. The boy would have everything.

The child *must* be a boy. Vettius would not countenance otherwise. Varres' parting wish had been unfortunate indeed.

Abroticus thought so too. Memories of his homeland were squeezing from his mind the contentment of the early hours. Soon, if he allowed, depression and half forgotten sadness could settle in its place.

Where was his charge? There, leaning on a stone drinking fountain, with his left hand pressed where so many hands had rested before, Varres was tracing with his other hand the outline of a horned bull.

Ech, horned bulls again. It was to buy horned bull of a different breed that Abroticus had left his northern home ten summers gone. His bull was to enlarge his father's herd, to breed strong cattle to feed his father's people, and to raise calves for a herd for himself when he should take to wife the chestnut haired Rufina. Little could he have known that the uplands south of neighbouring plain would become suddenly involved in a war of the Brigantine Queen Cartimandua. Less could he know that the simple action of driving a cattle beast could make him the prey of the meat hungry legionaries of the Roman Ninth. Still less had he imagined that having lost his beast, he too would be kept and used no better than an animal. Twice he had tried to escape in the first days, and twice he had been scourged as a runaway slave. Even now his cheeks flamed at remembered injustice. After the second beating he had been manacled to a post for two days and was on the point of being whipped again when Tribune Varres intervened. His stripes had not healed when the legion returned to Lincoln and took with it the boy from the North.

Rotus watched his charge chatter to a companion. He seemed content and the girl certainly was not bored.

These had been terrible days, in the winter of '69. Again and again he had tried to find his way home and each time some informer had sold him back to the Legion, where he was scourged and beaten. Finally came the threat of crucifixion, the ultimate punishment for a runaway slave, when cold reason, native in his forebears, persuaded him to

13

give up trying to escape. Alive he might one day win home, dead he never would. Then Tribune Varres took him for his body slave, giving feeling and purpose to the insanities of life.

How like his father young Varres looked as he stood by the fountain declaiming to a rapt pretty audience of one.

So had the Tribune lectured to his slave on the subject of Rome and the Romans: most Romans were just and reasonable he had said, home-loving and proud of their womenfolk; exceptions were, as in his own people, few and therefore easily noticeable; cruelty was a native characteristic too, as among his own, but intelligent men suppressed the trait; even, the use of slavery was an effective system of imperial policy. This was difficult for Rotus to accept, but accept he did because his master made his reasoning acceptable. As time had gone by, only the thought of Rufina remained vivid and pain-making in his heart.

Rufina. . . .

Ech. Enough of nostalgia. When Varres became adult Rotus would go home. Rufina had said she would await his return.

But ten years? Her family could not afford to keep unmarried daughters, and the Red One had sisters. . . .

First things first, however. He and the young one must leave these pushing, jostling, odourous crowds and breathe fresh air.

"Master, I thought you were in a hurry. Why dawdle here keeping slaves and maidens from the water? Come, we make for the south-west gate and a cisium."

"A *cisium*? By Hercules, a *fast* chariot? Goodbye, Levitica; I shall be here at sunset two days hence. Quickly Rotus, come."

As the slave watched the slight young girl dart off, and saw the pink on his master's cheek, he smiled. So the boy was not such a child as he had thought.

"A cisium, yes, and the fastest horse I can hire, for we have twenty miles to go to Sorrentum and the boat we shall

14

sail to the island."

Do we hire a pilot with the boat or may we sail it ourselves?"

"Who needs a pilot? There were no pilots on the boat your father and I built on the Tanaus in one of his forays. Don't you want to learn to sail?" Rotus grinned teasingly. "I taught your father. I can try to teach you. Meanwhile if we could only get out of this hurley-burley we might make some haste. Stay close by me, and presently don't breathe too deeply."

"Why? Fresh air. . . . Ech, what is that disgusting smell? By Hercules, how can people live near this?"

"Not only do some people live near it, they even work among it. 'That disgusting smell', young man, comes from fish guts rotting nicely in the garum factory. People are actually in that building, pulping and pounding and sieving the loathsome stuff so that your good uncle and his like may have garum sauce at their next banquet. Hold your nose and hurry. When we pass the glass factory we'll be beyond the smell and you can breathe again".

By the time they reached the election notices on the wall outside the glass factory, Varres was purple in the face.

"Whee, I shall never eat garum again. . . . See, the road is clearer here, let me race you to the gate."

Minutes later they were racing behind a faultless chestnut along the road that passed Stabiae to Sorrentum. Stopping only to buy fruit and flagons of water, for there would be no fresh water on Capraea, they sped on to the tiny harbour where sailing boats were for hire.

A stocky man, grey-bearded and grey-headed, looked up from a boat. The silver armlet of a slave gleamed in the copper sun.

"Good day, Barbarian. So you have come at last to teach your master the art of sailing?"

"Good day to you too, Barbarian. Yes I have come, and will hire the best sailing skiff of your miserable fleet. See that it also has good oars, and no holes in the bottom, for I

15

wish my master to handle sails or oars, not bailing pots." The young man chuckled into the older face. "Still quite happy in this searing heat, are you, old friend? And content to twist a living from our unwary overlords? But do not try to cheat me, Britannicus; remember where I came from— where one day I'll return."

"Oh Abroticus, how I wish you safe return to that cool lovely land. For me, I am too old, too weary to make the journey, and now in any case, I have my woman and our daughter to keep me tied to this coast. I dream of our cool Caledonia when this wretched heat is too much for my dry old frame, but I find it easier to go under the vine shade there than to travel these many miles.

"Go lad, unhitch that dust-raising roadster and tether the chestnut beneath the shade—I shall feed her oats and give her a drink when you have pulled away."

Varres did not think to question the order from an ageing slave to a freeborn Roman boy—Britannicus was a friend of his friend Rotus—so he rubbed down the steaming horse and tethered it under a rough shelter made cool by interlacing vines.

Rotus paid Britannicus from a bag of silver tied at his girdle, then he bade farewell in the firm handfasting of their custom, and Varres saw fit to do the same, before he followed his slave.

"Go carefully, Abro'tus," said the Briton. "Go carefully, I say. There is something in the air to-day which I like not. Look to the lad."

"Farewell, friend. We return in three days. Do you look to our horse." Rotus waved cheerfully then set his sail to the breeze and they skimmed away.

So skillfully did Rotus head their skiff with what wind there was, it was not until they were halfway to their destination that it was necessary to add oar-power to sail. Little was spoken, for both were engrossed in handling their craft; but when they had settled to the rhythm of oarstroke Rotus laughed again.

16

"Young man, your father was not as ready or so nimble as you have been here. Indeed, he all but took a ducking, shield, helmet, plume and everything, but for the steadying hand of our friend Britannicus."

"Britannicus? Was he too with my father in the IXth Legion?"

"Like me he was a captive of the IXth for a time after one of their forays to the west, but he was sent to Rome in a triumph some years before your father was killed. He is of the Novantae people, while I am a Caledon, but since his uplands and my native mountains look somewhat alike he chooses to call all our country beyond the Roman frontier by the name of Caledonia."

"It has a rolling sound on the tongue."

"It has a rolling vista on the eye, strong and lively and ever-changing — and all as rugged as that island." Rotus had rested on his oars behind Varres' back, and was leaving the boy to pull by himself. Now he was looking over his shoulder to the massive crag of Capraea rising straight from the sea, green and purple and impressive.

"You let me do all the rowing while you've been admiring the view, you. . . . 'M'hercule, it is rugged, and rather beautiful, but I can see nothing of a beach. I had hoped to swim. . . ."

"You shall — and by the way, you row quite well for a beginner. I shall allow you the oars all the way back to Sorrentum when we return, while I merely watch the scenery."

Such easy companionship had always been between the two when they were alone, although all the customary formalities between master and slave were observed at all other times. Lucia herself had done much to foster this comradeship and would have been pleased to hear them banter as they finally achieved landfall in a secluded cove.

Meanwhile Lucia had her own problems. Marcia was ailing and made everyone aware of the fact. Poor Caecilius could do nothing right, her personal slave was reduced to

17

tears, the cook was badgered, the bailiff provoked to the limit, relieved his feelings on the kitchen boy, and even Vettius himself, making a brief appearance before bathing and dressing for a banquet with business friends, became the target of his wife's factious discomfort.

Lucia felt sorry for her sister, and tried to divert her sister's mind to thoughts of new gowns or cloaks or a visit to the theatre when she was well again. Nothing availed, least of all mention of the theatre, until with sudden perversity of her nature and condition, Marcia decided that both sisters must visit the Amphitheatre on the very next day.

"Now that the late Nero's ban on beast-shows has been lifted from Pompeii there are some exciting spectacles being held these days, I believe. Caecilius shall escort us to-morrow afternoon."

Lucia's preference was for the less exciting, a Greek play perhaps at the Odeon, or a Roman comedy, but Marcia was adamant: a spectacle at the Amphitheatre she would see or nothing, and the more bloody the better. A gladiatorial show would suffice, if the fight were to the death, but truly she would prefer a beast-show with a gaggle of Christians added to enrich the excitement.

At the thought, Lucia sickened. Armed combat between two matched warriers was one thing, but a 'contest' between a wild beast and a man was quite unfair, and as for watching innocent men and women—yes and children too—cooped up with ravening lions, her mind revolted at the prospect. Yet Marcia was no more bloodthirsty than so many of her kind. Even the parsimonious Emperor Vespasian had financed lion and bear hunts in the far reaches of his Empire, that there might be beasts for the entertainment of the populace, and the new Emperor Titus seemed most willing to outdo his father in the extravagance and bloodthirstiness of his productions in the circuses of Rome. In her own Herculaneum such vulgarity would not be owned, but here imitation was the sincerest form of flattery, and Pompeii was nothing if not fashionable. Wryly

18

Lucia wondered how long it would be before it was 'fashionable' to be Christian: fashionable instead of being as now, crude, entertainment for people with too much time on their hands.

From the surface of her mind Lucia chattered on through the trivia of social life here and at home, and eventually she was rewarded by seeing her sister relax, and even, at last, fall asleep on her couch.

A great longing came to Lucia for the peace of her own little home and the companionship of her son.

THREE

For Varres the day had been pure delight. After landing in Capraea they had secured the boat and soon found a sheltered hollow protected by an outcrop of high rock. There they left such possessions as they had before swimming in the cove and rubbing away the day's sweat with gritty sand from the shore. Then, meticulously, they divided food and water into what they considered was three day's ration, ate the first portion heartily, built a small fire to keep away insects, and, of a sudden, Varres slept.

Rotus lay, watching the sky. The sun was setting in uneasy splendour, in dusty ochre, dull orange, and a spumy sea-green, with angry edges that he had never seen before. In this country there was little time, about the evening meal, to admire the colours of fast fading dusk. At home, where Sul the Sun God went to rest in more leisurely fashion, there had been time, the day's chores and meals finished, to stand and watch opal turn to gold, to bloodred, rose then silver, and presage from the Sun God's signs what the morrow's weather would be. Then was the time to plan the next day's work. His father had been very wise in the signs of Sul, and had taught Rotus a great deal of this wisdom, but what this peculiar sunset presaged it was doubtful if even his father could have said. At least, if the next day were less sultry it would be good.

In August in "cool Caledonia" there would be cutting of turf for winter fuel, if Sul had promised dry weather; if wet with the gentle light but penetrating drizzle that often kept the air cool, there would be shearing to do indoors, or curing of hides or the fashioning of spears for the hunt, spades for the turf and knives for skinning beasts; and, if time allowed, for making bronze armlets, and trinkets for the womenfolk. Life was busy, active and varied. Rotus' father had been progressive these years ago — had he proceeded with the plans they made together for hoeing a little more ground every year in order to grow more grain? Had he kept in repair the new outhouses they used for shearing? Or, sick at heart at his eldest son's disappearance, had he forsaken such new-fangled nonsense? Worse, and bitter thought, had the intrigues of Cartimandua's wars and Roman partisanship ravished both his home and kinfolk?

Rotus rose, restless and uneasy, tortured by half-forgotten doubt. Foolish he had been to come to this rugged chunk of island away from the mindfilling routine of daily chores; foolish to let the sight of old Britannicus remind him of his father. Even the name Britannicus flicked chords of memory to set them twanging. True, the old fellow's native name had been quite unpronounceable upon Roman tongues, but the usually nimbleminded IXth Legion could surely have formed some kind of cognomen, even as they had Latinised his own name, as young Varres had foreshortened it in his turn. But the British man had been named just that, and strangely he had kept the name even after he was freed, just as somehow, he had omitted to remove the silver slave-band from his arm. Rotus himself would soon remove *his* bracelet when *he* was freed; indeed, he would give it to the Domina, as was the custom not to put on another man's arm, but to place with those other symbols of renunciation which she kept in her tiny prayer room.

Oh yes, Rotus knew about the secret room, the tiny cross and that scrap of faded tunic, the box of fripperies she had given up, and Lucia knew that he knew, but no word of it had passed between them since that day when each, in dire straits, had sought the comfort of Rufus — that one who had been with Citizen Paulus — in an ugly back street in Rome. Lucia had had great need in her widowhood for a god who could give life after death, clean simple and clear-cut, not fraught with complications as the after-life in Roman Hades; while the young slave, bitter and bewildered, had needed desperately any reasonable straw to clutch in the confusing welter of alien divinities. The god of Paulus as taught by Rufus was human and personal, and Rotus, then so young, needed someone personal. Had it been only the attraction of red hair that had made him follow Rufus in the first place back to that dirty street?

Yes, he would give his slave-band to Lucia. Meanwhile, night though it was, he would swim again, swim and swim that he might tire himself out completely and gain sleep at last.

The water when he cut its surface was still warm, uncomfortably warm even this late, cloying and hindering his stroke, sticky, even honeyed, as it clung to his hair and limbs. Determined to weary himself he swam on and on, and at last came to a stretch of water below sheer cliff where the waves ran cool. Here he floated gently, letting dark clear water lave away unhappy thoughts, until for very chill he had to strike out again clinging shorewards back towards his charge. Suddenly for a space, cliff face disappeared in the mouth of a grotto gleaming jewel-like beyond. Treading water in the cave mouth, Rotus gazed till his eyes hurt. If darkness were all around him in the open, this was not lack of light that he gazed on now, rather a glimmering surface of water like black crystal, or the shimmering irridescence of black silk with a thousand lights behind it. Now, for a moment, it was the colour of midnight sky on a frosty night with all stars run in one.

Impatient at his lack of words to do justice to what he saw, and chilled now to the bone, but excited, and savouring the morrow's pleasure of showing this solemnity to the boy, Rotus sped to their cave, climbed to their encampment, and fell into deep untroubled sleep.

Next morning he was awakened before dawn by a gentle prod from Varres.

"Up, lazy one. I wish to see the sun rise over the mountain, but if you are not awake before I eat breakfast, I promise you I shall have your share also. You know, I don't think Servilia gave us enough food for three days—I could eat all to-day's ration myself."

Rotus chuckled wryly to contemplate this dainty picnic preparation. At home, when he had been on the hill, herding or hunting, he had had a piece of meat, or a hunk of cheese and whatever berries he might find on his way; and at home, he had water from clear cold springs or streamlets. The stuff in this flagon was flat, tasteless and tepid, and the wine was little better, thick as was the earthenware pot that kept it. At home, heather wine, when they had it, sparkled to the last drop, because the water that made it sparkled too.

Like the water in that cave, it sparkled. They would see the sunrise, then row to the cave. In the gathering light before the sun rose it was an arduous task to gain a vantage point in the chunky crag that was the island, but at length they gained the head of a rock from where they could see the bay round half of which they had raced the day before, and dark on the skyline beyond was the mass of Vesuvius. As they watched a silvered fringe tipped the mountain's edges and soon the sun rose pale, watery and misted.

"It is like watered milk in Emperor Nero's bathhouse," was Varres' comment. "Before his wife had had her bath."

"What do you know of the late Nero's wife's bathing habits, young man?"

"Oh just what I've heard from Aunt Marcia's complaints. You know my Uncle Vettius is about as rich as old Croesus, wherever his money comes from, and Aunt Marcia gets whatever she seems to want. Once when we were staying with her—mother had sent you to Rome for some reason—or was it the time you took Servilia to her niece at Stabiae? No matter. We were having one of these horrible holidays at the Vettii farm—Aunt complained about the sun spoiling her complexion—as if it could—and mother suggested she dab on a little goat's milk. Then nothing would serve the Lady Marcia but that she should bathe all over in goat's milk as she had heard Empress Poppaea had done. When not all the goats on the farm could produce enough milk to fill the bath, and the slaves added warm water Aunt Marcia fumed and sulked, until Uncle Verellius persuaded her that this was exactly what Nero had done for his good lady."

"And was it?"

"I don't know, nor, for that matter, did my respected Uncle, but he did get dear Aunt Marcia soothed down enough to step into the concoction, where she fell sound asleep and very nearly drowned."

Varres grinned broadly at the memory of the household's panic. "So Rotus, I see that wretched sunrise as merely the bubbling of Aunt Marcia's—and the noble Poppaea's—bath water. I am disappointed. I had hoped to see red and rose and flame and ochre, all splendid positive colours, not this washy, milky blur."

"I have" said Rotus, "something to show you which should satisfy your liking for positive colours, but first let us cover our belongings. This could foreshadow rain."

By the time they regained their hollow, however, it was apparent that rain was not yet to come. The sun brightened to a saffron disc, to dull orange and to blood-red, mopping the last of its milky fringe and drying all trace of cloud from amethyst skies. Such a sun Rotus had never seen nor yet had Varres although, disappointed in his first impression, he was unwilling to yield that even this burnished coin of mutative metal was noteworthy.

"It is now like the nose of my Uncle Vettuis when he has eaten and drunk too much—but of different shape of course."

Rotus laughed. The boy was possessed of vivid, if disrespectful imagery.

The sun brought heat, glaring, piercing heat, so first the pair swam in the shallows of their bay. Then they took to the boat and rowed gently round the headland to the cave which Rotus had found the night before.

Jewel brightness of speckless sky and translucent sea brought no comment from either, for soon they were totally involved in the task of guiding themselves and their boat, without bump to heads or prow, through a hole in the cliff so low only fish could enter, as Varres proclaimed.

But enter they did, and stayed spellbound. To-day the water was blue, or was it green? Who could define this tinge of crystal? Rotus remembered a single translucent blue scale on the back of a fish he had once caught at home: a fish pink of flesh, but with scales of so many colours that no-one could say which predominated, yet each, separate, had its own bejewelled glint. Varres lived again a half-dream from his early childhood: saw the sheen of a lovely garment in a dark room, a garment made for his mother to wear at a banquet before his father left for Britain. That gown belonged to the days when his mother still laughed and sang and was happy; that it lay now folded with other articles of renunciation in the cupboard room, the lad did not know. The dream he knew and his mother's kiss that night, and the warm glow of his father's presence; and he remembered long, till the crystal water turned chill upon his spirit.

Awakened from reverie by a strange surge and slap at the mouth of the cavern they saw the green-blue turn grey, and then blue again, and it was time to go.

Outside the sea was grey and roughening, with a stiff warm breeze from the east, and the sun had again retreated into milky bath water. The wind sped them to the headland which they would have overshot had not Varres drawn on his oar at just the right moment to turn the point and pull shorewards again.

"Well done sailor," was but a murmur as Rotus took in sail and turned to his rowlocks, and indeed neither had breath to spare for talk as they pulled, for the wind was rising against them with every stroke. At last they were ashore and gasping.

"I did not expect this when we set out. Nor did you, for you foretold rain".

As if to refute the boy's cheerful jibe, a few stray drops fell, the, after an interval as if for further comment, rain poured down, drenching them at once. Yet it was not cool. Even as it fell, the moisture steamed and a dark mist banked over the bay cutting them off from the mainland.

Varres lugged their boat to their hollow, turned it over, propped one side of it on two separate boulders and grinned triumphantly.

"There, dull one, shelter. I am surprised you did not think of that yourself." He crawled under his invention and beckoned. "Welcome to the country-house of Varres of Herculaneum. The threshold, I must say, is unpaved, and the door is . . . well, non existent, but the atrium is of excellent proportions, and airy. Enter Rotus-of-the-far-lands, and tell of great deeds."

Rotus complied, and while the rain continued to fall heavily, he sat beside the lad spinning tale after tale of his better days with the IXth Legion in Britannia. Tribune Varres was always the hero of these tales, Rotus sometimes the dutiful servant, sometimes the bungling buffoon: always there was excitement and cheerfulness, but never a mention of the people of the north. To hear the Briton then, one would say that Cerialis and his legions had enjoyed hilarious holidays around Olicana in the fast high lands of the Brigantes, and that for Legion IX a foray was a joyful picnic, and a skirmish a cheerful test of strength and wit. Roman behind his large shield prodded and poked his short sword at his opponent's little shield, while the Briton stolidly whacked his own long blade at legionary's bull-hide protection; and Varres' imagination delighted in the picture. The earth trembled as Roman catapult lobbed boulders at a British fort, and the air filled with smoke as victory fires arose from winning side.

The rain ceased, as did the stories, and it was then that shaking earth and smell of smoke were no longer of the imagination only. Dark mist on the bay had retreated to show, far east, the dull glow of another sunrise; yet now the sun was high above.

With one accord, man and boy raced to their former vantage point, and looked the way of the mountain.

Smoke spumed from the top, white, then pitted grey and red, then white again and with a vicious spit. Their rock trembled; flame licked where the smoke had been, and the sky glowered red and angry once more, till wiped by a hissing spotted mushroom rising high, before it spread.

Varres laughed somewhat sharply. "That's like the face of my friend Sempronius when he had the spotted fever. M'hercule he was no beauty".

Rotus could not respond. Uneasiness of the night before settled again upon his heart; what this strange happening was he did not know, but that it omened evil.

"Indeed Jupiter is angry to-day", the boy was rambling on. "First he washes the sun in bath milk, then spits on us with his rain, and now he is rattling thunder bolts till he has set the mountain on fire. He must be in a temper, eh Abro'tus?"

A torrent of hideous smoke and fire rose from the mountain top, spouting high into inflamed skies and pouring down like vomit with sickening stench.

"Old Jupiter must be sick". This cackle was an effort, and too late the Briton smiled as dusk settled on the lad's doubt-clouded face.

"The towns . . . that stuff must be falling on the towns. . . . This will stop very soon, Rotus, won't it? They will be all right at home — city walls are strong? My mother will be all right?"

"Of course, master. Your Uncle Vettius will let no harm

27

come to any of his household."

A third stream of fire and smoke shot skywards, and for minutes was beautiful to behold; then it fell, pouring down the mountain side and sending a spray of red and black in all directions, clothed in choking acrid smoke. Rotus pushed Varres to the ground behind a rock, but no hard thing came their way, only the permeating shrouding smoke.

"We must go to my mother; she will need me". The boy ran downhill and upturned the skiff that had been his "country house". Rotus followed, though in his heart he knew that there was nothing to be done as yet. Whatever was happening in the three towns, would be over before they could be of help, yet the boy must work his hands to keep his head from worrying. They would launch the boat and let him row.

The water when they got to it in gathering gloom, was turgid and seething, with an underswell that drained the tide, then lashed it back upon the shore. Grimly Varres laid his craft upon the surface, only to find the water had ebbed and the boat was dry on gritty sand. A second more and it was pummelled back against the cliff had not Rotus placed himself in the way and braced his body to the boat, before the water receded once more. The strength of both was barely adequate to haul the skiff back to safety before the swell pounded again and would have broken both them and the boat.

"It's no good, Rotus. We must wait. We can be of help to no-one if we kill ourselves." The lessons of life were coming hard, but surely, on this man-making expedition.

Now the wind had risen to a gale driving from the east and covering both sea and land with ash and smoke, so that only in the lee of a broad crag was there clear air for bursting lungs. There they lay together, separate in thought, alone in the fear that the other might share his fear, until at last, in the darkness that was not night, they fell asleep.

FOUR

Twice Rotus awoke, fearing that his master had choked in the thick air, and twice he drew the boy closer under the crag. The earth still shook from time to time but their rock seemed solid enough, and anyway, it would be quicker to die under falling stone than to suffocate or drown. As the boy had said, they must wait, until whatever was happening had finished, until Jupiter had done with playing out his tantrums.

When, at last hunger woke them to yet another half-light, the earth was still and there was no sound from the east; neither was there anything to see in the gloom but an angry ochre splash that might be sunrise or yet death-fires. The sea was quieter and the wind was down. If this was not the dusk of nightfall they might try again to launch the boat. First, though, they must eat.

Servilia's carefully prepared provisions, though well wrapped after use last time, were tired and tasteless, and both water and wine were warm.

"It is not becoming any darker, so it would seem this is daylight again, such as we shall have of light". Varres pondered over his meal, having little relish for it. "I would suggest that we launch the boat to-day, but that I fear we have lost one oar. I cannot remember that I brought one back from our infortunate launching yesterday". Embarrassed at what seemed his childish inadequacy, he lapsed into the stilted rhetoric of the pedagogue's schoolroom and Rotus felt for his embarrassment.

"Didn't you, though, you scoundrel? Well, what's to do? Do you make one to replace what was lost, do you scull across the bay single-handed, or do we first make a search?"

As they trod carefully downwards a light dust kicked up around their feet, itching at heels and ankles and stirring again the acrid smell of the night before. Of the missing oar there was no sign. though both peered carefully through the gloom. At the water's edge a thick grey scum surged and lapped, leaving long spittle-licks on cliff and sand alike. No more was the fresh clean pool of their first day's bathing.

Varres saw the oar first, lodged upright in a rocky cleft beyond the strip of sand. He was the onus of losing it, his, therefore, to retrieve. Hitching his tunic high, he plunged through the spume to wade the few wretched paces and bring back his trophy even before Rotus turned from the ledge he was searching. Ech, but this scum felt filthy on his legs; how it clung, and itched. A pace further, and his knees tingled, two more and he would have the oar. The smooth round wood was within his grasp when a foot slipped and he was down under a grey crust, and choking in sulphurous stench. Wildly he flailed arms and legs and broke surface with a blanket of filth on head and face. This would kill him, but get the oar he must. Now with legs only, he thrashed the sucking water, and with a supreme effort jerked the wooden handle from its lodging. With a smack that sprayed scum again into his eyes, the oar hit the surface, but it was his. He had retrieved his loss.

"Well done, young man, you have the eyes of an eagle, if the face and head of a grey owl. Come, let me take that filth from your hair, and find the change of garment Servilia prepared for you. Hew, but that scum sticks".

Varres broke from the ministering hands to cough his lungs clear. "No Rotus, leave me. I must serve myself, for to-day we are comrades, not master and slave. In any case, I cannot put on a fresh tunic before I have washed myself clean of this stull, and you know there is no water for that. Or would you have me use the rest of that epid wine? Doubtless if his wife once bathed in asses' milk the noted Nero would have swum in wine. ' Do you know? No? Now, *that* would have been an interesting fact to have learned in school. When we return home, I personally shall enquire whether Nero did or did not bathe in wine. I . . . oh, love . . . Hercule. . . ."

Tears did not come, not then, but the nervous babbling ceased, and Rotus, in his own growing wisdom, made no comment. Instead he carefully cleaned the dripping oar, found a piece of sandstone and rubbed down the other until it felt like new. "We shall do your one, friend, when it dries, which will be after we have checked this cobble for leaks".

There were none, since Britannicus was an honest hirer, and Abroticus had been quick to protect the craft against the rocks, so when work was done and the gloom had lifted somewhat, in the face of an eastward wind, they set off once more to carry the boat to water.

Again their efforts were baulked. Across what could be seen of the bay a huge monster of the sea reared and plunged its way to the mainland, as if rushing to devour what was left of yesterday's fires; then in full attack it halted, arched its broad back, fell and sank into the ocean, where it hissed and bubbled its fury into exhaustion.

"Neptune must be angry too, when he lets such a monster loose so near land. What can ail the gods these days?"

Varres stared fascinated at the cauldron of the bay, and Rotus left his questions to the air. Once, in that first terrible winter, he had seen such a movement on a bay just west of where he had been captured, and he had prayed that it was his own god Mapone come to save him. But Mapone had not come, nor Cocid, nor had the Divine Mother seen fit to heal his stripes when he was scourged, but had let them fester, so Abroticus in his mind had spat upon his father's gods; and when Metricus the engineer had said that the thing was a

31

tidal wave, and explained what he meant, Rotus was not averse to believing him. Meanwhile this was a time to be practical. Roman gods were not practical as far as he could see, nor for that matter were his own native ones; as to this new one, he had no evidence, but certainly his followers seemed practical fellows enough. What had been those words of Paulus? . . .

"Well, lad, if the gods are showing temper, we had best not infuriate them further. As you said, we can help no-one by killing ourselves, or letting old Neptune's monster kill us. Once more, shall we wait?"

"I suppose so." The boy still stared out over the bay, from which the mist was clearing gradually, and his face wore a look of concentration which had never graced the schoolroom. "If that were a monster, I can't see why it stopped halfway to its prey and vanished. Could it have been frightened by something on the shore, or did it suddenly change its mind? If the great god Neptune, king of the seas, sent it for some purpose then it would have to obey orders by completing that purpose, wouldn't it? Or, maybe, Jupiter gave another command to his brother's monster? Then whom would it obey, Jupiter the king of all gods, or his own master Neptune, king of the seas? Ech, but this is confusing. Probably that monster thing got confused too and just gave up".

Rotus laughed. His young charge certainly had a bright imagination — and a mind to sift old traditions for himself. In due course he too might see practical sense in the new god, but it was not yet time to speak of this.

"I think the monster became aware of your powerful cogitation and has slunk away before you decide that he is merely contrived by imagination and the wind. Come, if we must stay, we shall explore more of this island".

FIVE

The next day dawned clear. A film of ash lay over the island, and thick chunks of curded scum had settled in crannies by the water's edge, but there was easy access for both boat and rowers to a sea once more calmly green. With only a slight sir of wind to belly the sail, they had to rely mostly on power of arm when at last they set off for the mainland, but each in unspoken urgency laid to with a will. Deliberately neither looked over his shoulder until the sun was well above them and their journey two parts done.

The central sweep of the bay was still misted, seeming bleak; Misenum at the north point was invisible, but cosy little Sorrentum nestled as ever just beyond the southern coastline, and to-day its familiar serenity was reassuring.

By his jetty, when they finally got there, Britannicus was again working at his boats and, at the little house behind, his wife seemed preoccupied in one of her endless chores. The chestnut pony waited patiently under the vines.

It might be as if the last two days had never been. Yet as they pulled the boat up on the dark, gritty shore they could see a deeper darkness that was not there before, both on the beach and in the eyes of the old man; and when they looked more closely it was that the woman was scraping, cleaning, rubbing chattels as if her life depended upon her efforts.

"Greetings, Abroticus, you have returned. We shall eat.

Lad go tell the woman that we follow".

Rotus knew his friend's curtness for a warning, and searched the old face uneasily. Brown eyes that once had known lights of honey and amber, to-day were sombre and . . . mud-coloured, Varres would have said. There was no fear, for that force had been spent long since, but only bleakness, shock, an infinite compassion.

There was little he he had to tell: the three towns were gone, swallowed in the brimstone and ashes of the mountain's explosion, and none who were caught there had survived. Suffocation, it seemed, would have been the easiest end. There had been officials from the capital this morning in Stabiae, the least affected of the three towns, and doubtless these government men would have all details tabulated that might be required. Meanwhile, they must see to the boy.

The meal was frugal, but it satisfied. When they had eaten, the boy was told, quietly and without fuss. For a moment he sat, then rose and went out, and when Rotus would have followed, the old man shook his head.

"There are things a man has to face by himself—don't you remember, Abrot'us?"

Rotus nodded. He was remembering, but not the incident his friend alluded to; he was recalling the farewell of his Domina on the bright day when they had parted, the farewell and his fervent reply. He *would* take care of the lad, even with his life. There would now be no manumission, no freedom to return to his home as yet, for his master would need him longer, now that he had no adult of his own to turn to.

"In a space" the old Briton continued, "my daughter will go to the lad and fetch him in. But as yet he has his pride to save". Rotus nodded again. The face of the young girl and that of her mother were all compassion.

At fourteen, not yet a man, what was the lad to do? Where would he live, how would he eat? Her relations, probably, all had perished along with Lucia in the

34

holocaust, and of Varres the father, there had been no brothers or sisters to mourn his parents' death in that other earthquake before young Varres was born. From the ruin of their once fine farm there was no inheritance, and though Lucia's little household had lived in moderate comfort after her husband's death, it was from the beneficence of the Emperor Vespasian that this was so. Whether Titus would continue his father's generosity much longer had often worried Lucia in the last two months, especially since the new Emperor seemed so extravagant in other ways, but now, with the Lady Lucia doubtless dead, who would plead her son's cause? Who would listen to a mere slave, a Briton at that?

For the first time in many years, Rotus was overwhelmed by the sheer injustice of life, and was filled with intense longing for his own people.

At some point, the young girl had gone to find Varres, for when her father spoke again and Rotus found heart to hear him, she was not there.

"My friend, this house will be your home and the lad's as long as you need a roof; but there is little here for an intelligent youth, nor yet for a homesick young man. Oh yes, you are homesick now—I see it in your eyes—so this is the time to *go* home. Find a guardian for the boy, and get you going, before some rich fellow takes you for his slave. Remember, not all Roman households are as liberal as that of your good Domina, nor are all Romans as fair-minded and just as Tribune Varres was. It is seldom good to be a slave in this Empire—nor yet a freedman without a patron".

Rotus shook his head. Only half of what his friend said had any meaning for him, and with half of that he could not agree; he had pledged his faith to the Domina that he would look after her son, and that was that.

Young Aurelia returned. There were tears on her face, but she looked straight at her father and nodded. The boy would come directly. An hour since, she had found him, sobbing, on a crag that looked towards the towns, and with

35

the intuition of the young for the young she had laid her head on his breast and sobbed with him. Together they had wept for the passing of each previous generation, and for the loneliness of being young. At last he had calmed, and gently stroking her hair, had talked his heart out, till dried of all tears, he had as gently dismissed her.

"Tell them I must think . . . and that I'm hungry."

Gladly the older woman heard these words and bustled about for here was something she might do again for that poor child, but Rotus felt more helpless. The boy was still child enough to admit hunger even in the midst of grief. Often there would be hunger to come for them both, but for himself he did not mind. How could he keep the child in food? If only he had taken with him the bag of money he had been saving. Perhaps he might find it if he returned to the house? Tomorrow he would go back to Herculaneum, to see what could be found. The denarius which Marcia had given her nephew would not last long nor would what was left of Lucia's money. Now his private hoard could be a great help if he could find it, and, anyway, they must return the chestnut and the chariot to their hirer at Pompeii.

"It's no use friend". Britannicus laid a hand on his shoulder. "There is nothing to be found. The whole place is engulfed, swallowed up in lava." But Rotus did not even know that he had spoken his thoughts aloud.

"We must return the cisium and find my money. Then we shall bury the Domina".

The Briton shrugged helplessly and looked at his wife. She whispered "Let him go; let them both go—it is the only way they may understand," and so no more was said till Varres came back. He came gravely, but not in grief, and stood to his full height, looking straight at his slave.

"Rotus, Aurelia told me what she and her father saw this morning: what has become of Pompeii and our own town, yet I must see for myself—if anyone still lives, my mother will, and I shall find her. . . ."

"But you cannot go near the fumes and smoke. My father

36

will tell you. . . ."

"I believe you, Aurelia, but I must see for myself. Rotus, will you come with me?"

"Indeed master. I was to ask leave of you to myself."

"Then we go together, to-morrow." There was the dignity of the Tribune in his voice. "But not as a master and slave: you have called me 'master' and asked for leave for the last time. It seems to me that with no household and no womenfolk I shall have no need of a slave, but I shall have great need of a friend. My mother was to free you when I became a man, or at least when I had beard enough for shaving and to consecrate to the gods; but I think that is a foolish custom and"—his voice cracked and rose slightly—"I have now little belief in our Roman gods. So before these our friends, Abroticus, bondman of my father the Tribune Varres, I free you". Solemnly he repeated the ritual and yet again, and after clasping the man's right hand in his, so that their forearms locked, he made to remove the slave band from the broad muscular arm. At first the silver bracelet would not budge, and the boy looked up startled, as at an ill omen, but Rotus merely rubbed oil on his arm from the housewife's cooking pot and eased the thing off. In its place a pale indentation showed up clearly against the brown of his skin.

"It is the custom for a freedman to return his slaveband to the one who was his master"—Rotus looked gravely at the boy. "Do you take this from me, that the ceremony may be complete".

Tucking the piece of silver into his girdle pouch Varres saw the old Briton turn to his wife, but did not hear his mutter, "Better, I think, to have kept it on. It showed a kinship one might understand".

By dawn next day the two had exchanged wine flagons for lighter, portable skin bags of water, had exchanged Servilia's picnic basket for a napkin of new bread and another of apricots, had washed and dressed in their clean garments and were bidding farewell to the kindly

37

household, for they were anxious to find what trace of Lucia there might be.

"Remember, my home is yours whenever you have need", Britannicus gripped each firmly by the hand, while his wife bent each dark head down that she might kiss them both, and Aurelia stood quietly aside. Then Varres took her hands, kissed them, and her lips, and whispered "I'll never forget you Aurelia".

As the chestnut trotted off leaving the little group behind, Varres looked embarrassed, and pink flared on his cheeks and ears; against the suffusion a spring of dark hairlings glistened. Rotus handed over the reins.

"Can you coax some speed, man, from this malingerer?"

SIX

Stabiae was deserted in an aura of sulphurous stench. Any inhabitant not instantly killed by flying rock or molten lava or falling buildings would have had to run fast indeed to avoid being choked. What had happened to those who had had the sense to foresee the danger in the eruption? Had they escaped, and to where? Or, calm in the assumption that disasters always happen to other people, had they remained until it was too late?

At least one father had tried to herd his family to safety and had been overcome by the fumes, for at one point the road was blocked by four splayed bodies, each holding a pathetic bundle. Varres turned sick eyes upon his friend and was startled to see that he wept. Could a man weep too, as well as a boy? Carefully he edged the cisium round these poor corpses back on the road, and found that his own throat was thick with threatening tears.

"Please drive, Rotus, as fast as you can. The stench is choking me too".

It was hopeless even to try to approach Pompeii. There was no town, only a dark deep sea over the hillside and the plain below, covered by rank and stagnant air. At first no landmark of any kind could be seen, no roof, no temple, not the rim of a block of flats. Gradually, as their eyes grew accustomed to smoke and distance they began to distinguish the outline of rooftops here and there, of sturdier buildings. None was of a building they knew.

The direct road to Herculaneum no longer existed either, so they turned seawards to the pleasant line of coast fringed with summer villas of the rich. Even here it was difficult to breath freely, so it was not surprising that every villa seemed deserted. Each small estate was dead. There was activity, however, on the water where a fleet of small boats plied from galleys off-shore. Each boat disgorged pairs of men to search the villas and bring out survivors, or the dead.

From a jetty, they watched for a time as the little boats poised lightly on the water, each steadied by a single oarsman, and very gently did big clumsy sailors load their macabre cargo of dead and dying. Few indeed were the rescued who seemed to have any strong spark of life.

Varres chuckled, "A lot of little Charons on a very big Styx" and was at once ashamed of his levity. Now it was that the enormity of this tragedy occurred to him. His own bereavement he had met and understood in the hours gone, but this was more than his—it belonged to an entire region, to a country. His throat burned; his jaw muscles tightened for he must not weep again, not in company.

Rotus called to a rescuer coming in, "Ho, sailor, how is it at Herculaneum?"

"Haw," the man spat a dark slob of spittle back into the water. "Dust and ashes everywhere, in my hair, in my mouth. These poor smothered devils are thick in the stuff. What did you say? Herculaneum? By Jupiter, if it is like this here at the sea, what can it be like close to the mountain? No chance of getting the corpses out there, fellow. It's only here near the edge of the mess that there's hope of rescuing an odd survivor, and m'hercule, they are *odd* survivors". Gently he eased a limp body from a companion's shoulder and carried it back to his boat. "Steady, oarsman; hold her steady. We'll take two more dead or one half-alive before we go back to the galley. By Neptune, what a cargo we ship this day."

Momentarily he rested by the cisium and stroked the horse's mane. "Ech, but you are a beautiful beast. Where were you in this fiendish holocaust? There won't be many left at your stable, I warrant, after that day's business. A sorry, sorry day". He looked closely at Varres' set face, and at Rotus, cocking his head questioningly towards the mountain. "Someone of his. . . ?" Rotus nodded, and the sailor clucked sympathetically.

"You'll find nothing in Herculaneum, friends, nothing at all. Best you go back where you came, and the gods go with you".

Another sailor hurried up. "Did you know, Aesticius, that they found the commander Pliny further up the shore? Dead. Suffocated."

Varres stirred himself to ask, "Pliny, the Naturalist and writer?"

"Aye, son, the same. No doubt he was writing a few notes about the nature of these particular things too when the fumes crept up and choked him. Should have stayed with his fleet, the silly old codger. Come, Aesticius; one more house to search at this end, then back to Misenum".

Again Aesticius patted the chestnut's rump, and raised a hand in salutation. "The gods go with you in what you seek, young man".

"They tell me," Rotus paused, "that there were government men out yesterday. . . ?"

"I believe so, son. The Emperor and a fistful of Senators and candidates drove by, and they say that Titus was seen to weep; but when I saw them, the dirt on their togas seemed to be their main concern. Pshaw," he spat again, "how important it is to seem to be clean before an election. However, the Emperor has decreed that we search out all survivors from the three towns and take them to Rome where they will be compensated from the public purse. I doubt whether that poor wretch will see much good of *my* taxes by the time we get her to Rome". He turned to help a companion with his burden. "Gently mistress. Take short

41

breaths at first till we win to clear air, then we'll have you breathing freely again. There! We'll back to the ship now, oarsman, and smoothly as we can".

"Perhaps we should go to the city Rotus, but first I must see what I can of our own town. Perhaps it's not so bad as the last. Perhaps mother went back when the trouble started. Perhaps she went back to Servilia. Perhaps . . . I don't really suppose so, because she would not have left Aunt Marcia, and *she* couldn't travel fast what with the baby. . . . But I must *see*; Rotus."

"So must I. We shall see together".

At first the going was slow, as the road was full of rescue parties from the boats, and, further on, odd pathetic little groups of survivors endeavouring to lug precious possessions with them. Here and there lay bodies, or abandoned belongings, and who could blame the stragglers who tried to possess what seemed to belong to no one else? Later the road was clear for a time, but as they progressed the air became even heavier and more choking, and there were again the dead who had been overcome three days ago as they ran from danger. Varres looked at each body but none was of his mother, and wildly he vacillated between hope and fear, until they came upon Servilia.

The old slave lay with contorted face buried down in the folds of a toga, a boy's toga, purple-edged. In one hand was a little skin bag, in the other an apple.

Then Varres wept, and not alone.

At last, they wrapped the old nurse in the toga of her beloved charge, with a silver coin between her teeth, and placed her in a rough hole beneath a rock, shielding her from the eagles by a mound of stones.

When they turned to leave her, the things in her hands had dropped and lay where the pony had followed. In the skin bag were five gold coins and a handful of silver, along with a small gold amulet that once had been Varres' mother's.

While the two gazed on the unsought benefice of this store

42

of money, the animal gratefully acquired the unexpected nourishment of the apple, and even the strictly honest Varres saw the value of good horse sense.

"If the gods were worth believing in, I should say this is a gift from them. Take the bag, Rotus, and tie it to your girdle. We shall need money when we get to Rome".

The habit of obeying lay strong in the new freedman but it was not mere blind obedience that made him take the money. Just such a sum as this was what he had hoped to find in his room in Lucia's house, but when now it seemed that not even the house itself would be found, it would indeed be foolish to refuse old Servilia's last act of service to her young master.

"Where could she have got the money from?" Varres asked. "The amulet, mother gave to her as a gift one feast day. I remember, because Aunt Marcia was with us and she was very angry that mother gave a piece of gold to a slave".

There was relief in talking, for the man as for the boy.

"A *mere* slave, I think your aunt would have said. She certainly did not approve of your mother's kindness to us as 'mere slaves'." Rotus' tone was dry. "I remember how she raved when my superior, the Procurator and his wife by slave law, the cook, were freed to set up house near your grandfather's old farm and to have their children recognised under Roman law. The good Marcia ranted and scolded, when the Domina said with supreme dignity, "I cannot afford to feed so many slaves", your dear aunt replied, "You should beat them more, and they will eat the less".

"Ech," Varres grunted at length, "She could be a virago when she was vexed".

"She would have approved even less", Rotus continued, "if she had known that our Domina actually saved money for us towards our manumission. Each December at the beginning of the Saturnalia she gave me a silver denarius, and again in June at the feast of Vesta she gave me another. Likewise Servilia received one denarius in March at the Matronalia, the feast of Juno, and another on the twelfth

43

day before the Kalends of October, the birthday of Romulus, as they say".

"Why did she choose these days? Was it to give an excuse for a little feats every now and then? I used to love a 'little feast' . . ." For the first time since their return to the mainland the boy's face was brightening with interest, and seeing this, the ex-slave smiled and exerted himself further in companionable reminiscence.

"I believe that might have been one reason, but your mother had a keen imagination and saw little pictures in many things, just as you do. Servilia received her gift on the Matronalia because the Domina knew that the old soul loved you as her own son, and I suppose there was a similar reason for using the other date too; you know, you and Romulus both important babies and so on".

"Varres laugh was thin and cracked, but it was a laugh. "Idiot. But what about your gift days?"

"Oh", the tone was still light. "She probably thought I'd like to get drunk during the Saturnalia; then again at the feast of Vesta she subtly reminded me that there was a young lady waiting for me at home". For a second his eyes darkened, then deliberately he laughed.

"I never did get drunk, so my money is intact in my room, where I had hoped to find it".

If either noticed that they had spoken of Lucia and "home" as in the past and finished, neither mentioned it to the other. The slave woman's end was a fact, however, and as such was accepted.

"Dear old Servilia did us one last service then by bringing us her money. She was a good nurse to me.

But now, Rotus, to the capital. Servilia would not have left the house if there was any chance of remaining there in safety, nor would she be alone here if mother had gone home. It may yet be that we shall find what we seek among the survivors in Rome. In any case", he made his voice as matter of fact and adult as he could, "we must try to return this cisium and the horse to an owner, somehow".

44

SEVEN

It took longer to reach the capital than they anticipated since the roads were jammed with refugees, with many, like themselves, in search of relations, and with petty officials going everywhere at once and nowhere to much purpose.

Whenever they overtook a group on foot either Varres or his new freedman made careful enquiries about Lucia, and in return were asked many a heartbreaking question. "No, we have not seen . . ." attained the momotony of a Greek refrain as it bandied from one side or the other, but in this particular drama there was no need for masks: tragedy was on every face.

On the third day they overtook a solitary young man limping heavily by the verge, and long after they had left him they were haunted by their total inability to help. Indeed they had offered to take him in the carriage, but he was dully stubborn. "You have room for but one. Take another who may have some cause for living—I have none".

In age rather more than midway between their own, he was completely bereft of life or will to live, and for a breath, Rotus felt impatience. "Oh come, man. . . ."

"No. The gods have taken my home, my parents, wife and child, my dog even—why then did they not take me? When they sent the rock at my hip, why did they not kill me outright? Would that Jupiter allow me to perish by the road

45

and let me go to my Valeria". The eyes which he turned again to them were without the will to see.

"Go friends. Others may wish to live".

In silence Varres rode on asking no questions of wayfarers, and leaving replies to his companion. Others he saw were in sad plight too, for everywhere there was the tale of dead or missing loved ones, but none was so completely alone as that young man, none so utterly unwilling to survive.

"Surely he has little spirit", was the boy's first expression of long, long thought.

"Rather, it may be that his spirit has been quenched by shock, and numbed by pain". For a second's insight Rotus saw again the spiritless thing that he himself had been ten years ago, before Varres' father had befriended him, and now he wished to be a friend.

"We should have made him come with us, if only to find a physician for his leg. When we get to a place to turn round I think we should go back to make him come. You can hold him down if he is recalcitrant".

Varres nodded, half-smiling, in agreement. To be able to help anyone at all would salve his own anxiety, but even his youthful inexperience saw that it would be of little assistance to take one person — all they had room for — from any group of companions already formed. What comradeship they had, they needed; it was all they had. He choked.

"I'm lucky, Rotus, that I have you. . . ."

"And I, you . . . and that you have spirit". The sincerity of the words was carefully masked by his chuckle. "See, beyond that woman there is a widening of the road. Shall we turn there?"

The woman, bent and dejected, was heavy-laden; as they passed, they saw she held a child.

"Valeria?" The word came unbidden, surprising even the questioner. A tear-worn face jerked up, young and momentarily alive, but when the glimpse of hoped-for recognition died, the eyes dulled and she drooped again.

46

The child whimpered in slackening arms.

Varres leapt down, and repeated his question eagerly. "You are Valeria? Your husband is so tall and so wide — " his hand waved measurements — "his hair is black and curly and he has a mole below his left ear?"

Dull eyes widened and the listless young head fell and rose as if pushed by a force beyond its own volition, but the whole expression was uncomprehending.

"Oh please say 'yes'". Urgency filled the boy's face. "He has another mole on his right forearm and. . . ."

"Yes, yes. But he is dead, killed in that horror there".

"No, he is not".

Afterwards Rotus could not decide which surprised him most, his ex-master's perspicacity, the girl's sudden animation, or the speed with which Varres turned the horse and cisium and raced off down the road by which they had just come. All he knew for that time was that he must remain with this girl and child and try to reassure her and then later they would find attention for the young man's injured leg.

The baby whimpered again, restless and afraid, caught in the ferment of doubt and hope, fear, bewilderment and longing in his mother. Mutely the girl handed her child to the big Briton, and while she unclasped the travel cloak and the brooch on the shoulder of her gown the small black head nestled softly where before had been a silver armlet; tiny fingers gripped his large hand, and awkward but not unwilling, he let a finger rest on the child's groping mouth. It pleased him to feel hard gums draw upon his knuckle and for a foolish moment he pretended that the child was his. Then the mother was ready. Soft fullness gave satisfaction hwere his finger had none to give; and it was thus, suckling, that mother and child were united with their man.

Varres was delighted with his success. The swift ride had whipped the blood in his veins, and rejoiced his spirit, and as he raced back with Valeria's husband safely aboard his delighted cries "We've found his wife" brought answering

47

smiles, and infused new hope in all who heard him. When
the young man tumbled from the chariot to clasp his family
to him, it took all the lad's sense of occasion to keep him
from cheering aloud. Instead, he drew Rotus aside and
whispered delightedly, "He has come alive now, hasn't he?
And because of us. He might never have found them but
that we chanced to pass by. Oh, he's a funny little monster,
that baby".

Annoyed perhaps that his mother had temporarily
forgotten his needs, lost as she was in her husband's eyes, the
baby howled, and belched, to Varres' even greater delight;
and so it was that he found himself holding the child while
its parents locked themselves in each other's arms. Nature
decided to speed up the proceedings and the second howl
came from Varres. "Rotus. Valeria. Oh I wish I had not put
on my clean tunic".

Valeria was all apology for her infant's innocent manners,
while Rotus chuckled at the boy's look of discomfiture. The
laughter that followed covered every emotion; relief, strain,
happiness, anxiety, love and the prick of envy that Rotus
had felt as he watched the little family. Had *he* had a
guiding fate in his misfortune or a stroke of luck of a
beneficent god to guard him, what family would *he* have
had now? His four promised red-heads, probably, or three
and a black poll like this one.

Of what use to ponder? He was now twenty-seven, not old
by any means, but not a stripling either, for beside this
young father he felt old. No doubt Rufina had not waited
but had mothered some other one's red-heads by now. He
turned sharply to the cisium to find what was left in the
napkins of bread and fruit.

"Like the little one, I am hungry. Let us share what we
have. Then Varres, young man with the perceiving eyes, do
you find a way for transporting all five of us to Rome
together".

It greatly pleased Varres to be consulted as an equal
before a pair of young adult strangers, and when his

solution of transport problem was acclaimed and adopted with enthusiasm, it was an effort for him to refrain from puffing out his chest in pride. The couple — who were still no doubt exhausted after their ordeal, although sustained by the reunion — were to ride all the way to Rome. Rotus and Varres himself would take turns to drive, and to walk, two miles, the one to set off on foot before the small carriage, the other to drive on the specified distance, halt and leave the cisium in the care of Valeria's Gaius, continue on foot the next two miles while the first caught up in the chariot; and again, on the specified distance, the change would be made. This was to continue until they reached the nearest carriage gate of the City.

Rotus was hard pressed not to chuckle at this extra-ordinary likeness to the official, verbose, slightly pompous manner of the late Tribune Varres, as his son laid down instructions, but at the same time he was gratified that again his charge had successfully assumed responsibility.

Varres insisted on being the first to set off on foot, which he did in a blithe jog-trot, carefully counting out the first few hundreds of the required two thousand paces, but of this he soon tired. There were still too many travellers to be questioned about his mother, too many answers to give to inquiries, and too often the temptation to stop and give cheerful comfort by telling of one family already reunited.

During his turn to drive, he had to pull up beside one of the tall columns which along with tombs and temples now lined the roadside, in order to give way to a centurion and his military marching south. Perhaps they were on a mission of rescue, but the face of the squat little centurion under its gleaming helmet and bobbing plume was fierce enough for one about to attack an enemy fort, and Valeria expressed the opinion softly that she was glad she had not been rescued by a grim old faggot like that; whereat Varres finally allowed his chest a little puff of pride.

Rotus, some distance behind, recognised the military

insignia and his mind went back once more to his homeland and the possibility, now much more remote, of ever winning back to his own people. Had he known what was in young Varres' mind after he too met the soldiery, perhaps he would not have been so dejected, for by skips and bounds and the light bobbing of a helmet plume, the boy was indulging in thoughts of his great ambition, to visit Britain by way of his father's Ninth Legion. When his turn came to walk, he marched stiff-backed and with head held high, on an imagined route to the north, away and beyond known territory to the cool lands and opal mists and brave stories of his good friend Rotus. There when he could reach the frontier, on a craggy hill smoothed by purple heather and amber bracken, and jewelled by a clear running stream, he would bid farewell to his faithful companion and speed him homewards to the beautiful Rufina.

So direct and attainable are the ambitions of the newly grown.

The second of these two miles was somewhat tiring, what with the responsibility of manhood's decisions and the ache of a soldier's straight back, but once again at the reins for the last thousand or so paces he found renewed enthusiasm in the plain joy of swift movement.

At the Porta Capena, where he had agreed to wait for Rotus, he drew up with a flourish, and tossing the reins to a hovering groom gave explicit instructions as to feeding and tending the horse until he and his friend should require their carriage again. Dearly would he have liked to add ". . . when we go upon the Emperor's business," but instead he rifled awkwardly for payment at his girdle pouch. The tie-thong, hard after its recent dip in Capraea's ash-thickened water was stiff to his probing fingers, but his urgency to impress was strong. Suddenly the thong yielded and broke, splilling purse and contents to the ground. With them went all of his new-won self-possession, and chagrin flamed his cheeks.

It was Gaius who picked up the slave-band and returned

it along with Marcia's coins, and if he fingered the silver armlet rather longer than was necessary Varres did not care or see. The ebullience of his recent hours had vanished fast in mortification under the eys of three grinning soldiers, and it was with the utmost relief that he recognised the presence of his freedman. Rotus paid for the horse's fodder, tossed an as to the smirking groom and shepherded the others through the city gate.

Inside he gave a little of Servilia's silver to Gaius, and bade the family farewell.

EIGHT

Rome was a seething ferment of people. There had been crowds in Pompeii on the day they had left Lucia there, and Herculaneum often had been congested too, but never had Varres seen such a multitude of humanity all seeming to be busy at once. He was well content just to stand and look about, but Rotus had other intentions. He knew from previous visits where he wished to go, or rather, where he thought Lucia would go if she were in Rome, so he hurried the lad through such quieter streets as they could find, until they reached a shabby little leather shop in an odorous diety street. Varres wrinkled his nose.

"Not another garum factory, Rotus? We've done nothing but sniff peculiar smells since we left home."

"Not garum—leather. The smell comes from the tannery behind the shop. Hold your breath if the perfume offends you."

"Perfume?. . . . *Now* where are we going?"

They had entered a passageway between the leather shop and a toolmakers, and were climbing to an upper floor where the smell, though still obvious, was not so overpowering.

"We shall not find my mother here".

"Perhaps not, but we will find friends who will know whether she has reached Rome. Be patient; what you will see you may not understand — only trust me. These people are friends of your mother."

Disbelief gave way to speculation, speculation as to what Aunt Marcia would have to say if she were taken to this place, and Varres had reached the satisfactory conclusion that for once his respected aunt would be dumbstruck, when a woman drew them within doors.

"Abroticus, brother, you are welcome; and your friend with you. You have news of our sister Lucia?"

"No, Aretria, we had hoped that perhaps you might have news for us. You see. . . ."

Varres listened only to the beginning of the explanation. He knew already what he and Rotus had been doing these last days; what he wanted to know was what his mother had been doing, and where she was now. The lady Aretria spoke of his mother as 'sister', but to his knowledge he had no other aunt but Marcia. Certainly this calm charming woman would be a pleasant aunt to have, for Aretria was tall, gracious and though not beautiful her face had both a serenity and a liveliness about it that intrigued him. Perhaps she too had a gift of vivid imagery, could see many pictures in many things. It might be well to listen.

"No Servilia would never have left her mistress even in the gravest danger."

So Servilia too had been known here.

"We must assume then, brother, that Lucia had not gone back home when the calamity struck. Have you thought, however, that Vettius may have taken his household to the coast or to his farm before it happened — as a treat, perhaps."

"His farm has gone too, I saw as we came" Varres ventured quietly, "and if they went to the coast the fleet will find all survivors and take them to Rome. That, sister, is why we are here."

The 'sister' slipped out, but it pleased Aretria to hear it, and she drew him towards another room. "Well considered, young man: now you shall eat. Fabia usually finds

53

something for us in this poor old unhappy city."

In the room that was the kitchen another pleasant woman beamed a welcome from above her cooking pans, and soon served large comforting plates of fish with plum and quince sauce. There was no formality about the meal, although to the hungry Varres it was delicious enough to be a banquet, and there were no offerings made to household gods. Indeed he could see no lararium where libations could be offered, but that, Varres surmised, was because this room where they ate was the kitchen. Aretria did, however, bow her head and speak over what seemed to be an incantation, but this was finished almost before the boy noticed.

What did bother him was why she had called Rome a "poor, unhappy city." Why, Rome was the centre of the world, the mistress of civilisation, the acme of all that was good, beautiful, cultured, rich and powerful, the focus of every hopeful young Roman eye. Only the like of Rotus thought that there were other places more to be recommended. Yet his honest young spirit had to admit that there were parts of Rome—he had been through them to-day—where few of the beauties seemed to abound.

Honey-and-cheese sweets, and cherries, were following each other rapidly into Varres' mouth as he mused, and it was not until the pile of cherries stones toppled that he realised how much fruit he had eaten, and blushing, he hastened to apologise.

Fabia smiled broadly. "I am but glad to be able to feed the son of our sister Lucia. Eat as you will, and fill that man's frame—there is much for a strong man to do in this world."

He reddened again, pleased to be called a man, but annoyed at this ridiculous blushing. He must ask Rotus about this 'sister' talk these people had of his mother.

For that, however, there was little opportunity that night, for Aretria insisted that they rest there until the morning, when they could go to the forum and ask their questions, and indeed Varres was glad to have a couch to sleep on, after so many nights on the ground, so that when he finally lay down he was fast asleep at once.

Rotus talked late with the two women until he too fell asleep where he was. When Fabia drew over him a soft coverlet and noticed the mark where his armlet had been, she sighed. "Were better he left if on, to be seen a slave could be a safeguard. Poor gentle Barbarian, and poor, poor Roman lad. We at least have made our decision and gladly, but he had not yet had that chance."

Then the two women sat awhile, in silence, with their hands clasped, and there was peace about them when they arose.

In the morning, there arrived a visitor, whom, too, the women called 'brother' and whose talk was of a martyrdom in the Circus to appease the god Jupiter and to amuse the survivors from Pompeii. Unnoticing of the white faces around him, Varres listened carefully, for here he might find his mother, at the Circus. . . . The word martyrdom meant nothing and he was too shy to ask; an entertainment of some sort no doubt, paid from the Emperor's purse—he was a lavish man this Titus, one heard tell. This was something a fellow ought to see while he was in Rome. How his mother used to love plays at the theatre when his father was alive. The boy's thoughts ran on, happily unaware of the tension around, and only when he heard Rotus say goodbye to the women, did he rouse himself to add his own salutations and thanks.

"Lucia's son is welcome at any time," Aretria affirmed, but only Varres was surprised when Rotus said firmly, "Thank you, but we shall not return. There is too much risk for all."

In the entrance passageway, the boy stopped short. "Rotus, risk of what? I see no risk."

"Risk of suffocating in this smell. Come on," and though the words laughed, his eyes were sharp on the street and the people around. "Come *on*. We must find these government officials who are said to know all about everything."

No one could ask questions and hope to hear answers in the jostling marketing crowd at this hour, and anyway Rotus seemed in an extraordinary hurry to leave behind the smells of that dirty street. In the business heart of the city, broad streets and open squares promised easy movement, but here too there was congestion. Crowds of people there were, on foot, in litters, even a few, bolder, on horseback. At least one man was leaning heavily on a staff, Gaius, with Valeria and their baby was trying to push his way towards a temporary rostrum under the arch of Augustus.

"Ho, Gaius", Varres called, pleased to see someone he knew in this motley throng. "Where are you going? Ha, little one, soiler of tunics, do you know me?"

The family delighted to see their benefactors, added to the general hubbub with greetings and excited talk.

"We are making for the Arch yonder", Gaius volunteered. "where a quaestor and his clerks are dealing with compensations. We have just come from the Arch of Tiberius after putting our names on the official list of survivors".

He pointed down the wide space fringed with public buildings to where, beside the Rostra, rose the memorial to Tiberius' triumphs over Germanicus.

"Now up here we shall be allocated a patron who will look after us until our compensation can be paid. I could wish they had not made us walk so far".

Rotus looked keenly at the man's white strained face, and demanded, "Have you seen a physician yet about your leg?"

"Yes. He told me to be thankful I am alive, heaved a joint back in place, gave me some salve and relieved me of one of your denarii".

The reply was rueful but he grinned cheerfully.

The light tone was infectious, and careless of the glum and the gloom around, Varres beamed, a man again, among men.

"I am delighted to help at any time, in any way. But", he recoiled in mock dismay, "I shall *not* hold your monster of an infant again, Valeria".

Not a few people turned to look at them as their cheerful laughter struck through the general air of gloom, and one man at least stood still, surveying the little group. He was short, fat and sullen, and bothered, it seemed, by a perpetual itch under his dirty toga.

"Will you come with us to find where we are to live? If we know who will be your patronus too we shall be able to return your money when the government gives us our doles".

"No need to return the money—take it as a gift. And no, we shall not need a patron, for we shall be away almost at once. However, I must look at these lists of survivors". Such self-reliant declaration surprised Rotus but pleased his independent Northern nature; there was much of the man already in this bearding boy.

Amid their farewells, neither noticed the fat little man's head jerk first to the left and then to the right, nor saw two unprepossessing strips of male ugliness detach themselves from the fringe of the throng.

The short-legged one who followed Gaius in line to the quaestor's desk was wistful but bravely smiling and most eager to make conversation.

"You are fortunate indeed to be together, young people. All my loved ones have gone, gone in that terrible calamity". The brave smile faltered and a tear squeezed from one beady eye. "Not even a friend have I. . . ."

Valeria quivered, for something about the man repelled her, yet she who had received so much practical compassion did not wish to seem unsympathetic.

"Your friends laugh much. They are happy, lucky fellows. Perhaps they too have their families spared?"

With a shock Valeria realised that she did not know: so engrossed had she been in her own renewed happiness she had not asked whether all was well with her benefactors; indeed she merely assumed that it must be, since they appeared to be so cheerful.

"We truly do not know. They took us in their cisium and

57

lent us a little money, but that is all we do know".

"Lucky, lucky people. Money, a chariot . . . and a horse as well of course? They must be men of means".

Something irritated Gaius about these whining presumptions and he saw from his wife's face that she would not be sorry to be rid of this companion.

"I think not", he said shortly. "More like are they slaves. One carried an armlet in his girdle pouch. . . ."

"And the other has the mark where an armlet has been. If this misfortune to the rest of us has set them free, then it is good. May the gods attend them". Valeria shifted her baby's weight and moved forward to her place at the table. Behind her, the wistful brave smile was suddenly exultant.

At the Arch of Tiberius, further down the packed Via Sacra, Rotus and Varres waited patiently to see the lists of known survivors. Of all fears that are born in the mind of man, the ones that most rarely find release in expression are those that touch on death and dying; so the man who sees death coming, for himself or a loved one, is dumb except to trivialities.

"I'm glad that we met Valeria," was all that the boy had to say.

Behind them ferrety eyes missed nothing, but there was little reward for straining ears. Rotus too, had his own thoughts and fears, mostly to-day for the kindly household with whom they had spent the night, and of what was to be at the Circus. A harrassed little government clerk eyed them sharply.

"Masters, *please*. Others are waiting . . . You wish. . . .?"

"To find the name of the Domina Lucia Aemiliana Flaminia, a widow of the Tribune, Varres". Rotus had not intended to give this title of 'mistress', but the habit was not easily broken, and his mind had been preoccupied. It seemed unnecessary now to add "The mother of this boy".

Lucia Varres was not on the list of survivors. Perhaps to-morrow. . . . Names were coming hourly. . . . Yes, they should return, but truly if nothing were to be learned by

58

to-morrow it would be of little use to stay.

Briefly Rotus pressed the boy's shoulder as together they turned away. If he had expected tears, he saw none, rather a calm, if hurt acceptance.

"We will come back to-morrow, but after that, there will be no reason".

The long limbed ferrety one pushed aside a little child in eagerness to hear, and the child wept.

Suddenly they heard wailing, an ululation of grief that in all this dejected throng had not till now been heard. Towards them, along the Via Sacra advanced a procession of such noise and pageantry as seemed impious among the leaden fatalism that lay upon the crowds already in the forum. At the head of the procession came men in gilded masks, followed by lictors bearing their official bundles of rods, then women, in mourning, with dishevelled hair and clothing awry, and it was from this group that the loudest wailing arose. Finally, pulled on an open bier, and covered with flowers, came the leading actor of the pageant, the deceased. Varres was about to ask a bystander whose funeral this was when he caught sight of the mimics who capered about imitating the habits of the departed. One was giving a creditable presentation of a tyro civilian in command of a disciplined fleet, while another was deeply engrossed in a book from which he was loudly dictating notes to a slave-clerk beside him.

"It's Plinius, the writer", Varres whispered and hoped that his friend was impressed with his knowledge. These antics were ludicrous in the extreme—as indeed they were meant to be—so he could not refrain from laughing. Immediately he felt guilty, for this surely was no time or place for levity. Yet laughter bubbled again, as the mimic, engrossed in a monstrous, unwieldy scroll, tripped over the end of his toga.

Rotus was scarcely amused. To him the pageant was unworthy, more barbaric than his native "barbarian" rites of burial. Wailing women and capering clowns—ech, how he wished to be away from here. But now the way was barred, for the procession had halted before the Rostra and masked representations of the corpse's ancestors were swarming up to take seats on the curule chairs, while there in front of the platform was young Pliny, the dead man's nephew, clearing his throat to begin a eulogy about his uncle.

There was silence now, and the crowd hung on the youth's words, hearing in the praises he voiced a fragment here and there that seemed suitable to each for his own bereavement. In the solemnity came a breeze of healing and relief, until the procession re-formed, masks, mimics and all, and the howling pageantry resumed.

When the last of it had disappeared Varres drew a deep breath, halfway between laughter and irritation.

"I wonder what Pliny Senior would have thought of that ridiculous performance had he been able to see it? There should be some more peaceful way than that of reaching the other side of the Styx. Perhaps how we buried Servilia should be enough?"

NINE

There are men who can turn almost any disaster to their own material advantage, and Rome was by no means free of these in the days that followed the eruption of Vesuvius. Emperor Titus was swift to establish congiary to those who lost home or land, and by the time Varres finally decided that his mother must be dead, most survivors had obtained compensation, in money or parcels of land, and had embarked on the beginning of a new life. Not so the more gullible: by these, doles were paid over to tricksters in exchange for non-existent homes; land was given up in favour of subservience to a patron; some unwary actually sold themselves into slavery. The unscrupulous were busy in pursuit of their own ends, and there was little they could not turn to suit their purposes.

Gaius and Valeria were lucky. Their patrons gave them hospitality for a few days then had them taken to their newly acquired patch of land north of the city, where he supervised his own slaves in building a house, tilling and planting, until all was to his own satisfaction. Then he returned to Rome, and in the glow of his new beneficence, the young couple forgot their own idle remarks to a stranger beneath the Arch of Augustus.

The fat man with the itch did not. With the promptitude of the excellent business man he was, he had acted on all information his two henchmen could rake up and almost at once had acquired for himself every runaway or masterless slave who appeared in the city. These he was hiring at enormous fees to till new farms or build new houses, and after he had finished what he deemed his 'contract' there would be little left in his victims' purse with which to do any more.

The pale mark on the strong arm of Abroticus made the Briton a most interesting study for Adipatus the itching one.

In the interests of economy Rotus hired lodgings in a tiny side street in the Subura. Here, after an excursion into the streets of this teeming slum to buy food, they decided to remain indoors until it was time to return to the Forum on the next day. After all, as Varres sagely put it, they themselves had a better right to their own heads and purses than any other rascal in the area.

This street smelled every bit as badly as did the one where Aretria stayed, but here the stench came from excrement and decaying rubbish; by comparison the aura of the tannery was pleasantly healthy.

"You said that the risk at the lady Aretria's was of suffocation, but this, m'hercule, is worse, much worse. Rotus, the risk at Aretria's is of *what*? and for whom?" The boy would not be denied, and so, much time was spent in that quiet room in talk of the new god and the brotherhood of those who believed in him.

"My mother was one of them? And Servilia? And . . . you too, Rotus? Why did none of you tell me?"

So they came to the most humiliating reason to be given to youth: "You were too young".

"Too young to decide for myself what I must believe in? I have already decided what I want to become — I'm going to be a soldier in my father's Ninth, to fight in your famous Britain". If the boy wished to goad Rotus with his brief spit of vexation, then he failed, for the man's reply was calm and friendly.

"Good. Then I shall reach home all the sooner. You can be happy in my Britain".

The moment passed like others of its kind, and soon they were planning, eating, talking and setting the world to rights as the custom is when two bright young minds come together in companionship. On the next day, it was decided, they would return to the Forum to look for Lucia's name, because they must make sure of her situation. Then, if the gods had been more benevolent than Varres really expected, they would claim congiary for the Domina and find a home for her. If the gods — or her own God — had not been kindly disposed, they would immediatley inquire about joining the army. Rotus had the strongest doubts as to whether the age of fourteen was too young for enlistment, but since neither of them knew much about the process, it was agreed that they could only learn by asking, in the proper quarter of course. The question of claiming compensation for themselves was discussed long and deeply, for the greedy markets of the Subura had eaten much of their small store of money, yet each was staunchly independent, firmly averse to accepting any form of 'charity'; and so the matter was left that whether they sought financial help would depend entirely on how soon they might join the army. Oh yes, they would enlist together — a freedman would be as acceptable as men born free — as long as they both could join the Ninth Legion; and so, happy in their lack of knowledge, they set their hopes on the simplest way of reaching Britain.

Finally, just before he fell asleep Varres remembered. "My mother has a cousin Aemilius who lives among the rich on the Caelian Hill. She may be with him".

The next day too was hot and sultry. The crammed choking streets of this part of the Subura stank with the effluvia of another night's waste, and shoppers sweltered and cursed as they jostled around the goods on sale. Varres grunted. Aretria was right; the dear, beautiful Rome of his young

63

dreams was old and unhappy, and putrescent. Even the broad graciousness of the Forum and its environs, to-day again packed with dejected, anxious crowds, had nothing of beauty to show to the casual eye. True, marble gleamed in pure lines of elegant buildings, basilicas soared and arches curved proudly, above the heads of the crowd, but to survive in this hacking, jostling, exasperated mob, one had to keep one's eyes on the next man's feet, or at best on the back of the fellow in front. It would be good to be free of people.

There was no trace of Lucia, nor of Marcia nor of any of the Vettii. It seemed incontrovertible that they had all perished in the wash that poured from the mountain. Varres tried to pray to Juno for the wellbeing of his mother's soul and found no words to say: if the goddess all powerful had care of women from birth to death, did her duty now cease for Lucia? Perhaps the new god had a special care for the time after death? He wished he could ask Aretria.

But there was an urgency now to proceed with their own lives. If Varres would make his final check at the house of cousin Aemilius, Rotus would enquire as to enlistment in the army.

As it happened just eastward of the Caelian hill there was a cavalry camp, where doubtless someone could tell him the procedure. The quickest way to where they were going lay through rubble and dirt and huge piles of small red bricks among which workmen swarmed with the seeming purposeless activity of an ant heap, but there was no lack of purpose in this huge site where old buildings were rapidly giving way to new commanding public works. One, a half finished luxurious bath-house reminded Varres that he and his clothing were anything but fresh and he expressed a need to swim and buy a new tunic.

"But if we may enlist straight away there is little need for a civilian tunic. I can wait till after you come from the barracks."

Neither saw the pair who picked their way, grumbling, round rubble and bricks and across the path of Fat Adipatus paid well for information and better still for goods to hand, but neither raw-boned Edurus nor Decius of the short legs and long body was fond of too much activity. Indeed this last task set by the fat one was proving too arduous by far: apart from trailing these mountain goats ahead there, over all this rubbish and rubble, in a stifling day like this, had not Edurus spent all of the afternoon before in the moil of the Subura, waiting to catch sight of them again? And had not the legs of Decius worn even shorter on the Via Sacra from the earliest hours this morning? Faugh, this pair must be dealt with immediately and brought to Adipatus. Then there would be money to spend again, at the Circus Maximus to-morrow perhaps, and at the Lupanaria of course.

By Jupiter, their quarry seemed to be making for the Lupanaria now. Edurus sped on, followed, in gasps and spurts, by Decius. If they were to catch these two at all it must be in a quiet spot: behind were too many workmen, ahead, in moments, there would be too many women. Meanwhile the two in front were gathering speed also, in a hurry to attend to the final details of their plans.

Only a blowsy Sabine in front of the bawdy-house saw the strange procession approach, found it laughable and stayed in hope of fun. She heard Varres call, "Here again, within the hour" as he turned right and disappeared towards a number of imposing dwellings, and Rotus turned left towards the barracks. Edurus stopped in dismay.

"Come on", Decius caught up, puffing, "come *on*. If we take the big one first, we'll easily get the small chap later".

Rotus stopped to find his bearings where two roads met, and in that instant Decius' voice was smooth and friendly, his hand firm on the Briton's arm. "Greetings, stranger. You seem to need of help. May we be of assistance?" The fist of Edurus was firmer, less friendly, on the mark left by a silver armlet.

"A slave mark. You've been a slave?" His voice was over-smooth. "The life of a runaway slave is no sinecure they tell me: you do indeed need assistance".

"I do *not*". Rotus turned to protest. But the shackle was clipped fast. Round his neck was an iron collar, secured to Decius' waist by a heavy chain. Rotus lashed out and Edurus fell, before Decius tried the well-proved trick of his trade and yelled "runaway, runaway slave. Help with a runaway slave".

Rotus ran. Jerked off his guard for an instant Decius stumbled and was hauled along, still shouting "Help — runaway slave".

"With pleasure", the Sabine laughed, and struck. It's impact on Decius' head left a deep imprint on the large bronze pot, and the Sabine laughed the louder. "He'll sleep now, till we get that chain off. Come in here quickly and let me find a file. Julia, Valentia, Pennulina, see to the fellow on the road". She chuckled delightedly again. "My friends will be more than pleased to deal with the long ugly one — I think perhaps they have a few scores to settle. Meanwhile, keep still while I work, and hold this in case you need it".

She held out the bronze pot which had to be used once more before Rotus was freed, and the sound it made on Decius' head reverberated most pleasingly in the little room.

"Now we shall leave this one also to my friend Valentia — by the gods, we mislike these two in this house".

Rotus looked at her raddled kindly face and dared to ask, "Why do you stay here then?" She shrugged. "It's a living, I suppose. There are worse jobs". Then, very gently, she kissed his cheek. "Go lad, go home where you belong. This mark makes you prey for all the tricksters in the city and each of them is vicious. If you cannot go home, get you to the Catacombs on the Appian Way — there you may live indefinitely. All gods go with you".

Back in the street, Rotus found he was still holding the big bronze pot.

Varres was delayed: Aemilius, used to the longdrawn fawning of obsequious clients, could see no urgency in the

66

visit of a mere boy at this time of the forenoon. The boy, whoever he was, could wait. Fret as he might, Varres found no way to speed an interview, nor could he find anyone to answer his simple question: was his mother among this household? The tight-lipped Greek who seemed to be secretary or clerk or merely regulator of human traffic in the crowded vestibule, would say no more than "The master will see you in your turn".

When finally a message got through to the master that the son of a cousin Lucia was waiting to pay his respects the reply came back: "Let this new kinsman bathe and change his clothing and then he shall have the midday meal with the household". There was still no reply to his question.

Furious, Varres wondered whether to give up his quest and return to Rotus. "Back within the hour" they had agreed, and now his friend would be waiting. On the other hand, he must be absolutely sure about his mother, and if he left now he would lose what attention he had finally managed to gain in this interminable line of clients. So he let himself be taken to the bathhouse of his cousin's palatial home and submitted to a thorough cleansing and a change of tunic. This bath was not unwelcome: indeed he revelled in the routine of oiling and scraping and soaking in good hot water, and found the bathslave cheerful and pleasant. Yet not he either could tell whether Lucia was in that house, for as a slave of the male bathroom he did not meet any females except in the slave quarters at mealtimes. Certainly there had been no talk of a new lady, but one could not really judge by that.

The good fellow would have gone himself into the street to find Rotus and explain why Varres delayed but that a querulous young voice demanded his immediate attention.

Rotus was returning the bronze urn within the Lupanaria when Varres finally dashed out to find him, and the boy was at last in the presence of Aemilius while Rotus was kicking dust in the street with impatience.

67

After that interlude with the two hucksters of human flesh, Rotus avoided all who came his way. Certainly these were few, for the day was extremely hot. The blazing sun struck sparks from marble buildings and paved roads burned beneath his feet. A red mark chafed on his throat where the good Sabina's file had slipped, and another stung where they had prised open the lock of that shackle. Ech, waiting around in this heat was a trial of any man's patience. Should he try to make for the barracks again? Or might there not be others there recruiting men for anything but militia? If the soft-hearted harlot were right, he was well to put back his slave bracelet, and be seen to be owned already; but Varres had the armlet. Why did not Varres come?

The sun was beyond its greatest heat when the Sabine came swiftly to find him. "For the mother of gods, go man. We cannot hold those fools any longer. If they find you, they will have you branded. Go, *please*. I shall look out for the boy and tell him where I have sent you. I promise, but *go*".

Rotus kissed her and went. Behind rose the shout, "Runaway! help: catch a runaway", as he sped up side streets over an open space and into the wooded top of the Caelian Hill.

The wood on the hilltop was cool, but Rotus dared not delay to enjoy the shade. If he could reach beyond the next clear space and win into the street below he knew he could lose his pursuers; but there, too, there would be those nearer who would take up the cry without question: "Runaway. Runaway slave". Roundly he cursed his new freedom, and the impetuous action in which he gave up his symbol of slavery. With it still on his arm he would be safe from such predators as the short-legged one. For a spare breath he allowed himself to surmise how the good Julia and friends had settled scores with the two, and hoped they had had sweet revenge.

At last he reached the city gate, and the great road that led to the south, where it was not difficult to become a nonentity in the purposeful crowd. Nor was it difficult to join a funeral procession as it entered the burying vaults he was seeking, and in turn to lose the procession when he was ready to be lost.

TEN

Varres was caught in a net of adult good intentions. The wife of Aemilius had had her cook prepare an unusually large meal for that time of day, and expected it all to be eaten. Eggs, fish, fowl, followed each other with the leisurely progress of a banquet and though Varres sampled each course, he carefully avoided the sauces, of which one, he was sure, was of garum.

Aemilius, who could refuse his own son nothing, was most anxious, he said, to do his best for the lad who claimed to be his cousin's son. Kinsman or not, the boy was an orphan, victim of the punishment Jupiter had seen fit to send on the people of Pompeii. Poor child: here he must stay until fully recovered from his ordeal—or longer if he liked—and he must eat well and grow strong like the son of the house.

"If fat is strength", Varres considered irreverently, when Aemilius had spoken, "it would have been better to have called him Hercules" and was delighted to learn that Aemilius Minor had the added name of Crassus. Whose sense of humour had added that, he wondered: not that of the boy's father, for Aemilius Pater was kindly indeed, but restrained and oppressively sober. Rotus would be amused by the name's aptness.

Rotus . . . Poor Rotus would be waiting in the street and he would be hungry. He, Varres, must go.

Aemilius, however, would hear nothing of this. Varres must finish his meal. A slave would be sent to find Rotus and take him indoors for a meal too, but Varres himself must enjoy the good food, and the company of his cousin.

Indeed young Crassus was very amusing, and it was good to be in company of his own age again, and to laugh at schoolboy jokes. He and his friends had had much fun at their own schoolmaster's expense — as had every lad who ever went to school — but surely the grammaticus of this able mimic must be the funniest creature ever to hold a stylus. Varres was laughing heartily when the slave returned to say that there was no one on the street except a woman from the Lupanaria. The elder clicked his teeth in disapproval but sent the slave back to keep watch, whereat Crassus' mother egged her ebullient son on to further entertainment. Not only his tutor, but his father's friends, senators, and even the Emperor Titus himself came under the scurrilous lash of junior's tongue, to the indulgent amusement of his parents. Suddenly Varres tired of laughing — the schoolmaster is legitimate prey for juvenile buffoonry, but not the civic dignitary, and this was childish nonsense. He stroked his fuzzing chin and thought of his mother, and of Rotus. A man was waiting outside somewhere for him to begin on man's work, and he must go. He must.

Aemilius was not pleased. Here was a boy who brought out the most entertaining in his own son, a boy who might well become a permanent companion, while out there, if he were there, was an ex-slave bent simply upon his own purposes. Aemilius never yet knew of a slave who would not escape if he possibly could, and this was the chance of all chances for the Briton. He was astonished at the reaction of young Varres when this last point was put into words.

"Rotus is a man of honour. He would not break his word".

"A slave has no *honour*. He is a chattel. You are innocent of men if you believe that slaves feel or think like *us*." It was the young one who spoke, and there was no trace of

71

good-humoured banter in his voice now.

Varres in turn was astonished but courtesy checked his tongue, and with the utmost politeness he thanked his hosts for the meal and the tunic and bade farewell. The last words of Aemilius chilled him.

"Come back to us, cousin, when you have proved that I am right".

The Sabine had waited for hours to deliver her message, but no young lad appeared in the whole length of the street, and now she had work to do: a woman must live.

Varres too waited for hours, pacing the dusty paving with embarrassed feet, searching the face of each passer-by in the gathering dusk, and becoming more and more impatient with Rotus, with Aemilius and with himself. Would that he had never left his freedman's side. Why, *why* did he not come? He, Varres, had a responsibility for his father's slave: he must see, somehow, that the Briton achieved full and legal manumission, if not return to his homeland. On the other hand, could Aemilius possibly be right? Would Rotus welcome escape? Why, oh why, *why* did he not come or send a message? Might he possibly have returned to Aretria? Had he learned something of warning to Christians?

The hours passed. The street was deserted except where men entered and left the building nearby in a steady trickle of numbers. As he scrutinised each man, Varres would have asked news of the friend he sought, but that he feared to involve himself in anything that would take him from his vigil: and he heard of the dangers attendant on meetings of men, that took place in quiet streets. With night, he curled himself below a pillar and slept, and it was there that the secretary of Aemilius saw him next sunrise.

That Aemilius left his morning gaggle of hangers-on, to fetch the boy himself, might have pleased poor Varres if he had known the importance of being a patron, or been less miserable at the disappearance of his friend. As it was, he again submitted to bathing, a change of tunic and the prandial mimicry of the son of the house, without pleasure, or annoyance or pain. He was numb. His mother's loss he had borne, and become a man in the bearing, but this, his friend's defaulting, he could not comprehend. Of his companion and mentor of eight happy years he now had nothing but a silver armlet.

The catacombs were dreary, dank and cheerless, as befitted their gruesome purpose, but in their ling passages and dark recesses was safety from even more grisly prospects.

Having left the funeral procession with which he had found his way in, Rotus at first remained in a shallow recess not far from the entrance, until the familiar cry "Runaway" sent him further among the vaults. Here in the darkness he began to fear that he might never again find his way back to daylight and the chance to meet Varres when he came. Here too, he realised that he was hungry. The Sabine at the Lupanaria had said that he could live indefinitely in this place . . . not unless he found food, he thought wryly, and there was little chance of getting back to provision merchants until these two delightful gentlemen gave up their chase. Perhaps she intended to give Varres some provisions when she directed him here — if so, he wished she would hurry.

In musty darkness it was easy to let his mind wander, to pick around problems that ought to be urgent, to feel rather than to think. From time to time he wondered vaguely why he should be so necessary to those two thugs, why a woman like his rescuer lived in a place like that, why Varres had delayed and what kept him now, and what was to happen next, but for most of the time he merely felt — cold, hungry and infintely depressed. He dozed, and dreamed vividly that he was back in Fabia's kitchen enjoying her fish with plum sauce.

When he awoke it was to the knowledge that he was not alone. Somewhere, and very near, someone — two people — stood paused, expectant. He could hear nothing, strain as he might, only sensed the merest tingle on still air. He himself ceased to breath, but as his stomach knotted, he was sure that the movement went out to the intruders. Surely not his ears alone heard the thunder of pounding blood? The whole city must hear it, be drawn to him. A long moment hung endlessly over the tension.

Then a breath hissed into sound. "We're safe. There's no-one out there".

Rotus sat down before his knees gave way. The voice was that of Aretria. Were some of the group in hiding here? Was the rumour of a martyrdom becoming more than a threat? Who had betrayed his friends? Had Varres perhaps gone back to their house and let himself be followed? Was this why the boy did not come? Where was he now? So much required to be answered, yet if he spoke now he would frighten the poor woman more than she was already: if he followed, the brothers would feel themselves betrayed.

The dream of Fabia's cooking was still with him and he was hungry. At last he happend on the group, led more by his sense of smell than careful trailing.

"If your nose brought you to my cooking again, young man, I am flattered". Fabia had brought a steaming dish. "But I must remember to use only what is odourless. It would not do if the soldiery smelled us out because we yield to our appetites". Behind the light words there was anxiety that brought sober agreement from the others. The man Rufus seemed to be their leader, along with one whom they called Marcus, and there were in the gathering a few whom Rotus had met before at Aretria's house.

When he had told of his anxiety over Varres, a young man volunteered to go and search for the boy.

"I shall leave now, so no-one will see me, and be inside the gates at first light. No-one will notice a waggoner's boy taking hides to the tannery, or a builder's slave walking around with a hod of bricks. By to-morrow night when I return I shall be master of all sorts of trades and stuffed full of information." He smiled airily and was gone.

"We came here", Rufus explained, "that none of us might unwittingly betray any others, and because too, we have more to do for the brotherhood than feed the Emperor's lions. Titus wishes to appease his gods for their anger in Vesuvius, and how better could he do that than by sacrificing some of their rival's followers? I believe the aediles are preparing a memorable spectacle at the Circus to cheer the bereaved, the survivors, and the pampered lazy who are disinclined for work. But they are finding it very difficult indeed to recruit fresh meat for the animals. As you see, we have our retreats; and", he nodded, smiling quietly, "the brotherhood enjoys a battle of wits with the establishment, in a worthy cause". The smile dimmed. "Doubtless other sacrifices will be acquired from somewhere since we don't wish to co-operate, so all unattached people are well to remain out of sight for a time, you also Rotus. As for the boy, our young Stephanus will see that it is well with him.

For that day, therefore, Rotus slept, ate and talked with the group, and listened when Marcus prayed, while he summoned all his patience to await the return of Stephen at nightfall.

The youth came late, and alone. All day the little group had gone about their several chores, appearing and disappearing by routes known only to themselves, meeting at set times to eat and to worship, and at all times they seemed placid, and cheerfully serene. When a lookout reported that outside it was dark, Fabia prepared warm food again, and the rest settled to wait with calm expectancy. Only as the hours dragged on was the slightest unease to be sensed: a man might stop what he was doing, to wrap himself in a silence of his own for the merest breath; a woman would drop her head as she sewed, and mouth her own peculiar comfort, or lock her eyes with a companion to read unspoken words; and with each tiny private prayer Rotus felt stiffen in his mind the courage to endure.

But the lad came late, and alone. Rotus wished he could

pray for himself.

"Your friend is with his cousin Aemilius, safe on the Caelian Hill. There is no risk for him in that household—except perhaps of over-eating—for the good senator is a worthy and upright citizen, true to the best of the city's traditions—but stodgy, very stodgy, and totally without humour". Stephanus spoke lightly but he was distressed for this man's distress, and having spent all day in the city with sharp ears and eyes wide open, he was well aware of the various risks for all his friends. Baulked of a large haul of new converts to sacrifice at the Circus to-morrow, those responsible to the Emperor, and no less to the mob, were scavenging the highways and bye-ways for people who might never be missed. Even the labour force of the fat Adipatus was plundered, to that master's huge annoyance.

"I believe he is scratching himself thin with vaxation".

But Rotus could not smile.

Of the solitary, only those who were survivors from the three towns were left alone in their sadly independent state, for it was for the benefit of just such that the spectacle was being held. Rome was not a place where one ought to be alone, so Varres was safest with his cousin, and Rotus with the brethren here, awhile at least. In time he would see that this was true.

A youth of bubbling spirits and calm courage, Stephanus was sensitive too. Disgust and revulsion, sickness of spirit were on the woman's faces as they realised from where were drawn substitutes for themselves in the arena, so invading their thoughts he embarked on a vivid description of the day's activities. In a bundle of hides he had reached Aretria's house in time to warn off a new convert and send him to his father's farm. Rufus' cousin had been marketing when Stephen was butcher's lad for an hour, and was now on her way north with her family. A pickpocket on Via Sacra lost all his purses when, by the greatest stroke of misfortune, he bumped into Stephanus' fist, and a widow

76

from Stabiae blessed the mother of gods when two of the purses dropped at her feet. The heavens rained silver on several needy before that night fell. The public bathhouse being built in honour of Titus became two bricks the greater and half a wall the less, when the builder hired a new mason; and the Greek secretary of the patron Aemilius wore himself out translating the needs of a client newly arrived beyond foreign seas.

At last even Rotus was laughing and Stephen had earned himself rest.

ELEVEN

It was not as play-acting foreigner that Stephanus finally
had searched out a friendly slave in the house of Aemilius in
order to leave a message for Varres himself, but as an earnest
young man urgently seeking a comrade. The slave was most
amiable, and the message easy to convey, but as was usual in
that household, no contact could be made with any member
except through the master, and the Spaniard knew his duty.
Likewise he knew the punishment for disobedience. So when
Amelius was told that the friend of Varres was safe, but had
been delayed and would return for the boy in a few days, he
merely omitted to pass on the message. He had, after all,
spent a long afternoon persuading the boy that his former
slave had gone for good and was now probably well on his
way north to his homeland. It had been a difficult task, for
Varres was stubbornly loyal to his father's body-slave and
believed firmly that everyone, freeborn or not, was possessed
of that virtue called honour; but Aemilius persevered, for
here was an excellent companion for his highspirited son, an
educated boy who, unlike expensive Greek freedmen would
need no fee and seemed also to have a fairly frugal appetite.
Tutors had been none too willing, of late, to remain in the
Aemilius household, because they said young Crassus was
difficult, wayward, unruly — "a vicious little beast" one even
dared to call him. That one, Aemilius reflected with
satisfaction, had paid well for his opinion. Aemilius

persevered: Rotus was a deserter, a no-good; he had procured Varres' money and had departed; he was now showing his true colours; his treachery, merely subdued for so long, was obviously native. He was a blackguard.

At the moment then, Varres was in his house as companion of Aemilius Crassus, and seemed to be settling down. There was no need to unsettle him again with a trivial message from a mere slave.

Poor Varres had no alternative but to seem to settle down. What else could he do? One day he would join the Ninth Legion and go to foreign parts, but not now to the Britain of Abro'tus, not to the land of a traitor. Aemilius had done his politician's work well.

Meanwhile Crassus was a pleasant enough companion. His fund of stories was inexhaustable, his mimicry was amusing, if somewhat over-bold, and always he could find something of interest to do in an exciting city. Usually he was not restricted by his father, but for some reason Aemilius had refused them a visit to the Circus to-morrow. So Crassus today was indulging in sulks. For a boy of his own age, Varres deemed this to be childish but he kept his counsel to himself. It was not wise, he was learning, to be perfectly frank in this household.

In a few days they were to go to see a performance of the story of Daedalus and Icarus, which was bound to be exciting, so Varres concentrated on looking forward to the play.

Back in the gloomy cold passageways of the burying vaults, Rotus was tortured with impatience. True he took comfort from the fact that Stephen had left a message for Varres and from knowing that the lad was in good hands, with the wherewithal to eat and sleep in comfort, but he was wearied with having nothing to do, and he longed for the open and clear fresh air. Carefully hiding his impatience, for he knew that under their calm exterior his companions too had their tribulations, he helped with whatever chore there was to do — and indeed there was little enough to be done to keep everyone occupied. He trimmed and filled lamps, that Aretria might see to sew and Marcus to paint a picture on the passage wall, and then there was nothing to do but stoke Fabia's little fire in the far recess she claimed as her kitchen. At night a young man left the company by a way known only to himself and from somewhere replenished the store of fuel for a cooking fire, so Rotus employed himself by stoking, and more often than not was blinded as his eyes watered with the smoke.

These good people had made the very best of their cramped retreat, and the place held the warmth of friendship and care for each other, if not of physical comfort. Someone had wrapped a cloak round Stephanus as he slept, after his day's activity; an old man shivered, and his companion drew closer for warmth; the hand of Marcus faltered on his picture and there was soneone to encourage and admire. Yet there was nothing they could do to help the time pass more quickly for Rotus.

Yet it did, even those despairing hours before the dawn. That day, the one fixed for the wild beast spectacle at the Circus, the whole group remained together, in prayer, in meditation and what Rotus heard them talk of as "communion". He tried to listen and to understand, but there were gaps in his knowledge of the foundations of this faith, and he was depressingly concerned over Varres. Yet compassion for the victims in the arena he could surely understand, and he joined in supplication for their souls.

At first it was not easy; his father's gods Cocid and Mapone had never seemed to answer prayers; the almighty Jupiter of this great city and his brother Neptune of the seas had more power to destroy, one saw, than wish to save; that new god whom this group worshipped had allowed his very own son, they said, to die the usual death of a criminal or runaway slave. Not even the bloody-handed Mars could neglect his own offspring like that. Yet it was of this very crucified that they spoke as a friend, as one they numbered among their companions whether they had known him in

80

his life or not. Indeed the strength of their faith seemed to be the assumption of this friendship, the feeling of his presence with them even here.

Gradually, as they prayed, though he felt no "presence" yet, the mind of Rotus gathered peace and he was no longer under strain. In time he too was able to project his spirit upon the martyrs at the Circus and will that for them also there might be peace; and when, after all the purpose of his life-force had strained to touch these other beings in their distress, and limbs and body, throat and mind tingled to concentrate his spirit upon theirs, at last he felt the presence of that friend.

All that day Crassus sulked. There were no jokes, no stories, not one impersonation. Meals were dignified and infinitely tedious. With sharp native Roman wit made sharper by comparison to the lack of it in his father, Crassus was the life—and death—of his family's fun. Varres felt that he knew this very well, and made full use of the knowledge. His parents blossomed as he joked and teased, and wilted in his silence. To-day's silence wore a shroud of Stygian gloom. Varres would gladly have left him to his black mood and wandered off on his own, but Aemilius forbade him to go out. Never before having been forbidden to do anything without a good reason, Varres was dismayed, but wisely refrained from query.

Finally he took refuge in the bath, and in conversation with the good-hearted slave there. Form him he learned of the afternoon's doings in the Circus, and was promptly, most violently sick. Together they cleaned up. Unaccustomed to no more than bare orders and not at all to courteous help from a young master, yet the man recognised a great need that the lad should use his hands. The bathroom was cleaned till the tiles sparkled, and Varres could speak calmly about what he had heard.

"You were not there, Servilius?"

"Indeed no, young master, but the others talk of it in our

quarters. Some love the sight of mauled flesh and the smell
of blood and the screams of the terrified people."

"It's so cruel. I'm surprised the Emperor allows it".

"Not more cruel than crucifixion or stoning or scourging
to death—all quite in the fashion". The slave's tone was dry
as he oiled the lad's shoulders and back. "They say that
Titus enjoys these shows every bit as much as his people—his
father certainly did—although I myself believe that he
really feels it would be weakness not to. I know the master
Aemilius is not popular in some quarters because he will not
go to watch, and yet he too is a cruel man when his own
authority is crossed.

"But I talk too much. Aemilius is a good master".

Varres wanted the slave to talk for somehow in this man's
presence he was not so sure that his friend had deserted him
entirely, but he could not bring himself to ask what he knew
to be an unfair question; "Would *you* run away if you
could?" Instead he played safe with "Where do you come
from, Servilius?"

"My father was captured in Gaul, but I was born in
Rome. My mother too was a slave of Aemilius' father so I
naturally became part of the household. My parents died in
the year of the great fire in Nero's time."

"Now there was a cruel emperor". There was no harm in
denigrating the silly short-sighted old Nero, for had not
even Vespasion the father of the present emperor insulted
Nero's memory by altering his statue? Indeed old Nero was
good for a few ripe jokes, of which Crassus had a huge fund,
so he, Varres, the shy innocent lad from the coast might also
make bold with the name. "I've heard tell that he made
torches of some Christians once, to illuminate his garden?"

"Yes, my parents were among them".

Appalled, Varres gripped the firm hand that oiled him,
but all he could say was "I did not know".

The slave shrugged. "It is over. I was a child then and am
now a man. I have my slave-wife, and we have a child
Servilia—an easy name for a child born in slavery—and as

yet we are content. We eat and sleep and have each other; and our master is a just man on the whole. What more need we wish for?"

He took the strigil and gently scraped oil and sweat from the boy's body.

"Now, master, while you soak I shall fetch another clean tunic. It is well that Crassus has so many".

Varres could not let the subject rest. Of course, one did not ask who was or was not a Chrisian; from his stay at Aretria's he understood that one did not betray one's own beliefs in unfamiliar company: Rotus had said there was risk: yet he might, he supposed, ask why such treatment was meted to the followers of another god.

"After all, one more god would scarcely be noticed among all the gods we've already got. *Why* are they so cruel to Christians?"

Servilius considered carefully.

"Who could know? For myself I believe in all gods and no gods. Can one really trust any Supreme Being who can allow cruelty and hate and destruction? As for these Christians, my father believed firmly in their crucified one although he let it be known I was too young to be mixed up in a new faction. That is, I think, how most people view this sect, a political faction and threat to the government. Whether they are or not, I don't wish to know, but they themselves strengthen that impression—if they would yield to worship the Emperor's statue and the statues of Rome's gods, then no-one would care much what else they worshipped. But they are stubborn, and when the mob—or the senate—wants a target for spite and ill-will, there they are, obligingly being traitors by refusing to worship the Emperor. Ech, one is easier in mind not to think too deeply; and more comfortable not to listen to talk".

Varres was thoughtful as he dressed and went to the triclinium and his dining couch, and the possibility of Crassus' funny stories, that somehow were out of place when a city had dabbled in blood. But Crassus still sulked.

83

TWELVE

A few days after the show at the Circus the city had returned to normal. Survivors from the eruption of Vesuvius had departed for a new life, with state money in their purses, or had settled unobtrusively with relatives. Many found work on the massive rebuilding projects that the Emeror had on hand in Rome, and only the swollen ranks of scroungers and those who rejected the indignity of the pastime called work, showed that there had been an influx of outsiders to the city. These scoungers had enjoyed the entertainment provided and were waiting around for more, while they lived quite comfortably on state benefits, and spent most of their time watching builders at work and despising them for their energy.

Gradually groups of Christians in retreat filtered back to homes and occupations, but not until their scouts like Stephanus decreed that it was safe to do so. For Rotus it was not yet safe: Edurus and Decius and others of their kind were still on the prowl in the cause of their master's labour force.

As each further morning brought continued delay Rotus chafed and fretted, but while Marcus and Stephanus remained behind with him he could do little but bear the tedium and be grateful for their company. At length, after a complete day and a night ranging the usual haunts of the rodents of Rome as he called the two he was trailing, Stephen returned with the news that Adipatus and his gang had moved out of the city to where there would be much building going on, on the land given to survivors, so it seemed now safe for Rotus to take up his life again too.

Never had fresh air been so invigorating. Memorials along the Appian Way sparkled and gleamed to match his mood, and the crowd at the city gate were all splendid fellows, enjoying like himself, the joys of the open. Marcus had stayed behind finishing his picture of the lady he called Mary, Stephanus had vanished as he ever did, but Rotus was in no need of company. The world was his friend and he knew where he was going. The Caelian Hill to-day was beautiful, tree-crested in the sunlight and emerald smooth on the southern side. To the east and north lay the city; pure of line and marble splendid, burnished with the culture and assembled beauties of the whole world over which she ruled: gracious and bountiful and eternally virtuous. The word snapped his thread of maudlin thought. Where was the virtue in a city whose people wallowed in reeking bloodbaths and wanton cruelty? Rotus looked down to his left, half expecting to see the Circus stained red under his accusing eye, but it too shone gem-clean, a hypocrite to the sun.

Disgust settled upon his earlier mood. The sooner he met Varres and took him away from this cesspool, the healthier they should both be. Downhill and to the right lay the street where Aemilius lived. This would not take long.

In that street were also, to the shame of the censorious upright Aemilius, the villas Lupanaria, the houses of generous women. A pair of their least popular clients, newly laden with money, had spent the whole of the last two days in one or other of their rooms and now the women were heartily tired of both their manners and their money, and quite out of sympathy with the plea that the two had deserted their employer in order to patronise them. With scant regard for courtesy or trade, Edurus and Decius were being turned out of doors.

Decius saw Rotus first and his yell was part spite at the women: "Runaway. At last, at last. Runaway. Runaway salve".

The women did their hampering best and the men not unnaturally were tired, but the Briton had been caught off his guard and lost time in knowing where to run. The way he had come was steep and open, to his left a group of idlers lounged at the foot of a basilica, ripe for an amusing ploy—any moment they would join the chase. Behind, the street was empty, and there was a corner soon.

Edurus loped on, his long legs gaining ground as Rotus hesitated, though the Briton, once started, made speed. One street, the corner and another short street fled under his feet. In the next might be somewhere to hide. Decius, with more power in his lungs than his legs, kept up the cry "Runaway", behind Edurus who was pounding after Rotus, and those who saw the procession, joined in for the fun and noise. "Runaway", a man joined the cry as he left a city bathouse, and threw his toga over Edurus. They fell. Parcelled in the garment, they rolled and roared as "Runaways. We've caught them" rose from the next in line. Pinioned to the ground beside Edurus, the merchant swore and kicked, loudly lamenting the rent in his toga.

"Here is the slave. *I* caught him".

"*There* is the slave. He's still running".

Decius panted up, cursing his short legs, his night's work, his companion and the whole world's company of fools. 'The man we're chasing is *there*".

Across a demolition site, leaping waist-high piles of rubble and dodging among workmen and tools, Rotus fled, with the baying pack behind, till all of a sudden he was at the entrance arch of an Amphitheatre, where he bolted—only to be caged by tiers of tiers of seats. He had no intention of spending the rest of the day scrambling over and along these before a tightening net of pursuers, but where to go? The arena offered a short cut to an exit straight across but in its fresh sand he would leave a track not even the doltish

Edurus could miss. Behind, the rabble was increasing, for the long one was an entertainment to hear, and above the laughter and cursing, the shrill yell of Decius persisted, "Runaway. Follow a runaway slave".

"Sshhst. Come in here". A strong hand hauled him through a slit door, down steps into what looked like a guardroom. Shields hung on the wall and swords ranged on a rack. A man in uniform lolled at a table.

"Hey, Balbus. Run around the perimeter and deploy the rabble out there. You need an hour's training anyway this morning."

The man Balbus grinned, slid off leather kilt and corselet, shook his brief tunic and went out by a larger door. Shortly there was the renewed bellow of "Runaway. Ho, there's the runaway".

Rotus relaxed on to a couch.

"I see you really are—or were—a slave as that mark shows. But you'll have your reasons for getting out of that life and none of them are my business. Here drink, and rest awhile".

The wine was strong—extremely strong. In its heady draught swords, shields and barrack room danced a languorous greeting to Bacchus, the soldier became to turn a satyr, a nymph, a stolid be-laurelled Caesar. Rotus drooped. The shouts from outside had passed long since. Then they came again, faint and flagging, and died away.

Some time later the soldier returned.

"I led them a merry dance. Twice round the Theatre and in and out of a few entrances and now off towards the river. A swim will cool them down. Now who have we here?"

As the room steadied it was not difficult for Rotus to explain to these men and to recount all his history, save the days spent in the Catacombs. On his encounters with the rodents of Rome their comments were pungent and military, and Rotus warmed to their frank friendliness.

"I intend in the long run to join the army for overseas. Perhaps you can give me advice?"

"Oh, we are not soldiers, as such. We're a bit like yourself, prisoners of war, now in the Emperor's employ. I am from Gaul myself. We are gladiators trained for the entertainment of our very unworthy captors and the pleasure of the rabble of Rome".

Balbus grinned. "We don't work ourselves too hard, although we let the population believe that we do. It's not a bad life really".

Rotus' eyebrows showed surprise for he had heard of the rigour of a gladiator's life. To submit to the "burned, bound, beaten, killed with steel"—was that not their initiation vow?

"But dangerous surely?"

"Is not all life dangerous? You yourself were in danger by merely walking a street. No, it is not too bad. My partner and I have been matched for a year and we still fight hard enough to impress our public without inflicting but the lightest wounds. One draw of blood each for a contest is our limit—enough to keep the crowd happy—and the rest is feint and tackle, and a deal of subtle showmanship. Of course, my partner and I", Balbus squinted at his friend, "are very skilful with our swords".

"So were Flacchus and I". The Gaul's cheerful face dulled for a moment. "Why, we were partners for a whole season longer than you two, and it is only because the public were in a particularly dirty mood that day, that Titus was forced to give the thumbs down when old Flacchus slipped. He knew I was sorry. It was a quick death blow and he died like a man".

The trump that Balbus dealt the Gaul was of sympathy and friendship.

"It was indeed bad luck. You and Flacchus were well matched and you worked till you each knew the other's every move. You will be hard put to find another like him, one who will have the wit to cheat the blood lusts of the mob and still put on a convincing show".

Gallus sized up the stranger beside him, gently sucking his

cheeks.

"I am not sure that I will: my size and my weight I imagine . . . good limbs and shoulders, and strong thighs . . . long legs, for evasion. A bit out of training, and flaccid, and certainly cannot hold his wine, but a fair enough specimen of manhood".

He turned Rotus' face to the light.

"A profile to please silly women . . . and enough sense in my head for us both. Eh, Balbus, do I still lack a partner.

"Ho, Briton, wake up. Surely the wine has not drowned all your wits? Do you not see that I am offering you free food and lodging, a fine uniform as disguise against those scavengers, company wherever you go, and an easy life for at least a few weeks until you make up with your friend again? Faugh, the man's drunk yet or dolted".

Still staring at the Gaul, Rotus ponderd. The trundling winch that was his stultified brain was almost audible to the two at the table, but wisely they did not comment further. Somewhere behind his glassy eyes pricked a glimmer of understanding.

The fumes cleared and sense came, and with it cool native Caledon thinking. Suddenly captured by the effrontery of the proposition, if not by the dangers implied, he laughed and beat the table.

"Reporting for training at once, sir . . . if you have a spare sword?"

The wine flagon emptied and another took its place, before Balbus was despatched to find a uniform, and the approval of the trainer. With the second flagon, the first of many risks appealed to the Briton.

"Will the trainer want to know why I am here? He will see I am an absolute tyro—I wasn't even a soldier when I was captured".

"Listen, friend, in these barracks we are all liberal minded men, making a fair form of sport out of what is usually a bloody, beastly entertainment. No-one will turn you away seeing how you . . . shall we say . . .

volunteered—and a good strong captive costs a lot in the market these days. You will be given time to hide your ignorance and train in the techniques of the sword, and together you and I will work out a performance that will display all the skill the public wants without being too hard on either of us".

Balbus laughed as Rotus gaped. "Look, tyro, the people want to see skill—there's little thrill except for the really bloody-minded in seeing a killing too soon. On the other hand if we can prolong a fight with skill worth watching and neither man down, then they become wearied and call for the next pair. That way we live to fight another day. The wine is finished. I'll find the trainer".

His friend considered Rotus carefully.

"Of course, you must first gain proficiency with your feet: if you fall, then it's kerchiefs, or thumbs, and no question, and there are not always enough ladies in the seats to wave kerchiefs for a handsome profile. Flacchus was good-looking too, but he crossed the Emperor's lady. You must smile sweetly on them all, and on none too sweetly".

"Meanwhile, things may never come to a contest for you. What with wild beast shows and a waiting list for execution, there is not so much demand these days for us simple gladiators. I believe three criminals are for finishing in a day or two in what is billed as a spectacular mime—we do not need to see it and, of course, these Christians seem to need keeping down from time to time, as here the other day.

A memory did not please him, and he brooded for a time.

"When you rodents have stopped scratching the gutters for labour, you can flee from here as nimbly as you came, and make your way to the soldiery abroad. But don't go without telling me—I might wish to travel too".

Rotus was still agape at these new and extraordinary circumstances when Balbus returned with a uniform and accompanied by the barracks' trainer and a doctor. The doctor looked at the new recruit's teeth, prodded his biceps and stomach and padded off humming softly to himself.

The trainer was more energetic: he sized Rotus against the Gaul, prodded his biceps and his stomach, read over the rules of the establishment, explained the oath he must take, sucked his teeth like a ruminant cow and decreed,

"We shall call you Britannicus. It will look impressive on the bills".

THIRTEEN

Aemilius Crassus was in the foulest mood.

He had bullied his body-slave into describing in minute detail all that he had missed at the Circus, and with each spilling of blood, each torn massacred limb, each scream of terror or pain, he had revelled in the description and demanded more and more. Bloodlusty himself, and delighted that for once he could please, the slave piled terror on terror, agony on tearing agony, and drooled over pulped, palpitating flesh with the sensuous cling of a lover. Crassus hung on every word.

When he tried to recapture the scenes for his companion, Varres would not listen but went off to swim in the public baths.

Then Crassus changed his tune and ranted about his father: the old fellow was a fool, a mean stingy, stodgy old-fashioned fool who refused to move with the times. What other man of his position would keep his only son from the Circus? Who but an old stick-in-the-mud would deny his heir an essential part of his education? Never let him do anything that was *interesting*, did mean old Aemilius Pater. Was ever a son as hard done by as poor Aemilius younger? Did not Varres agree that Crassus was martyred by his fool of an old-fashioned parent?

Varres said a loud "No" and went off again to go

swimming.

Crassus sulked for nearly a week. His mother fussed and petted, father bribed and cajoled; and the brat, delighted, still refused to smile or eat. Mealtimes were dull, sober offerings to any god there was of Silence. Gloom hung again over the tables, daring the parents to eat while their child was in no mood to do so.

Varres watched his companion and began to dislike what he saw. He longed to leave the child-ridden household.

Even the prospects of seeing Daedalus and Icarus in a "spectacular scene in mime" had lost its appeal. All he wanted was to be away from here — at Aretria's in spite of whatever risk, or with Valeria and her husband and infant; with old Britannicus by the sea at Sorrentum, anywhere, but away from this pouting spoiled, bearded bullying baby.

That was it. He would bide his time, plan with care, and go to Sorrentum. While he planned, he would wait for that play about Daedalus.

When the day came, Crassus was all humour and gaiety again, as if his sulks had never been. His kind, good father was taking him to the play at the Circus, to an official's seat at that, and there was a place too for his good friend Varres. Busy with conjecture as to how actors could be made to fly on the scientist's exploratory wings, Varres paid scant attention to the gloating emphasis that it was to a Circus they were going. Plays he thought were at the theatre, but perhaps this was to be a performance of such a grand scale that only the Maximus would hold it.

His seat on the bench was baked hot with the afternoon sun, but anticipation prickled his skin so that he barely felt this discomfort. In seats reserved for magistrates, he and Crassus were the only young people, while above and behind, crowds, old and young, men and women, and even quite small children jostled and sweated and clamoured. Crassus had had his slave fetch a picnic basket which took up room on the bench beside him, while he nibbled at its contents. Now the slave had been sent home, and Aemilius,

93

on the muttered excuse that there was a client he had forgotten he must see, had slid from his seat and made for the nearest exist.

"Soft old fool" Crassus commented through a mouthful of fowl and eggs. "Want some?"

Excitement kept Varres from eating. The noise was terrific. Behind them men from the back streets elbowed and pushed, a crowd of the vast collegiate of non-workers jostled and called rude comments, children fought and scrambled; before and around, magistrates in the officials' seats talked buiness and greeted acquaintances, while their wives and daughters posed and preened, and discussed fashions in falsetto affectation. In a welter of new experience Varres was fascinated, if confused, and deeply engrossed in sorting out these fresh impressions.

Crassus was crashingly bored.

The lady Lepidiana, two tiers below, had spent much time on her toilet that morning, and the slave-girl responsible for her hairstyle was now lying down exhausted in her quarters. Crassus had a mind to improve upon the slave-girl's work. A pheasant's egg, stuffed, made little impression on the mountain of curls, but a honey-cheese sweet landed with a soft melting spludge and oozed over the lady's ear. Her husband turned with a scowl which melted, too in Crassus's beatific salutation. The dandy Naso had painstakingly trained his cultured curls to draw attention from a somewhat prominent nose, whose bibulous colouration he covered with a thick layer of powdered chalk. This Crassus dislodged with a deft peppering of soft grapes. No charming smile could turn Naso's wrath, and when he threatened to report Crassus to his father the boy was subdued for a time. But to his left, and downwards, the polished dome of his father's colleague Calvus offered strong temptation and he had eaten many cherries. Stone after stone popped merrily off the shining pate before Calvus located their source, and his fury too was vociferous. Only the appearance of the long awaited trumpeters stemmed his flow of words. Varres, out of patience with the childishness of his companion, pretended he was not with him.

He was engrossed in the inventor Daedalus of the ancient myth busy on the arena below, fashioning his axe, his wedge, sails, mobile toys, and a statue that took movement to itself. Beside him, Icarus his son was restless and impatient, though his nephew Talus became almost as clever as his uncle in inventing. The two busied themselves very convincingly. Varres was spellbound.

"So instructional," cooed a matron from the seat behind and Crassus loudly snorted.

Daedalus' increased jealousy of his nephew's ingenuity visibly increased until it crescendoed into frenzy, setting the audience tight and breathless in their seats. Up on a high crag poor Talus was driven, the audience with him in suspense, till at the top with a mighty shove he was pushed to his death below, and relief broke from the seats in a throaty "Ah." Daedalus fled from this crime with his son to Crete — a few paces along the arena — where he worked hard on the labyrinth of Minos, and was sentenced to death for his pains. The despair of young Icarus as he waited for his doom, Varres felt, was acting that would melt the hardest heart. Even Crassus muttered a feeling, "Poor fellow." Then hope was born with the idea of making wings, but even as he worked on his feathers and wax Daedalus emanated a palpable fatality. Varres felt with him inevitable doom, and marvelled at the actor. The wings were strapped on, instruction given and the pair catapulted from their prison. Icarus straight towards the golden orb of the sun high on a soaring pillar. Varres gasped; the machines of the theatre were marvellous. Down dropped Icarus on moulting wings to plummet on to the arena, and lie dying by slow painful spasms. Oh truly, such acting deserved the laurel crown; what a wonderful lifelike portrayal.

Meanwhile Daedalus had flown lower and landed more gently in Sicily, further along the arena. Borne down with grief, leaden with despair, at his son's death, of-course, he trudged wearily to and fro, back and forth, till Varres almost wished he might find relief in death at last. He did, in the claws of a ravening bear, and this death too was long and horrible.

Varres screamed. Jolted and appalled, he rose from his bench and shouted "Stop it, stop it. That bear will really kill him." but Crassus pulled him down and hissed,

"What did you expect, you fool? This is a public execution."

A long time later Varres struggled back to consciousness. The seats were empty except for Crassus at his picnic basket and the lady Lepidiana with her slave; all traces of the play had gone from the arena except a trio of browning splashes where three corpses had been. Varres fainted again.

"Where is your slave? Your father should never have left you: I shall speak to my husband about his negligence".

Crassus smiled sweetly at the lady. M'hercule but she could scold.

"When my husband returns he will hire a litter to take this poor boy home. *Then* I shall have something to say to your father".

Two gladiators crossed the arena prepared, it seemed for practice.

"Ho, fellows. Come here and help us".

"Lepidiana the emperious" Crassus thought, mincing her words to himself for future enjoyment. Aloud he was charmingly deprecating.

"My father will be most grieved."

"And so he should be." The gladiators arrived. "Young men, we need your help to carry this boy home. We won't wait for my husband — probably forgotten me anyway — I should not suppose there will be a litter anywhere to be found in this totally inefficient city. Take the boy. Slave, the basket, and you boy, your support please, on these steps".

Gallus and his new partner saluted and turned to the inert body. Only the Gaul heard Rotus gasp, and was quick to whisper "Careful partner. Take things calmly, eh? Don't put the boy at risk?"

There was a thick dark fuzz on the young face that lay heavy on his shoulder, but the pallor beneath, wrung Rotus' heart. The child had grown, and shrunk, and was neither man nor boy. As the street sloped into the hill of rich men's houses, Gallus took over his friend's burden and in the moment of transfer Varres' eyes flicked open.

Rotus whispered "We're both safe, friend. Have no fears. I shall come for you as soon as I am able", but the lad's eyes were shut again, his body limp.

Lepidiana talked on.

At the house of Aemilius they laid the boy on a couch and were dismissed. Rotus would have spoken again, left a message with the other boy or his mother or a slave, but the Gaul spoke first to prevent him.

"May we come back, good Domina, to enquire for the boy?" he begged, furning lustrous Gallic eyes on each woman in turn.

"Of course, of-course. Whenever you like. My thanks. Now go." Lepidiana replied, for who paid regard to the wife of Amelius?

"Now what did your husband mean by leaving these children alone in that frenzied mob on a suffocating day like this? Upon my word, some men have less sense than . . . a . . . a lump of cheese. Which reminds me, good lady, that I have a word to say of your son. . . ."

The magistrate's wife was in full voice. For lack of her usual audience, her husband, she made good use of what she had, and started all over again when Aemilius senior appeared.

Out in the street Gallus sagged in feigned exhaustion. "By Jupiter, no-one could match that one in a fair fight. She would talk a champion to a standstill."

"So that is your young Varres? A sizeable manling and no light weight. I could make a swordsman of him too. . . ."

"You should have let me leave a message. . . ."

"Which might never be delivered? My good fellow, as I told you at our last practice, you must not make your moves known to the whole audience. Keep your tricks where they are fully appreciated. Now, *my* approach has brought the solution you wanted. We may go back there when we wish, to pay our respects to the boy—and none of that lot will know of your interest."

"But your permission came from the wrong woman."

"I know, I know. One of my subtler moves. The lady of the house herself might have refused. Now in the face of that disapproving virago, she dare not. I have a feeling that the talkative lady Lepidiana is delighted to have a chance to bully that household for quite a time to come. She'll be there when we return to-morrow—would you care to wager?"

She was there on the morrow. So were her own private doctor, her secretary, her hairdresser and her cook; but Rotus and Gallus delayed by the small matter of a surprise inspection by the Emperor himself, reached no further from the barracks than the nearest tavern when dusk fell.

The following morning, early Aemilius and his entire household were on their way to the hills to the more remote of their summer homes, and Lepidiana, furious and frustrated, had not the slightest inkling of their where-abouts. Her wrath fell on Gallus when he came to pay respects.

Alone in the horsedrawn litter in case his condition might be catching, Varres hovered in a half-life of dreams and tortured wakefulness. Wild bears, the volcano, a poor demented man-bird, and a sullen over-fed schoolboy jostled in and out of grey scum rivers that were his wakeful mind. At times he felt that Rotus was again with him, holding him as he would a child and his words were soothing and distinct: "Have no fears. I shall come for you as soon as I am able." Then the face of his friend would vanish into that of a helmeted stranger, or of Aemilius peering at him to ask if he were better.

Poor Aemilius was troubled. Goaded to distraction after a day of the garrulous, over-bearing Lepidiana, his wife had been on the verge of the weeping sickness on the day before, and only a firm promise that they would depart before sunrise, had seemed to calm her. Now she sat in the raeda amid hurriedly packed luggage, exhausted, drab and plainer than ever. Crassus was sulking, worn out too, with the effort to persuade his father that his behaviour at the Circus had really been exemplary, and hurt to the heart, he insisted that his parents actually took the word of old Nosey against his, and believed that painted harridan and the silly bald-headed senator. Indeed, he was too hurt, he said, to speak any further.

Aemilius was more troubled, however, by this malady of his new ward. The doctors had no idea what it was, or even if it were catching. As for the expensive charlatan brought in by that domineering crone of a wife of Lepidus, all he could rake up from a muck heap of theories was that the boy was possessed of a demon or two.

Aemilius turned his horse once more in order to peer into the curtained litter. This time the lad lay inert, staring dead-eyed at nothing. It was a quiet demon, now, in possession.

Before, the man had been afraid at the screaming, tearing, terror that filled the young frame from time to time, for he once had had these fits himself and knew well what set them going. Why else did he avoid the Circus, or leave before the beast shows commenced? A man of authority, and kind, well-meaning to a fault, if somewhat inflexible of mind, he was ashamed of his lack of blood lust, and so, afraid to see it in another. Thus he grasped at the theory of the demon, and paid the medicus sweetly to give it and go away.

None of this would he tell to his wife lest the bold Crassus might hear, so Varres rode in a litter alone, as one with a catching disease.

99

FOURTEEN

Rotus fretted and fumed and all but quarrelled with Gallus. To have found his charge and so soon lost him again was infuriating in the extreme. As his temper showed through his swordplay his trainer was anything but pleased.

"You ram-headed, flat-footed, ill-natured son of a blue-painted barbarian, *think* what you are doing. You must watch, judge, assess, *think calmly* before you make a single move — or it's wet flesh you'll be on the sand. Then off to the carnarium with you, and who will deem you a loss? Now *here*", he pointed on the practice post, "you aim to scratch, but *here* you aim to kill — or he'll kill you. In all things be cool. *Again!*"

After two hours of this Rotus had sweated his temper away and docketed his further setback as it belonged, among the natural hazards and frustrations of living outwith himself. Meanwhile a cup or two of the barrack-room wine had a mightily cheering influence, and Gallus was again the best of fellows.

Before they selpt that night it was accepted by one and all and by Rotus in particular that the only sensible way to get through life without very much trouble was to wait patiently for whatever turned up, and they all happily drank again to that maxim.

It was not, after all, such a bad life. He had companions,

food, wine, clothes, exercise and something of a position. Ruffians in the city stood aside when gladiators passed; ladies of fashion had been seen to look his way from daintily curtained litters; and when he was not exercising new expletives in the extravaganza of his invective, the barracks trainer even seemed slightly pleased with the progress of his latest recruit. Rotus worked hard and as the days passed he acquired more than moderate skill with his sword and a nimbleness of foot that surprised all but himself. For him this was merely a welcome return of the grace and speed of his early years spent on rocky hills.

When their trainer went so far as to comment on his progress, Gallus saw fit to add a word or warning.

"If you go on at this speed all the time partner, we'll be sent into the arena before we know it. Slow down, man, and give us time, as a pair, to work out a foolproof routine. I have no wish to be flattened by a mere Briton". So Britannicus of the barrackroom curbed his enthusiasm and though he missed not a moment of practice or a word of the trainer's advice, he was careful not to make his progress too apparent. When they could, he and Gallus worked on their own private technique, criticised and encouraged by Balbus and his partner, and their scant leisure time they spent, all four, together. There were times when Rotus caught them looking at him with eyes of speculation, and was at pains to seem even more of a fine fellow than he was. Then the look would die, and their male activities progressed uninterrupted.

As September wore towards its end, the gladiators were kept strictly within their traning area, and hours of extra practice left them neither time nor vitality for other ploys. Finally, two days before October began, they were all assembled in the arena to be addressed by the Master of the Games.

"Men of the sword", he said, "men skilled and fortunate in the service of our noble citizens".

Gallus nudged Rotus. "This approach spells trouble—he

has a job on hand for us".

"Men of noble art, you are of the elect. You are the favoured of the Emperor".

"Ech", Balbus grunted from behind, "he talks too much, like all senators. There is oil on his tongue—would there were more on his palm, stingy clod".

"The Emperor has chosen that you, men of the mighty sword, will do honour to the tutelar gods of the new month. What better greeting may we give to Mars and his sister Minerva—who have in their hands as you know the guardianship of Mensis October—what better greeting, I ask, may we give than a show of the skill of their favoured warriors?"

"Pompous garrulous old ass", Gallus hissed. "Favoured . . . Iove! . . . Some favour to have to use our skill before the likes of him".

"Two days from now there will be held here in this arena, a mighty magnificent spectacle of gladiators—the men of the Eastern barracks against those of the West, omnes ad unum".

"Hercule, that means all", Balbus spat. "All on one afternoon. All to the end".

"All . . . before the Emperor himself". As if he had heard and was looking for the speaker the Praetor glowered around the assembly before adding, "And the honour will be yours, in the favour of the Emperor".

His chubby form bounced down from his rostrum and bowled away towards the senatorial exit, leaving his audience to their reactions, and their trainers.

The hours that followed left them limp, sweating and vociferous. The partner of Balbus, a large usually silent Helvetian ox of a man, produced a flow of imprecation that would do justice to their instructor, and kept it up all the time the quartet bathed, changed and ate. Rotus alone held his tongue. This was more than he had bargained for, but since he had chosen to follow, at least for a time, this particular way of life, then he must cope with all its hazards

102

as they came. Gallus would teach him a trick or two, in the form of combat expected, and then he could only hope for the best . . . or pray to what gods he believed in.

He pondered. *What* gods? A few months ago he would have said "This new god, this all-powerful, of Paul and Stephen and the crucified one", but now after all the chances and changes his fortunes had undergone, he was more inclined to believe in the Sisters of the Shears, the three blind Fates. In the days of his youth he had been able to *explain* happenings, or to find a reasonable cause — yes even the event of his capture those years and years ago. Now nothing had good cause attached in his life these days. The Christ's god or Mapone, the Mother of Gods or the Fates, all seemed blind to his needs.

When they were at last alone in the small cell that was their shared billet, the Gaul expressed his regrets.

"It's my fault you are in for this, but I did not imagine we would be on show so soon and in an all-in bout at that. It's so long since we've had one of these that I thought they had gone out of fashion. The Emperor must have got a number of new prisoners, all expert in sword play, since he wants rid of at least half of his old ones. Or maybe", he laughed ruefully, "he thinks to cut down on our food bills".

The description of what must be done in the kind of contest that was planned, did not cheer Rotus in any way, and although he was a man of as great heart as the rest, he had bullfrogs in his stomach all night and all the next day. When evening came, with its gladiators' formal public banquet, the bullfrogs were in full throat. At first he barely touched the delicacies set before the contestants — even an olive would have choked him, he felt sure. Then Gallus whispered,

"Easy man. You might as well enjoy what the Emperor has provided. In any case, if you show yourself to be nervous, that lot", he waved a tasty roasted dormouse towards the gaping herds of the public, "that lot of goggling fools will notice, and mark you in the arena. Then they'll yell till they see your blood. Eat, look calm, and persuade them that you are an uninteresting, bloodless old diehard, like me".

He helped himself liberally to the next course, and made Rotus do so to.

Long before dawn, they were awakened by the clamour, outside, of the populace jostling for priority of place when finally the gates would open. Apprehensive gate-keepers tested their locks and rehearsed their plans of evasion when the time of opening came. Why, early in September, there, at the beginning of the great City Games, two of their colleagues had been trampled under the surging rush, and their end had had little dignity.

Gallus and his comrades burnished shield-boss and sword, helmet and greave, and oiled the thongs of their sandals, while they listened to the clamorous, irreverent crowd, and with the work, Rotus gradually felt his spirits lift. His situation began to seem even amusing. Out there, an aimless gaggle of bird-heads scrambled to be entertained, to see some sight or other, some spectacle to pass their leisure, while within were men of courage, all wrenched in their time from former, busy, satisfying lives, now wasting energy in preparing to make the fools goggle. He chuckled: if Gallus and he were spared after this bout, he had thought up a trick or two for the next, to tickle their silly fancies, and mock all foot-licking officials . . . if they dared to use the trick. Of course, they'd dare. If he survived this day, he'd dare anything; if not, then he'd not. That was all.

The day's occupations wore on. The gates opened and the mob surged in, shouting, quarrelling and elbowing even when they reached their seats. The men of the sword broke their fast.

The rabble argued, made bets, conversed with cronies: the gladiators bathed and purified themselves for possible death.

Refreshment vendors in the arena sold their goods and returned to replenish their stocks; the swordsman offered some gift to the god of his choice, and readjusted his deep leather belt the further to protect his loins.

The rabble fought with their neighbours and clamoured for the show. The Emperor and his train took their seats, while the crowd shouted at them too and did not curb their curses. At last the fanfare brought a lift of quiet on its tail.

A river of burnished metal flowed over the fresh sand, over and around, then divided before the Emperor's box. Two hundred swords rose in salute and two hundred voices rumbled, "We, we are about to die, salute thee, Caesar". The crowd roared approval.

The river of bronze flowed smoothly back and away, leaving only a pool in the centre. Two men alone were left, one holding a net and trident, the other a sword and shield. The fight was sharp and vicious. In moments the man of the sword was netted and lay stuck, like a pig. An attendant, black, and dressed as Mercury, trailed off the corpse and raked the sand as another pair came on. Of these, one carried a gleaming crescent blade and small round shield, while his opponent wore a bronze sea fish on his helmet. Their contest lasted longer, but finally the fish fell to the wicked scimitar in a spray of jugular blood. The mob wallowed and roared and gurgled; the Emperor's lady smiled.

Pair followed pair in the heat and dust and the scavenging Mercury hauled and raked and sweated.

Another retarius with trident and net appeared, skipping and clowning, grinning impudently at the imperial box. The crowd yelled. The gladiator hard on his heels had the strength of two and was nimble with it, but the mob was clearly on the net man's side. To-day at least, his impudence would save him. He sprang and danced and pricked his forked spear beneath the other's guard, yelling obscenities to the delighted seats, and leering at the Emperor's women. No bawdy-house tout would have got away with such jests, but the crowd, and the Emperor's lady, loved him. The gladiator fell, the trident in his groin.

Trumpets sang for silence to greet the bout of the day.

Swiftly, two sides lined up with only four paces between. On the right of Rotus was his partner, Balbus on his left, and on his left again, the powerful Helvetian ox. Straight in front were four of the Wests, all good fellows, comrades of a roystering night or two, and experts in barrack ribaldry. When the trumpets brayed again what was left of the two hundred marched neatly to fighting order, beating a final prayer to Atropos in the tread of compliant feet. Rotus and his three comrades stepped smartly back and to the right as some twenty swordsmen of the First Order side-stepped to meet a like number of the same from the Wests, on the edge of the prescribed four paces. The crowd silenced, and some even stopped munching, the better to comprehend the design of this novel formation. Twenty men of the Second Order lined up several paces behind on each side, and behind these again at a similar interval, were the Third, with, finally, the Fourth, the Tyro Order, with Rotus in their number. So too, surprisingly were Gallus, Balbus and the Ox. As eight ranks faced each other grimly the mob settled to savour the possibilities in this sport. Why, a First Order swordsman might have to fight his way through three opponents and even then not be downed — or be felled by a mere tyro from the rear rank. Oh indeed, this was gambling sport this afternoon.

The Emperor's kerchief fell. Sand powdered and rose under fifty riffling pairs of feet as the four paces shortened and the front lines met. Sword fell to sword in half hearted dints; feet danced, weapons glinted; now and then a man grunted. A brave show of busy-ness swallowed snatches of time.

Gallus nudged his friend. This moment-wasting tactic might possibly pay off. Skill and technique would please the Emperor, but would it appeal to the mob?

Light blow and parry, thrust and retract held the spectators for little longer than a long-drawn breath, a breath of disgust. On their feet and yelling, they assured the Emperor, his lady and every mother's son of the swordsmen

106

that, by Iove, if this was the stuff they would see, they'd be into the arena themselves, by the gods.

"Pity they wouldn't", Balbus croaked and swore his finest oath.

Down the line an unfortunate slipped, a sword tickling his hairy bare chest. The mob sighed in an instant of hope, but he was on his feet in a flash and waggling his own sword at his opponent's chin. Titus looked grim, his lady scowled. Trainers took the message in the imperial eye and found their own ways to pass it on. If the contestants continued this tomfoolery there were hungry beasts at the ready for a meal. Death at the sword, with honour, were better than that.

The lines stiffened. Metal clashed and sang; men muttered. Over the recurrent thud of sword on hide, and hiss of slicing air, a low rumble ran of grunts and imprecations. Boots gritted on sand, leather slipped on loins; sword points scraped and slid on greave and boss. The tide of bronze heaved stormily, flanked by steady silent pools.

On each side three lines of reservists stood erect, motionless, intense. The best of the opposite side would be their opponents, so it was well to observe and absorb and endeavour to prepare.

The crowd in the seats were happy. They commented and guzzled and cheered.

A man of the Wests went down, to be speedily dispatched. The black Mercury raked him swiftly aside while his counterpart of Class 2 took his place.

A woman's voice screamed joyfully, "Habet, habet—he's had it. Well done, Easts; let's see more".

Rotus glanced at Gallus and swallowed.

"Eyes *front*, man; don't let them see you are nervous. Just pray that we four reach the fighting line together, for that way we may protect each other".

"Can we? I mean protect each other".

"Of course". Ballus produced a hoarse chuckle. "I forfeited a First Rank bonus for the pleasure of having you

107

fight beside me".

The Ox hissed, "Shut up. We'll forfeit even the Tyros' benefit if you bring the Goad up with his whip".

"See, two Easts down".

"That's your line and mine, Gallus. Us soon, m'hercule; may he preserve us".

The front ranks were falling steadily now, replaced at once from the line in reserve. Black Mercury had called in his assistants and all were kept busily raking. A sickening smell rose from the sand to make Rotus' stomach lurch and the back-benchers crow with delight.

Titus thought of his Empire and problems imposed by the mob; if only this fashion had never started, of feeding the worthless with blood, he might not nowadays be nauseated by the sight of good meat at meals. Ech, this pandering to the masses was a strain and becoming a bore—to say nothing of depleting his coffers. If only these men would make haste and get this blood-letting over and done with, for this afternoon at least.

One man only of the First Order still stood, a stalwart of the Wests, fighting his way through to the tyro of his late opponent's reserves. The Easts were reduced to the remnants of a sorely depleted Second Order and the bulk of an unreliable Third. Soon, as Balbus had whispered, the fight would be theirs; theirs the sand or the laurel.

Rotus did not know that he prayed, did not see Gallus squint at him under his helmet. The mob were yelling, "Habet. Cut his throat. Show his blood", then Rotus himself was on the fighting line. Dully in his bursting head he recalled his trainer's advice, sought to use tricks he had learned from his partner. Warm reek filled his nostrils, his stomach; lead trickled in his veins, but his sword arm was not of his own possessing. Dimly aware of his comrades now beside him, and some fellow in front beyond his shield, he let his feet and his arm live their own lives, himself seeking only to avoid metal and metal. There was a music in the noise, as of a singing wind in his former happy hills, a tintinnatus of summer water gentling over moulded stones; or the male-throated crump of autumn seas talking to the shore.

Sweat beaded his back and trickled on his loins; his leather girdle clung and chafed, the grip of his shield ran wet. The figure before him loomed larger for a breath, cleaving the sunlight to splintering golden fragments of pain, and vanished in a haze of sweaty dust. His sword arm threshed again, to the right, and the other fellow sank. Rose-grey mist eddied and swam; the music swelled and rolled; breath hissed, and splintering agony tore on breast and arm.

Suddenly the Emperor had seen enough. Whatever the mob or his court might feel, he, Titus, had had a sufficing. Trumpets blared the finish.

Sand rose as an unwary tyro fell, buying a moment's surprise with his heart's blood, then the dust rose again as a pitiful remnant raised swords to the Emperor's box, and turned to march away.

"Te salutamus, Caesar", a voice slurred insolently over the crowd's dissatisfied roar.

"Hush man. Hush. Mother of Gods, not here, not now. Hold *up*, man, till we reach the barracks".

Gallus' shield pressed hard in the Briton's side, and Balbus' sword arm into the other, while, behind, the hot metal of a shield boss urged him on. "Keep going, man. We're nearly there. They must not see you stumble".

"No? Caesar, we salute you; Caesar son of a skinflint . . . we salute . . . We about to die, salute . . . Jupiter all powerful, God of all gods, why should we? We. . . ."

The shield pressed harder, lifting him up and on. Sun, swords and jostling rabble melted in a livid pool of pain.

Rotus awoke to find Gallus and the doctor torturing the flesh of his breast, and he fled thankfully back to oblivion.

In the shapeless misted days that followed only the doctor was clear, for he brought wakefulness and tearing pain. Once it seemed that Stephanus appeared and held long

109

council with Balbus, the Gaul and the Ox, and their voices held the purring of the wind in many trees. Rotus cried out as they swam and sank away and the medicus chuckled, "Yes, Rotus, lad, we come in all guises in the brotherhood".

FIFTEEN

The remoter of Aemilius' farms was pleasantly cool after the torrid city and the hot, dry, jolting ride to the north, but the lad Varres had little will to enjoy his surroundings. When at last the fever left him and the hideous nightmares ceased, he was listless and depressed, and missed his home and parents with a gnawing consumptive ache. Worst of all he felt the desertion of his companion, his father's trusted henchman, the slave he himself had freed.

In the early days of the fever, young Crassus had left Varres severely alone, as indeed had the household, for fear of taking whatever disease he had. They were kind in their way, and gave orders daily that the boy should have what he wished at the hands of a slave, an expendable old fellow from Crete, but they were none of them willing to expose themselves to his malady.

The Cretan slave was kind, amusing the boy as he might with tales of his home, or irreverent anecdotes about his masters, but even at his guileless stories Varres found it hard to laugh. The old man was worried: the boy was still such a child in some ways to be left at the mercy of the world and of such as young Crassus.

It was Fundanus, bailiff-slave of the farm, who suggested that Varres might care to help with the horses and find healing in the growth of things. Aemilius uttered no

111

objections to the possibility of extra free labour, and when the Cretan asked to join him in the bailiff's quarters, "to feed and look after the lad", the lady Aemilia was relieved to agree. This kinsman boy of her husband's was a responsibility she could well do without, especially since he was proving to be no companion at all for her son. Dear Crassus was a lively lad: of course, he had times of waywardness, but what young man of high spirits had not? This Varres had no spirit.

So Varres moved into the bailiff's quarters and lived there among his family.

Varres was content. Fundanus and his conserva were very kind, their daughter reminded him of Aurelia at Sorrentum; the old Cretan had less work to do and more freedom to tell his stories. The horses were beautiful.

Mellow September wore to an equally mellow October as Varres began to live in a peace of mind had not known since the day he had sailed to the island. The ploys and skills of farm life fascinated him and he learned quickly, careless whether the job he did was for a free-born lad to do, or for a slave. There was indeed healing in helping things to grow.

On the day when Stephanus arrived, Varres was grooming a chestnut stallion. The perfect beast was spirited, perverse on occasion, even wicked, but he had a feeling for the boy that Fundanus saw and recognised. Such a pair would make a wonderful team in a race, he thought, in a race or in a battle. But Aemilius would not agree that the boy should ride.

Stephanus came quietly, with Fundanus, and it was clear that the two were friends. When he left, late, Varres was happier than he had been for weeks. The little god of merriment never far from the scout of the Catacombs had awakened a mate in the orphan youth and they laughed together, greatly pleasing the Cretan. There was no malice in this laughter, no ill-will; this was a real companionship for his charge. That Rotus had not deserted him brought the greatest joy, and Varres asked several times that Stephen repeat what he had heard from Gallus and the doctor and seen on the barrack room cot. Now he was impatient to return to his friend so that they might make their way north together.

Stephen the irrepressible had a plan, full of possibility, that even Fundanus finally agreed might work—at least he gave it his blessing. Varres gasped when he heard it, then laughed, and kept laughing, a deep throaty rumble that became part of his moments alone and now he was even more impatient to get back on the road to Rome.

Crassus was easy prey for his persuasions, for he was bored with country life. The Circus and the public baths, some new scandal on which to try his wit became delights he could not wait for, as Varres fanned his desires with neatly conjured suggestion. Mindful of Lepidiana, he wisely omitted to mention Circus to his father among reasons for returning to Rome, concentrating instead on affairs of state, the senate and the need for all wise members to keep an eye on the expenditure of this Emperor. Titus, one heard, spared no public expense—was it not for the like of shrewd, careful, responsible father Aemilius to restrain too deep delving into the coffers of the state? Aemilius agreed, for it was from such as his very own taxes that these coffers were filled in the first place.

Soon they were all south-bound again, in various degrees of relief. Varres parted from Fundanus and the Cretan affectionately, with the merest glint of conspiracy as their eyes met, but as this friendship was not of the household, neither Aemilius nor his son deigned to witness its dissolution.

At last they reached the city. By the carriage gate a lean youth took their baggage, and if he grinned at their kinsman, none of the family noticed that either. Varres saw Stephen overladen with heavy baggage but Stephanus would have none of his help.

"Do you wish to lose me my fee?" he hissed. "A good fat fee from your guardian? Besides, this is a trade I have not

113

yet practised—let me become as adept at this as at all my other skills. Would you discourage my education?"

Crassus saw his cousin as very coarse, talking to a street boy so he tucked in his cloak and turned up his nose and hastened behind his mother. Aemilia sighed with relief to be back in the confines of her close town house. If her dear Crassus was happy, this Varres interested her not at all.

And Crassus was happy in the days that followed. He had an audience again, in his kinsman, an audience surprisingly receptive, a companion surprisingly enthusiastic. They went to the Baths, joined the talk of the day, wrestled in the Campus Martius, watched the world at play; rode, raced, drove; attacked any and every pastime with the verve and enthusiasm of long deprived youth. If from time to time Varres saw a wrestler, a groom, or slave with strigil and oil, and each met his look and passed the time of day, then Crassus knew nothing of it, for Crassus was either engrossed in his present ploy, or agog for the next diversion.

It was the groom at the riding stables who mentioned the show at the Circus on the day after next. There was to be that day, he said, a gladiators' show, a fight to the death, a fight where the survivors of the last big contest, wounded or well, were to finish each other off to the very last man. The Emperor's lady, in a spectacular rage after the last show, ordained it. The contest, the groom promised, would be interesting to say the least, surprising, if one liked surprises. Crassus waxed enthusiastic, and Varres was content.

Later, while Crassus entertained his father's friends in return for the promise of magistrates' seats at the Circus, Varres went riding from the stables. He and the groom found a great deal to discuss besides horses.

SIXTEEN

Britannicus the gladiator lay awake, his shield arm moulded to his chest. Whatever they had done to him in those days of swimming dark, left now a dull weight of pain. Balbus and Gallus fed him gently and held wine cups to his lips; the Ox sat by him often, merely watching.

As days passed, these men and the small sleeping cell became his world. The time before Vesuvius never was; the days after, a kaleidoscope of dreams. Long, long ago, there had been something in his life that was akin to this, something bound, like this by pain and sweat, but what, he could not remember. All that was vivid in his memory was a woman's face, beautiful, lively, compassionate, beneath a braid of bronze-red hair. One day he might find a name for this beauty, but not now; the effort to remember was too great.

The doctor sucked his cheeks and worked away. Balbus grinned cheerfully as he fed him; Gallus was there when his wound was dressed; the Ox gave his arm to clutch at in relief from pain. Days wore on, and pain gradually assuaged. His arm and his breast at last lived separately, but still his head was thick and his little world was a barrack cell. The men did their best. Even the trainer came once to visit and practise his invective.

"Do your people really paint themselves blue before a

115

battle?" Balbus echoed the trainer's mellowest oath and chuckled deeply. "Do they truly wear nothing but their shields?"

Through misted head Rotus found a laugh.

"My tribe fought only when we had to, and then we did not take time to think about it. We were too busy plying swords to be daubing ourselves with woad".

"But even the great Caesar called your people the Painted Ones".

"Even the great Caesar was nowhere near my homeland. Even Cerialis fell short of it by many days' march".

Talk tired him, especially talk of his home. The weariness of exile lay, with his wound, sore on his breast. But his friends were good: he must not seem surly or impatient.

"A few tribes of my Caledons do certainly go into battle stripped for sacrifice, but most of us prefer not to freeze to death".

"Is your land so cold, then?" the Helvetian found tongue to ask.

"Is yours? Are your mountains *all* snow and ice? Are there not days in your land warmer and more soft than these?" Rotus wished only to sleep, and indeed, by the time the usually silent Swiss had made an end to eulogising on the warm sun, and fresh, keen air of his native Alps, the Briton was deep in the arms of Morpheus again, and dreaming of a high hill stream, cool and sparkling fresh.

Refreshed and clear-headed at last when Stephanus came, Rotus was but mildly surprised to see him.

What astonished him was the extraordinary plan he had evolved, the complicity of his friends and the doctor. It seemed that he had not merely dreamed that the medicus said "we come in all guises in the brotherhood".

"Your doctor knows where I can be found — oh yes, we are old friends in the brotherhood", Stephanus said. "You do not remember that I came?"

"But vaguely. How did he know that I knew you? Surely I did not babble so much . . .?"

116

"I told him" Gallus interrupted. "In the arena you muttered a prayer to our Christ Jesus, not to Mithras, or Sul or Jupiter or your Cocid, but the Crucified of us all".

Rotus looked round the small company, at the Gaul and Balbus, Stephen and the Ox, at the doctor newly within the doorway, at each grinning placidly back on his surprise, and for the space of a heartbeat there was, too, in the room an unmistakeable Presence.

"But if you are of the brothers of Christ, why do you waste your time in this bloodbath, this pandering to the vicious in the mob, this entertainment of empty-headed fashion-seekers, this. . . ?"

The Ox stretched and stood. "It seems to us that Christ needs friends in all places".

"We three have not been long in the Brotherhood and much of the old life dies hard within us, but we persuade ourselves that we have helped not a few in distress to escape, or to meet death with assurance of life to come. Perhaps, too, we have inspired the odd one of the mob to admire skill rather than to scream for blood". Gallus gently turned his sword, as he burnished the gleaming hilt. "As our sturdy Ox says, Christ needs friends in all places—even men who live by their sword arm. One day he may need soldiers to fight in his cause, and we have wished to be ready".

"But now", Balbus broke in, "Stephen says there is need for us elsewhere, and, for myself, I think his plan has the most promising possibilities. I am ripe for a bit of adventure". He chuckled and thumped Stephen soundly. The young man grimaced and returned the blow, then, remembered suddenly that to-day he was the surgeon's assistant and this horseplay was beneath such a one's sober dignity.

Nevertheless he left the men in high spirits, convinced that his plan would work.

The Empress had been in a tantrum. Since the last great show at the beginning of October when her husband had suddenly called an end to the fighting for no good reason but his own bad mood, she had fumed and fretted and suffered. Her friends, delighted to find the means to prick at her susceptibilities, had idled around the subject, prodding, stinging, niggling at reasons why and wherefore, thoroughly enjoying her discomfiture; and so she in turn had nagged her husband as to why he had suddenly turned squeamish; whereat he in masculine fury demanded to know to whom he, the Emperor of Rome the Great, might be beholden for permission to make up his mind on such trivia. That "trivia" ignited the explosion: the tantrum lasted for days.

So the gladiators were to fight again to the last man, but definitely, that the court ladies and their Lady might be satisfied.

The crowd as usual thronged, cursed, quarrelled, ate, sweated, jostled. The men at arms made ritual preparation, and set their minds, it seemed, to die. The Emperor and his following took their places early, eager, on the face of things, as the rabble, to see the end in a blood and sand. Lepidiana, Naso and the Bald One made their several entrances with an impressive degree of pomp. Crassus, a picnic box, and Varres, took three seats behind.

Crassus beamed and waved and ate. Varres eyed the vanishing provisions ruefully while he tried to steady his pounding heart. Would Rotus have to fight his bout or would his wound keep him in his cell? Would any, or all, co-operate? Had Stephanus been able to do as he had said?

As the trumpets blared, a young nobleman slipped into the seat beside him, weighed down too with a basket of food.

Ritual approach and greeting gave Varres time to scan the contestants. Yes, Rotus was there, gaunt and bloodless but armoured and grim, with, beside him, shields locked before them, three men who could only fit Stephen's description of the Gaul, the Ox and Balbus. Varres tensed.

". . . te Salutamus, Caesar". Four pairs of eyes scanned beyond the Emperor in his box, as a soft honey sweet sailed over the head of the Empress landing gently at their feet.

118

The nobleman grinned cheerfully and tackled his tuck box again. The eyes of Gallus stilled. As the men marched away, the cloud of dust lifted on the first pair remaining to kill or be killed. This retiarius was clumsy with his net, the swordsman vicious but inaccurate, and in each was evident lack of desire to bring the bout to an end. Twice the sword might have struck for the kill and as often the net man missed his aim. Slow of foot and sluggish, they had not the heart to play to their audience. What had to be had to be . . . but not yet, if they could delay it.

The crowd grumbled and swore.

A honey sweet skimmed lightly over the Bald One's head to land on the curls of the wife of Senator Lepidus. Crassus was intrigued; that fellow on Varres' other side was a man after his own heart, an acquaintance to be encouraged. He delved in his own lunch box for a similar suitable missile and aimed it neatly towards the nose of old Naso.

As the net man fell, the mob's instruction to their Emperor was clear. Three spurts of blood greeted the trident's teeth, and the crowd signified approval. Varres kept his eyes on Crassus' lunch box.

The next pair were swordsmen of consummate skill, so the contest lasted longer, much longer, with even the youngest of the watchers held captive by their ability. Only Crassus and the young patrician were unenthralled by the bout on the sand, but then they themselves were fully occupied in a gently amiable contest as to who might land most delicacies on the piled hair of Lepidiana. The young noble was leading by part of a stuffed egg and pieces of cheese, when the trumpet brayed for the next two in the arena. Varres tensed. Here too was skill of no ordinary calibre, but one of the men was obviously unfit; his neck scarce bore the weight of the helmet above, his shield arm drooped, will power rather than strength holding muscles at strain, and, wide and unguarded, a scar ran livid over his chest. Varres' gasp was lost in his kinsman's crow of delight.

"He's soon for the finishing, that one".

The young noble was busy with cherry stones and the pleasing target of the Emperor's box.

Rotus and his Gaul parried and thrust in automatic, well-trained precision. Skill and timing, impeccable footwork and the result of long, hot hours of practice were holding attention and even gaining a little applause. But the wounded one was clearly weak.

The nobleman's aim became more accurate; a piece of jellied peach hit the Empress's ear, and of apricot, the Emperor's. Crassus, determined to show himself no laggard in similar impudence, opened fire with a handful of olives, a thrush stuffed with garum, and a small but strong Samian jar. His aim was perfect.

The effect was better than Stephen had hoped for. The Empress screamed fury. Titus swore, the ladies of the court went hysterical—perhaps, dared they admit it, with laughter—and the Emperor's bodyguard leapt up tiers of benches. A he scuttled between legs and sweating bodies Varres grinned wickedly to himself. Let the dear spoiled Crassus get out of this the best he could: doubtless his father would pay sweetly for his pardon. For a second the boy entertaineded a qualm over his well-enough meaning old cousin—poor Aemilius barely deserved this—but the moment passed as he raced after Stephen through the maze of gladiators' cells. Vaguely aware of large men pounding after him, he stripped like Stephen now to his tunic and in a second's delay when he tripped on a corner of cloth, the first man behind caught up.

"Hold, man, hold. Must you be so hard on an old friend when there's no-one as yet in pursuit? My wind is not so strong as it was on Capreae".

The reunion of freedman and master was no more than a fierce handclasp, a gulp of joy and a rumble of pleasure from four companions, then the race was on again.

"If they catch us now, we'll all be for torture and the lions".

Crassus, however unwitting, was in the throes of the most

unselfish moments of his life, as he became the focus of all attention. Lepidiana was in full cry, Naso and the Senator Calvus in strong support; the Imperial party was in high dudgeon, or hysterics, and Crassus, poor Crassus, in consummate confusion. Only one man dared to bleat, "He was not alone", words that melted in the heat of Lepidiana's tirade, and were lost for ever.

SEVENTEEN

The six swam the Tiber unhurriedly as other swimmers on this sticky autumn day and Rotus bade goodbye to his military shirt with as little regret as he had done to his uniform and shield on the way through the barracks.

On the further bank they dressed from a pile of tunics guarded by a little boy then strolled as to the next bridge back.

The river bank swept north and east enfolding the city in its curve, so they struck west on the road to the coast, whereon the world and its traders moved incessantly in search of adventure, fortune, or merely a new mode of life. It was not difficult to merge with travellers; the difficulty was not to seem hurried or anxious.

Beneath the citadel on the Janiculum they sat to rest, while a stream of carriages and carts moved on, and they rested still while fellow pedestrians plodded out of sight in the dust from their feet. Not till Stephen declared that they might, in a lull when no travellers were in sight, did they move down over the back of the hill to a sheltered spot, where, amid overgrown shrub and piling creeper, two horses, knee-hobbled, cropped patiently over a minute patch of dry, unsavoury grass.

"There will be two more in about another two hundred paces, and two yet further on. Meantime, you gentlemen, late opponents of the arena, take these mounts and be on your way with all speed. North-east you will strike the Via Aurelia well beyond the city walls. Halt as the sun begins to set, and if all goes well, the rest of us will have joined you before it has finally gone. Make haste, and the prayers of the brothers go with you.

"More than prayers", thought Varres, as he bade Rotus farewell once more. "Prayers, and plans and material aid. I wonder just whose are these horses?"

Stephanus and he took the last pair of horses and sped northwards after the rest. In all, their escape had been quite simple; Stephen's plans had gone without a hitch, even the co-operation of poor unsuspecting Crassus had been perfect, and now, within the hour all six would meet at sundown on the great road, north towards Gaul.

Things just then were not going well for Crassus. His pleas and those of his father had fallen on ears deafened by the fury of Lepidiana's harangue, of Naso's querulous tirade, ears too, somewhat clogged by the remains of a jellied peach. Calvus of the bald head and long memory had much to say about a previous occasion, and when Crassus had been suitably dealt with, in the presence of the Emperor's lictors, when the gush of his mother's tears had finally subsided and his father's shame had been digested, then, and only then, was the absence of their cousin noticed. By then Varres and his friends were happily at rest in the quarters of Fundanus, the bailiff on the farm of Lucius Aemilius Flaccus, father of Crassus.

From there the son of Fundanus, and two other young slaves, immediately set out to return the horses borrowed from a certain riding stable on the Campus at Rome, and Stephen settled to sleep with a conscience cheerfully clear.

Long before dawn, fed, clothed, mounted, and blessed, they were on their way again, with Varres on the beautiful stallion he had lovingly groomed not so very long ago.

123

Stephen went with them, for fun as he declared, but also to guide them over bye-ways to the north, and to bring back the prize horses of Aemilius to his farm, when some other form of transport was obtained. The eastern sky was brightening as they joined the Via Aurelia once more and broke the stillness of a beautiful sunrise with the ring of flying hooves. The horses, fresh and unaccustomed to the strain of sustained endeavour, took their heads and streaked through the crisp morning air like the mares of Diomede until slowed by steadily increasing traffic. Then for a time they ambled, and the company savoured the goodness of companionship and a new beginning.

Only Rotus sat his horse unhappily, for his wound ached, dragging with a weight of pain on shoulder and arm together, yet not even when they left the great road and cut off through open country, led by Varres at a vigorous rate, did he voice the slightest complaint; the boy was happy, he himself was surrounded by good companions, and every mile convered towards the northern hill was another mile away from Rome, its quirks, its pollutions and its sad social miscalculations. So Rotus kept on, grimly, with only a tightening pallor on his cheeks to betray, if one had cared to look, that he was not quite as carefree as the rest.

Full daylight brought heat unusual this late in October, heat that tempered the exuberance of the party and suffused the Briton's pallor with angry mottled fire, but they pressed on, following Stephen now, without question.

With late afternoon a new burst of energy seized them as off to the northwest a glint of sapphire sparkled, and disappeared behind a fold of land. Stephen shouted and they raced forward over springing turf round crags and boulders, with all the joy and enthusiasm of the morning, till of a sudden they were on a ridge above a cove. Below, the sea laughed up at them, as it licked gently around the feet of a village built terraced into rocky cliff.

"If we can find a way down to the shore", Stephen laughed, "there is a boat will take you to Massilia, in Gaul.

From there it should be easy to join levies enlisted for foreign service". Balbus and the Ox looked at each other. "They tell me they take anyone, just anyone, there to garrison the wild and blue-painted north".

It was then that they missed Rotus. Varres wheeled his mount and streaked back over the way they had come. The stallion's hooves took wings; his rider's urgency was in him too, and there was no need for knee or heel. The four behind were hard pressed to keep the pair in view.

They found the Briton beneath a crag, splayed naked, his head in a pool of blood. His feeble grin was twisted. "I knew you'd come Varres. . . . I was tired and lagged behind. The rodents . . . they've taken the mare. . . ."

Gallus and Stephen when they came, took charge of this fresh wound as the boy looked helplessly on and wished that he knew how to help. His stallion pawed restlessly, breathing puffs of hissing fury, tossing his gleaming head and mane, side-stepping with impatience; the role of onlooker was not for such as he, and the boy agreed.

Two miles on, the chestnut halted, sniffed the air like a hound and whinnied softly. Beyond the ridge Varres saw the trio, a long, rangy streak of manhood, a shortlegged stump of ugliness and a very reluctant horse. The Rodents of Rome were far afield on the business of illicit acquisition.

Varres had no time to wonder why. His mount stamped, trotted forward, and whinnied a gentle wooing note; then he charged. Round the trio he raced, round and round in a tightening, dizzying circle. The mare halted. Decius swore, hauled, pulled, and thumped her. Edurus pushed and kicked. The beautiful stallion slowed, pranced, waved his tail, wooed a second time with the soft call that was little more than a breath, and began his vertiginous charge again. Pressed to the beast's neck Varres enjoyed himself. This was a dance of heroes. The horse was in charge, not he.

Suddenly the whirling ceased. The chestnut nudged his mare from between the two men and edged her behind the shorter one, then he pressed his own head into the long one's

125

back and firmly urged him forward. Varres recovering his seat after the sudden halt chuckled to see what they were at. Slowly, inexorably, and—if animals show emotions—with the greatest of good humour, the two proud beasts were driving their victims forward, straight into a marsh. He was almost sorry for the men, till he remembered that these were the two, who had first separated himself from Rotus, who had delayed their journey to Britain, and had now almost killed his friend. Stephen had described them perfectly, and now here he had them at his mercy; or rather, the horse he was riding had them at *his* mercy. The situation had a delicious incredibility. How far would this animal push them?

Decius was up to his shins in morass. Edurus merely over the ankles, but he was squeaking the louder. The mare looked up to her mate and curled her lip over perfect teeth. It seemed she was laughing. In a moment her victim was flat on his face, drowning his curses in bog.

A roar of laughter from behind startled them all. The little mare reared, found her balance on the supine body; Edurus squealed the louder, for his friend or for himself.

"Call off your horses, Varres, and let the rascals flee. Rotus will live, but he needs a mount."

The Ox hauled Edurus to firmer ground, and helped Varres trail the other from his soggy bed. As he pumped the man's lungs clear of wet he whispered fiercely in his ears, words of a wonderfully curative effect, for the short one struggled to his feet, joined his friend and bolted. The stallion, riderless, followed for a pace or two, reared, applied a hoof to each back in turn, neighed furiously, and turned. It seemed that he too laughed.

"Come, beauties. Varres, the little mare needs gentling: if you ride her, her mate will follow.

"We spend tonight in the village by the sea. To-morrow, there is a ship. There are farewells to make".

EIGHTEEN

They did not take ship on the next day. The doctor whom
Stephen procured to attend Rotus advised at least three days
of rest, and the others, Balbus and the Swiss refused to make
their own way home until their comrade should be well
again. Gallus argued: was he not taking ship too, to
Massilia? Was Varres not also a companion for the Briton?
An ox-cart was waiting with provisions, to take these two
pig-heads over the mountains, and when the Ox reached his
home in Helvetia, Balbus would yet have a mountain ridge
to traverse before he reached his own land. The year was
trailing on, the days shortening; soon autumn chills would
blanket the mountains, snow would come to slow their
journey.

But Balbus would not listen.

"I intend to stay a winter with the Ox—what is one more
winter in so many?—for I have much to learn of his way of
life, if it is as wonderful as he claims it is. No, Gallus, we
remain here, until you three are safely aboard".

Stephen was likewise adamant. His friend the shipmaster
would wait—his cargo was of tiles and marble for the
Governor's palace at Narbo, and the Governor was in no
real urgency for a new roof. Government requisitions were
notoriously slow in being carried out: this need prove no
exception. He, Stephen, had much news to cull from his

seafaring friend, many acquaintances to renew in the village. He too would wait until Rotus was fit to travel.

Anyway, the horses needed resting before the journey back to Aemilius' farm.

Stephen had several friends in this village, friends who were kindness itself. No effort was too much for them, and they seemed to have links everywhere in their chain of contact. Indeed, they came in all guises in the brotherhood.

In the lodgings provided by a gentle old man, a relation of Aretria, they rested, and talked, and shared his frugal fare. Mostly they talked: of the ways of the world, of Rome, of her splendour and squalour, her culture and her cruelties, the Circuses, and love of God; and all of them learned from the gentle one the lessons taught by Paulus, who was Saul of Tarsus. They heard too, at first hand, of the man who was the Christus, as they listened enthralled to the old man's tales of what he had seen long ago as a lad. This man was the only one even Stephanus knew who had actually seen the Carpenter, and the account they heard was enthralling. In the old man's simple telling, the Presence again was at hand.

At last Rotus was deemed fit to travel and the five went their several ways. There was little for grown men to say except "God speed, my friend", but eye spoke to eye and fist to fist in the moments of their parting. They could, though, loose emotion on the horses. Varres spent long moments with the chestnut and his amiable little mare and in this parting he bade farewell to all the loves of the life he was leaving. Dim-eyed over the animal, he let his heart weep for his home and his mother.

Stephanus stood on a rock above the little town and waved his blessing until each group was out of sight.

Roof tiles and marble not withstanding, the boat heaved on a treacherous sea, and Varres and the Briton lay under the stern in the hideous anticlimax of seasickness. Even Gallus was somewhat dejected.

Massilia when they reached it at last did not relieve their morbidity. Dirty, smelling, seething with travellers from all over the world, it was also a clearing station for hordes of slaves awaiting shipment for Rome and places south. The bubbling good spirits of Stephen might have dispelled their wretched depression, but he was by then far south again, back in the home of Fundanus.

Dark skins and dusky, fair skins and olive, rich silks and tattered wools, patterned their immediate view; Gallish pimps and painted harlots, jewelled Syrians, vied for their attention; determined merchants haggled, traders cried their wares, messengers eeled through the crowd, and only the slaves stood still, stood on their little platforms, waiting hopelessly for whatever was to come.

Nowhere was there a soldier to be seen. "Ask the first soldier you see" the captain had said when they left the ship; "any of them will tell you the way to the parade ground.

Rotus refused to ask a civilian the way to the barracks, and would let neither Varres nor Gallus ask either; and still there was not a soldier to be seen.

As day wore on into evening and the reek of teeming streets became even more oppressive they decided to return to the comparative quiet of the ship to consult its master, and perhaps claim a bunk for the night. On the way, in a back street, they saw the first uniform they had seen all day, just disappearing into a tavern.

NINETEEN

Aulus Atticus was distinctly peevish. This accursed leg of his, which had taken him from the frontier fighting back to this sickening, stinking hole of a port was giving him one of the worst of his bad days, and the surgeon Phrenobalus certainly was taking his time about coming to attend him. By the gods, this was discomfort at its worst. And now, the great god Mars give him patience, there was this missive from the commander of the legion himself.

"One full cohort to be dispatched forthwith for shipment to join the IXth".

Where was *he* to get a cohort? and why him anyway? Why not one of the chaps at Lugdunum, or for that matter at one of the base camps in Britain itself? He had no spare men — he could hardly hold the men who had actually volunteered, far less the ones who had had to be requisitoned. Was not yesterday's defecting of a whole family of Narbon brothers not the very reason why he had ordered an entire company to be confined to quarters for a week?

But Phrenobalus the surgeon was not confined. He should be here to dress this infernal leg. M'hercule, where was the fool of a surgeon? Senior centurion Aulus balanced his vinestick thoughtfully then threw it down in disgust. Well he knew he'd never use it on the Greek — they'd seen too many campaigns together, and when he did finally condescend to come, doubtless the doctor would bring something to relieve the pain.

He did. Phrenobalus brought two large amphorae of sweet, non-issue wine, as well as his unguents and dressings, and before either man mentioned leg, or ache or reasons for delay, one complete jar of wine was consumed. Aulus began to feel better, and Phrenobalus had more stomach for his job.

"It was a mistake, you know, Atticus, to have this heal over before the bone was cleared. . . ."

Aulus gritted his teeth and tried not to give voice to his pain.

"Mistake nothing. If that other surgeon had poked and scraped as he wanted, I'd have been a cripple for life—*and* been discharged from the army on the spot. I'd a mind to serve out my twenty years and earn my pension, and, by Pluto, I still have, so get me patched and this pain eased, and say no more about it.

The leg dressed, they finished the second amphora in an increasing haze of warmth, understanding and comradeship, and lusty criticism of officers and all official missives, especially the last one from the north. Atticus made up his mind: he would send the Legatus all the men he could muster, all five centuries of them, and to Hades with official orders. Let the Legatus find the sixth century himself. One thing, though: the fifth century had only seventy-seven men, and it didn't have a surgeon . . . Well, never mind; a century should really have one hundred men, not the usual eighty—someone must have cheated there—so who cared if there were only seventy-seven . . . in the fifth shentury . . . an' no shurgeon . . . sheventy . . . sheven. . . .

He was having extreme difficulty with the number just before he fell asleep.

Phrenobalus stretched the centurion on his couch and departed. He must get some more wine. There was a piece of work he must do on that leg to-morrow, whether Aulus liked it or not, and they both would need to be fortified. The tavern near the quay supplied just the wine he wanted.

Within an hour of meeting the surgeon, Rotus, Varres and the Gaul were as good as accepted into the fifth century of the eighth cohort destined to replace a company of the Ninth Legion stationed in northern Britain. The three were jubilant.

Aulus Atticus, Primus Pilus, were he awake and in a state of comprehend, would certainly have used his vinestick upon the surgeon for such indiscreet babblings to three complete strangers, but Aulus was not awake, and the surgeon himself was scarcely fully compos mentis and so the three were recruited on the spot subject of course to two trifling conditions: that Varres, being under age, volunteer as surgeon's assistant, and second, that Aulus the Primus, agree. Somewhere, at some time in his sojourn with cousin Aemilius another birthday had passed over the boy, unnoticed by any but himself, but even so, he was far off being the necessary age of seventeen for formal military training.

"Nevertheless", the surgeon studied him over yet another cup of wine, "if you scrape that black fuzz from your face before you report to the centurion, and be careful to show at least one razor cut you'll pass for seventeen . . . if I say so".

That night, all four slept soundly in the fort hospital.

Atticus, accepted his new recruits gladly and wasted no time in having them take the oath. He would be a fool to do otherwise for were not five centuries each complete to the eightieth man, a force much nearer the required cohort than four centuries and seventy-seven men? To-day he could enunciate but had the greatest difficulty in trying to calculate, for the pain in that accursed leg was second only to that in his bursting head. What he really needed was another large goblet of the stuff Phrenobalus had brought yesterday. He dismissed the two older recruits to their own centurion, and sent Varres to find the surgeon.

"Phrenobalus!"

Varres turned startled eyes to his new master. The Greek grinned reassuringly.

"His leg itches a bit and makes him bad-tempered, but a cup of wine will soothe him down". He lifted the leather curtain of the inner room, where Aulus had taken to his couch.

"Well! Did I do well to find you recruits, Sir? Shall we celebrate your complete century in a cup of this good stuff?" He turned to his roll of instruments on a table and whispered, "Fill it high, lad, and keep it filled; and watch well his eyes. The eyes tell everything to a good doctor".

When the bandage was off, and the cup filled for the fourth time, the surgeon whispered to Varres. "Hold him if it's necessary, and keep careful note of his eyes; very careful note. Remember".

Aulus' eyes were shut. Varres caught the goblet as it fell.

The drunken slumber lasted only long enough to dull the first incision of the surgeon's tool.

The centurion heaved and shrieked, then bit his lip in shame and fury at himself.

"Give him something to bite on lad."

Swiftly Varres tore a strip of linen and stuffed it between the teeth of the sufferer, whose dark eyes momentarily gleamed gratitude then flamed agony at the second, telling incision. Instinctively Varres gave the man his hand to grip, and was rewarded by a faint nod of appreciation before the pools of his eyes flooded again with pain and his head threshed on the hard pillow. Gently the boy eased his free hand to the linen again and wiped sweat — and was it tears? — from the livid face, as his other hand lay crushed in the centurion's fist. Then, mercifully, the man fainted.

Phrenobalus grunted. "You've removed the gag have you? Good. This putrid mess would never heal without excision, but now that he has had the sense to faint I'll get it scraped clean of all this rubbish". He looked at the lad keenly.

"Fetch a large jar of cold water boy, to revive him when

I've finished".

Varres went gladly. His one surrender to curiosity had shown blood, suppurating flesh and a yellow-stained knife in the surgeon's bloody hand, and he felt sick. He'd have some cold water himself before he returned.

Phrenobalus grunted again. Young the lad was, and as yet squeamish, but he showed promise. Quickly he rolled the soiled linen from under his patient's leg and replaced it with a clean piece.

"Good fellow. You were speedy. Now, let me show you what I want done".

Varres' stomach lurched, but he dipped his fingers in he bowl of sour wine his master indicated and carefully pinched together raw edges of flesh as the surgeon pulled firm his bandage.

"Well done. Now let's both have some good wine before we waken our patient, for, by Jupiter, there'll be none for us when he's through with it".

Together, they slapped the centurion's face with cold wet cloths until he finally stirred into consciousness, then Varres was despatched to the furnace with a bundle of soiled linen.

"After that, take a walk round the parade ground", Phrenobalus chuckled, "and watch your companions suffer".

Aulus stirred restlessly.

"All right, old friend, your leg will heal now. A few days' discomfort as it knits and then will be the end of pain there for ever — you have my word.

"No, you did *not* disgrace yourself in front of your newest recruit, nor did he in front of you, but you can squeal now if you want to, for he has gone out . . . and is probably now being sick. If he admits to it I'll tell him it was the wine that made him so. But wine never sickens you, Primus. Here, we'll finish this bottle together".

Varres was not sick. He was engrossed in the doings of the Centurion of the fifth and his squad of men who with Gallus and Rotus were certainly being put through their paces, and seemed to be enjoying the effort. Their recent training for the arena was standing them in good stead so that their centurion was eyeing them with what might almost amount to pleasure.

Varres watched with delight. This was soldiering as he had visualised it, not that messy butchering he had just witnessed.

No, that was unfair; the surgeon was no rough butcher, and the mess had been in the wound before, not after, his administrations. In time, when he was old enough, Varres too would excell on the parade ground; meantime he would try *not* to let his stomach be master.

TWENTY

The Chief was a most impatient patient. Strapped to his couch by linen strips, so that excess zeal for duty might not persuade him to hobble to his desk, he required that all of his desk work, and much more, be brought to him. Varres, was at his beck and call for five whole days, and almost as many nights, fetching and carrying food, drink, potions, slops, unguents, messages, despatches, commands; shaving, sponging, oiling scraping down his patient, helping Phrenobalus to change bandages and keeping all the rest of the camp, even Rotus and the Gaul, from seeing their officer in such a state of indignity.

After a week, Aulus was sufficiently recovered to don his uniform and from his official chair, to interview lesser ranks, with a semblance of his former air of authority. Varres thankfully repaired to a hospital couch to sleep soundly and long.

Wakened by Phrenobalus to assist dress the leg again, he met a tirade that surprised even the longsuffering surgeon.

"Fools. Fools! Every one of them a fool. Senators, legations, Rome based generals — knuckle-heads the whole multitude of them. What do soft home-fed councillors know of the rigours of war, the needs of men on the field, the chaps at the fighting end of a campaign? Oh, these mule brains in the government make me furious — by Jupiter they

136

should fight a campaign one season and see for themselves what it's all about".

"Tch, tch. Calm yourself. Such ill-humour will burst your spleen, and that I can *not* bandage up. What ails you at the all-powerful of the government?"

Aulus' fury turned his face such a brilliant hue that Varres reached for the water jar and a cold compress.

"Ails me? You ask what ails me. Read this". He thumped a scroll on his desk and all but broke its wooden spine. "Just before you decided to carve a hunk from this leg of mine, you may just possibly remember—*if* you cudgel your pigeon's headpiece sufficiently—you may remember that I read you a message from the legate in Britain".

"My pigeon's head piece remembers well, good Aulus, and I heeded the message enough to get you three good recruits to fill up a century; but all this is of no interest to me. It is your sparrow's limb of a leg that exercises my brain, whatever size that may be".

Aulus had the grace to apologise, and to calm down sufficiently to have his wound inspected, and even to concede that it pained him now less than it had for months. Phrenobalus had Varres look closely on the wound and note how the edges were tidily drawing together.

"Not like that furrow of a scar on your friend's chest. Whoever tended that sword-cut was no doctor; a charlatan, well paid, no doubt, from some of our government's taxes". Varres about to retort that any friend of Stephanus was no charlatan, saw in time what the surgeon was at, for he looked slyly at the centurion and was rewarded by a second, though less vehement, outburst.

"Ech! Government! Officials—faugh. Oh, they lay plans and say what's to be what, and think what fine fellows they are as they do it, but do they know what they're planning *about*, or who is to do what, or *with* what? Here have I a request from the frontier for a cohort to be sent forthwith. I do my best to recruit the three maniples asked for, and am within a mere eighty men of doing just that". Phrenobalus lifted a quizzical brow over his bandage roll. "And what happens? What happens, I ask you?"

"All right. *What* happens?"

"That soft-headed set of officials we call a senate send a messenger who arrives to-day with the order that no troops move northwards from here until the spring.

"What I say is, if Agricola needs a fresh cohort, a whole fresh legion, ten legions even, for his campaign against those barbarians, then he should have them, and to Hades and the shades of all dead senators with what any government thinks".

The surgeon grinned: his patient at last felt something other than pain.

"I quite agree. What say you, Varres?"

The boy, surprised, nevertheless nodded with vigour. "He agrees too, Centurion, but then he is, like me, a mere pigeon's brain of a medicus. We cannot advise in the face of practical experience".

Delighted to be included Varres waited for more, but was despatched to the furnace with wet linen, and thence to join his friends for their session at the baths.

The surgeon let his patient rant on for a time. Giving vent to his ill-humour would clear his spleen of foul vapours, and that would be good for his wound.

It seemed, in brief, that the Senate had declared that all military bases were to maintain the status quo for half a year.

Ah, well, much might happen in that time, and Phrenobalus was philosophic. "Look at it this way, Atticus; by the spring you can have recruited your full three maniples, and you can have them trained to do you credit".

The sound Aulus made was not beautiful.

"Once you have full use of this leg again, you can lick your men into shape yourself, and when it is known that the garrison's commander is a first class man", he squinted from the bandaged limb to the centurion's face, "you will find recruits flock to your companies. At the moment the neighbourhood can be forgiven for considering this fort as a very second rate establishment".

Aulus popped with fury and reached for his vinestaff, but halted as he touched it.

"You're right, friend, as usual. I've been only half a commander, a one-legged crane, a thing of ill omen".

"But if you continue to accept my ministrations, I'll have you back on the parade ground, good as new, before the Saturnalia. I might even be able to certify you as fighting fit for another campaign—in all honesty to my profession—and you might lead your cohort yourself to the frontier of Agricola. "I have faith in my ability. Do you not have faith in yours?"

Aulus studied the doctor's face. By the gods, the man meant what he said. Mars hear him, what he'd give to be on active service again! According to Phrenobalus, all that was needed was patience and perseverance and faith in himself.

Rotus and the Gaul meantime had been sweating it out in full marching array and were more than ready for a refreshing dip. Varres met them on the way back to their billets, and, full of his newly developed care for the afflicted, offered to carry their equipment. The two gladly loaded their packs on him and walked on unemcumbered.

"Here! Wait. Come back". Varres picked himself from under the weight, dusted his tunic and bellowed in a tone extraordinarily like the centurion's. "Wait! Halt!"

"What on earth do you carry in these things?"

Rotus turned back laughing. "A few odds and ends we need for a day's march. Here, carry mine, and I'll take the other". Gallus obligingly held back.

Two stakes, a pick and spade rattled heavily against cooking pots as Varres thankfully dumped his load on the billet floor.

"Hey, be careful. My spare clothes are there. On my miserable ten asses a day I can't afford to buy another new tunic". Rotus put down carefully the gear he was carrying and even more carefully re-arranged his own kit, adjusting

139

moveables and placing his little hand-mill on the shoulder frame to give a comfortable balance to the load, and checking that his small bag of wheat was still intact.

"There, no harm done. But surely, youngling, your muscles are softening. Is the life of a doctor so easy then?"

The boy retorted with one of the meaner wrestling tricks he had learned from his cousin Crassus, and in the rough and tumble that followed he showed that his muscles were by no means unmanly. Rotus picked himself up.

"I was going to suggest to our centurion that you drill with us when your doctor friend has no need of your services. Now I'm beginning to regret even the thought. Your muscles are fit for most uses except the carrying of a march-pack . . . but then you won't need to march when we go north. You will be travelling elegantly in the hospital wagon with a litter of malingering patients".

"Gallus, I need oil and a new strigil. Will you take me to that apothecary's where you bought your last phial?"

The following week Atticus addressed his entire company in no uncertain terms.

"Old Skrimshank has bestirred himself," a voice rumbled in disgust, albeit tinged with pleasure. "Perhaps we'll see action now".

The edict was read; the grumbling rose: no action here, no march, no battle; still the same enervating boredom.

The harangue resumed. As it swelled and rolled, men stiffened, heads lifted, eyes lit. This was a touch of their old Primus Pilus for the few veterans of his company. To the listless, bored recruits of the levy this was a strange new officer worthy to command. Before the half year was out they would be, the voice affirmed, a cohort worthy of the name, a force in arms to be reckoned with, one Agricola could be proud of, and he, Aulus Atticus, would be with them — the great god Jupiter willing, and possibly Mithras too.

One had to acknowledge other chaps' religions as well, of

course.

The weeks passed, busy weeks for all of them, for Aulus meant what he said. Varres drilled with his pack when he could, but for the most part he was with Phrenobalus learning the arts and tricks of his trade. Gradually he hardened to the sight of blood and pus, learned the uses of potions, herbs and unguents, instruments and foments and gained ability to discriminate between true sufferer and malingerer.

For these last Phrenobalus diagnosed need for immediate excision of offending limb or organ, a diagnosis which brought wondrously effective cure.

Gallus and Rotus worked hard too and were soon marked down for possible promotion, a verdict which Gallus took with no very great delight. Now that they were actually in Gaul, Varres half expected him to make for his home, but as weeks passed and Gallus never mentioned home or family the boy surmised that it would not be till later as they marched north that he would find the urge to seek his own people. Rotus said nothing on the subject but observed his friend with compassion.

In mid-December the feast of Saturnalia brought a break from work. Aulus spurned the diversions usual at such a time, so the seven days of the festival were spent mostly in eating, drinking, singing and doing much as they pleased as long as they stayed within the camp.

Nevertheless, the festival brought its own train of minor upsets, mostly to stomach and head, and Varres was kept fairly busy dosing the sufferers. Suddenly there was a sharp rise in sickness cases and Phrenobalus and he were fully occupied. His right arm ached with wielding a pestle till, on an inspiration, he asked leave to borrow a hand-mill in order to grind more of his curative herb at once.

Rotus, out of uniform, was rolling a small tight pack when Varres ran into his billet to make his request. The Briton started, then shrugged and smiled.

"You might as well know, friend, I'm taking leave of

141

absence for a few days".

"But you know the rule—no-one leaves the barracks. You'll earn a flogging if you're caught".

"I shan't be caught. No-one will notice my absence with so many on sick parade".

"But why? Are you going alone?"

"I had not intended to implicate you. If my absence is noticed and you are questioned then it were better if you really knew nothing, but now you'd best know it all. Gallus has had news of his family. It is not good news, but Gallus feels he must find for himself whether it is true. You remember how we were after Vesuvius?"

Varres' eyes, bright with dismay and a touch of jealousy, dimmed now with sympathy as he nodded.

"So you are to help Gallus as you helped me? All I can say is 'God speed' . . . But you will come back, won't you?"

"Of course; and if there is truth in what we heard, I shall hope to have Gallus with me. He is as well with us here if he has no family to go to. Give us three days. Don't worry—there will be so much coming and going to your hospital, that no-one will notice where we are".

He gripped the lad's wrist and smiled warmly. "I shall desert you, only for my Rufina, if I ever find her.

"By the way, I think it was that special garum two evenings ago that caused this epidemic. Have the rest of the batch thrown into the sea; never liked the stuff myself".

When Varres broached this suggestion with his master he was told to detail carefully which of the sufferers did, or did not, take the relish, an interesting piece of research which culminated in having all the garum emptied into the sea and the crocks which held it smashed into the rubbish pit to be covered immediately under the watchful eye of the surgeon. Then Aulus used up precious parchment on an irate letter to the quartermaster-general in Rome on the subject of supplies to be issued for the next festival.

". . . Better the wholesome porridge of the march camp than banqueting folder that fills my hospital with gut-ache. Further supplies of laserpitium essential, immediately".

Phrenobalus smiled his satisfaction when he read the letter: the writer of this was his old self, fighting fit again. He begged parchment from his superior and departed to write a letter of his own.

Rotus returned, as promised, in three days.

Gallus did not appear on duty with his friend but reported to the hospital later with a very heavy head. Correctly judging the cause of his misery, Varres, pounded more laserpitium, that panacea for all ills engendered by food and drink, and advised his patient to stick to issue wine for the next few days. Gallus agreed ruefully, and went to his billet to sleep off his malady.

"He drowned forlorn hopes in a long carousel". Rotus explained. "His headache he will get over by tomorrow, but his heartache is less transient. It seems his father and brothers were killed in the same rebellion that made him a prisoner, and his mother and sister have disappeared; one says to the north, one says to the west, yet another that the girl married among the Nervii, taking her mother with her. Now Gallus has decided that he is best with us, and will remain a Roman soldier unless or until he hears other news of his people".

Rotus remained still for many moments, watching the young man. Varres waited for what he knew was to come.

"When we reach Britain, I shall begin to feel restless too. I hope and pray that I shall have better luck than Gallus".

"And when we reach the frontier . . .?"

"Then we shall see, shall we not? But I shall wish to search for my people".

Varres looked up from his mortar, and his eyes were clear. "And I shall wish you God speed".

TWENTY-ONE

So the Saturnalia passed. Held at the time of the longest night, this festival satisfied all creeds: the followers of Mithras rejoiced that the Sun God was renewing his strength for the coming season; the adherents of Jupiter, Best and Greatest, and his ever loving, squabbling Juno, pledged temporary allegiance to Saturn the father he had dispossessed, and the converts of the Christus were happy to celebrate their friend's birthday at that time of year.

Varres missed the talks he had with Stephanus about this new God of his, and his time with the Gaul and Rotus were never quite private, quite intimate enough to talk on a subject that had been known to hold risk. Once, when he tentatively sounded his master about belief in gods, the ring of the surgeon's answer brought the boy back with a jolt to unhappy days with Crassus.

"I believe in all gods and no gods", but Phrenobalus was more specific, more hopeful than Servilius had been. "I believe in some Power for good, above and beyond this self that is I — give it what name you will. I believe I have some of this power in my head and in my hands, and that I must use it only for good".

He spread his long fingers wide and studied them with care, as he would study the tools of his trade.

"I believe that you too have some of this power, that must

be found and trained and practised; but do not ask me what god it comes from. The Greek Zeus, your Roman Jupiter, Mithras of Persia, Isis of Egypt, or Mapone of the fierce lands where perhaps we shall go in the spring, all are but names to me. Certainly I feel nothing for your Minerva who, they say, looks after physicians. My respect is for the Power that is in me and beyond me and above me, that must be used for good."

Varres pondered. Aretia had spoken of 'caritas', desire for the well-being of others; what had Stephen spoken of? . . . the holy ghost? Varres struggled with this conception — a ghost, a shade, a spirit, an "anima", formless but powerful, able to pervade the soul at the behest of the god of Christ. Was this what Phrenobalus had meant? If only he could talk to someone.

Rotus knew little of the discipline of his worship, or on what reasoning to base belief. "All I know", he had once said, "is that I *feel* that Christ holds good for me, and so I believe in his God".

The Gaul, also an admitted believer, was at present in the throes of a deep dejection quite alien to his nature. His captivity he had borne calmly, and his days in the arena with a kind of obstinate enjoyment, as being an experience in his life to be used to the full, since it would not, could not, last. But now Rotus saw his depression, and felt for him, for might not he himself yet come upon a similar disappointment? There was nothing, however, that he or Varres could do, except perhaps pray, as he had seen the brotherhood do in the Catacombs for the victims in the arena.

Varres had other thoughts. He did not know how or what to pray to the new god, but he had learned how to minister. Carefully he made an infusion of cabbage leaves — his master had great faith in the revivifying effect of cabbage — and made Gallus drink it twice a day.

Atticus was in a quandary. His five scant centuries of four months ago were now rapidly reaching a total of five maniples, a cohort of the old-time size, full ten centuries no less, at which Aulus was both proud and disconcerted. Much more of this expansion, he reckoned, and the theorising ignoramuses of the government would send a nose-poking official to supervise his command, a tribune of the people, no doubt, a specimen of home-fed civilian-turned-soldier stepping carefully up the ladder of promotion to the senate—how he despised these non-practising, un-army officers. Yet, he himself hoped for promotion—to the fighting frontier of-course—and he wished his superior s to know that he deserved it. The matter of that irate letter to Rome gloomed heavily over his future.

As usual Phrenobalus diagnosed his condition correctly.

"I told you they'd flock to your standards when you were yourself again. Now they are coming too fast for your peace of mind, eh? Well, I have no longing for a civilian overseer either. We must hope for hard weather to delay courtiers and ships, until we are ready for the spring expeditions; A good strong gale could solve your problem."

The gales came, as every February in that part, and came with such ferocity that ships scurried for harbour from all directions. With them to Massilia came a merchant who had been in Capernaum. The harbour filled tight as steersmen could fill it, so that one might jump dry-shod from one quay to the other. The town, already overcrowded, threatened to burst its walls; so that some, unable to find sleeping space of any kind, returned to bunk in the ships.

Aulus considered the rabble, and prepared to shift his men's families within the walls of his fort. He it was saw the flames first. The wharves were alight, a boat was on fire. A few rapped commands brought his men tumbling out, carrying pots and vessels of every kind, and to the harbour at the double.

Varres turned out with the rest.

"You, surgeon" Aulus bawled. Phrenobalus was nowhere in sight. "You, surgeon, take the families within the walls, get women to help in the hospital, and you take charge in

146

there."

"Yes, you young one. Speed up".

Aulus leapt for a horse, with the senior surgeon suddenly behind him, and Varres caught only his master's words, "Oil for burns; oil and clean linen".

Varres stamped with vexation. This was not why he had joined the army. He wanted man's work, not nursing of women and children, scrubbing a hospital, clean, daubing a few scorches with oil. He should be with his century, putting out the fire down there.

Yet, orders were orders. Families had to be wakened, given billets inside the fort, women organised to help in the hospital, though with what, Varres was unable to see. The place was spotless.

The first few "scorches" came. A high wooden flat near the wharves had caught a spark that become a raging inferno. These patients were all who remained of a score or so of families.

At the harbour Rotus eyed the scene with horror; tight-jammed decks and thick-pitched prows fed the flames a ready banquet. The whole harbour was afire, a level spread of tearing, boiling flame, a furnace to sear the sky and cremate the very gods within. The pitiful potsful of water which he passed along the line, fell spitting feebly, to expire in breathy gasps on the conflagration. Yet they worked on: lines of men, from sea to harbour, passed buckets endlessly, knowing well the futility of their sweat, but seeing nothing else they could do to assuage the flames of their conscience. Gallus passed a vessel from his friend's hand to the next and as their fingers and eyes met for the moment Rotus read total, furious impotence in the gladiator's eyes.

Suddenly the Gaul's head jerked up, his ears pricked, as a hunting dog's and he ran.

Just beyond the harbour mouth and in the swell beyond the sea wall, abandoned to the storm by its captain, tossed a

147

galley as yet untouched by the driving flames. Gallus raced to it, his sandals barely touching the hot stones of the pier and, as a gull clean-sweeping the sky he dived into the sea. When he surfaced, the roar of flames and surge in his ears became the rumble of many voices seeking, questioning, wailing. Slaves still chained, were in the hull of the ship, uncomprehending but not uncomplaining. As Gallus touched the deck, a spark flicked over the sea wall upon the rigging, where it lay alive, unnoticed.

The nearest slave turned stricken eyes upon the intruder and swore to see him with empty hands. A man in front muttered a half-known prayer, a third screamed in hysteria.

"Get us out of here, man, for the love of all the gods".

"I shall, for the love of *God*" Gallus answered and tore a looseded plank from the ship's side. This he smashed on an oar, just short of the oarsman's hand, leaving him free of the main length of the blade. Before this could fall into the sea he grasped it, as a better scythe for other oars, and when each rower was freed he took his own oar-blade to another man's shackle before diving overboard. Even so, it took time to free eighty men and to encourage the last into the wind-tossed sea.

Rotus saw the galley's topsail scythe flaming downwards beyond the wall, and ran, as his friend had run.

Galley-men, with oar-pieces still at their wrists, were handling their liberator from the scorching wall as the Briton came upon them. Gallus' eyes were closed, his tunic, a charred rag, clung to his blackened frame, only an old sword wound stared livid, and a fresh weal lay on his shoulders. Rotus cradled him on the warm stones and called for a makeshift litter.

Slowly the scorched eyelids raised.

"No litter for me friend. I shall march from the arena, even if this is to be my last fight. Just give me a lift, as Balbus did for you, eh partner?"

He struggled to his feet and could not stop a scowl of

further pain.

"Your sword arm round me, Rotus, and I shall reach our billet with my head high".

The Briton's arm was gentle on the blistered back; his own eyes burned with tears.

"We fought well, you and I, but its thumbs down, I'm afraid for me to-day".

His heart too full for protest, Rotus laid his hand on his partner's chest, on the one hand-span not blistered raw. The heart beneath beat feebly but the voice was calmly glad.

"At least this fight was to some purpose, and it was not you who dealt the death blow".

The few paces were agonising before he collapsed, but his head was indeed held high, his mouth grinned.

"Tell Varres . . . this time . . . no cabbage water. . . ."

His chores done, his orders fulfilled, Varres searched the heavens. A glow, gold, crimson, vicious, suffused the stars and licked the velvet lift of the winter sky. Here was beauty, brutal, compelling, beauty that could bode only evil. The black hairs above his young writst rose with apprehension. Vesuvius had been beautiful too. Gradually more burn-victims came, scorch marked, pitted, seared, mostly civilians whose curiosity had brought them too near the flames, and Varres daubed on his oil with little sympathy. Then came soldiers, end-men of the water chains, forcibly relieved by Atticus and sent back for rest and medication. Blistered faces and hands, burned feet, weals lifted by flying splinters, needed and received more careful attention. Two of the local guild of firemen brought wrist wrenched when their sipho back-kicked as they struggled to prime its pump; two more had legs scalded when the water butt they threw on the flames exploded in a burst of steam. Varres worked patiently, gently; comforting, teasing when necessary; hearing tales of courage and endurance and hideous licking flames.

Phrenobalus came with Gallus.

"Your friend needs your help" he whispered as he passed the boy. "Your Briton and the litter bearers, much more than this poor soul. There is sweet wine in the locker there". The litter he then placed in his inner room where he drew the leather curtains firmly against all comers.

TWENTY-TWO

The merchant from Capernaum bought freedom for all slaves who had been in the galley, and when they buried Gallus he insisted that it be with Christian rites and under a tombstone inscribed "*Pro aliis, mortuus: Requiescat*".

Aulus made no demur against either gesture. A man's religion was his own private business, he declared, as long as his soldiering was good. One heard tell that in Rome the name Christian was not acceptable, but it was long indeed since he had been in the mother city, where fashions changed with the wind — or the government — and well Phrenobalus knew his notions of *that* body of numb-skulls.

As usual, the surgeon listened patiently. He himself was not surprised that the boy Varres and his friends seemed to adhere to the cult of the merchant's god, but then he was surprised by little these days, even the fact that those four chaps who had borne Gallus' litter, had used their new freedom to join up in another form of bondage, this beloved army of Aulus Atticus.

"That Gaul was worth four men: we are here to take his place".

To this too, Aulus made no demur. Indeed he accepted them gladly for again he needed all the men he could get. The latest missive from the senate read:

"To Aulus Atticus, greetings.

151

"On the Ides of March, Aulus Atticus, Primus Pilus, at the head of two full cohorts Marian (one thousand, one hundred men), will journey to Lugdunum with all speed; in which fort you will join a further four cohorts, before proceeding to the coast, in order to journey into Britain. There you will become part of a legion, possibly the Ninth but yet to be verified, at the fort of Eboracum.

"A holding force of two centuries will remain in Massilia. . . ."

Such official jargon. Aulus was gratified, delighted even, that he was to be back on active service. He eyed his surgeon shrewdly.

"Did I not say I had faith in my ability, and you should have faith in yours"? Phrenobalus parried the question in his friend's eyes for he had no intention yet of admitting to his own hand in the matter, the detail of a letter to the Senate.

"Now this holding company. . . . There are still several badly burned who could remain. . . ."

"I shall take only the unmarried. Soldier fathers have little enough time with their families, as you know as well as I".

The surgeon's eyes darkened. Both he and the centurion had families—Aulus' wife had been a beauty, and his elder son showed much promise—but that was before the Great Fire in 64. His own wife had been pregnant with their second child. No indeed, neither he nor the centurion had much to praise homefed officialdom for, when they let a madman like Nero loose on the empire. His own son—if son it had been—would now have been the age of the boy Varres there.

Well, these were days long gone, forgotten, were it not for that conflagration at the harbour. Better to forget again.

The doctor looked closely at the wound on Aulus' leg inch by inch, through a convex glass he always carried.

"A perfect piece of work, though I say it myself".

The next weeks were hectic. The married men to be left in

Massilia grumbled furiously amongst their comrades, while their wives made no secret of their delight; those still apart from their families had them sent for forthwith, and much work went into renewing, repairing and refurbishing of married quarters.

"Old Aulus is no skinflint with government money— perhaps the next legate will be meaner, so we'll re-roof and re-pave while we may". A legionary laughed and sweated as he worked, and shouted to his companion as he saw his wife approach, "But by the gods, I wish I were one of *those* lucky fellows".

"Those" indicated by his grimy thumb were sweating it out on the square and strongly questioning their luck. Under newly appointed centurions, of whom Rotus was one, new levy and old timers alike were drilled and bullied, tongue-lashed and marshalled until they were fit to drop; yet they enjoyed it all, in the main, for this held promise of action. Rotus demanded Varres' attendance at parades as often as he could be spared from his mortar and bandages.

"You must be able to carry your pack on the march, young doctor, if as you say you want to carry a standard one day, and you are better in my century than in any other".

"I want no favours. . . ."

"You shall have none". Rotus, though less sharp in the tongue than his colleagues was no less strict a disciplinarian, and it was with both pride and chagrin that Varres presented himself to Phrenobalus to have his own blistered feet doctored.

The surgeon chuckled roundly. "If you will mix your occupations, lad, what else can you expect, but ailing extremities, feet sore from soldiering and hands horny with healing?"

In their too-brief spells of leisure it became their custom, those who had been together to see Gallus put to rest, to seek out the merchant of Capernaum and listen to his talk. What he spoke of was exciting: this Jesus had let himself be crucified, that people might know he had died and been buried, and then had risen again with the promise that all men could do just the same. From this merchant Varres found answers to questions that troubled him, and help to understand the concept of Stephen's "holy ghost".

"To me, and I say to *me*, it seems that this is a spirit in my spirit that brings me to contact with the Power Supreme, the God of Jesus Christ".

On March 15th just after sunrise they left Massilia, marching three by three, in centuries, with Aulus Atticus at their head. The spun gold of a spring dawn played bravely upon their burnished bronze as they stepped smartly along the cobbled road, and struck sparks of envy from those who remained to hold the fort. Young sons of soldiers stood by their fathers, still, straight and proud of the force of which they had been a part, and desolate to be outwith it now. Wives, sensing their men's hearts, ceased to cling for a moment, and drew aside, having no part in this male emotion.

Varres saw none of the sadness of departure, none of the glory. His right foot had festered and he was indeed riding in the hospital waggon.

TWENTY-THREE

The River Rhodanus to their left hurried past, in haste to see
where it had come from, this molten streams of bright
metal, that sang loudly as it flowed. Aulus Atticus doubted
the propriety of the words his men sang, but heard their
rhythm beat a solid background to the miles they had to
march. Fifteen miles to-day before campdown, fifteen
to-morrow and the next day, and the next and infinitum,
would be tedious going indeed without the uplift of a song.

His men were still energetic when the day's fifteen miles
were behind them, and a few wished a push on a few
thousand paces yet, but their Chief Centurion was firm.

"Conserve your energy while you have it. There is a long
way ahead as yet". And so they set to, to dig a perimeter
ditch, plant the mound of earth that came from it with the
stakes each legionary carried, and prepare their evening
meal. Rotus made porridge enough for two and took it and
their ration of wine to the sick-waggon.

"I seem to have the gift of Fore Sight, young one. Did I
not say you would ride comfortably while the rest of us
march? Some doctor, you, who lets his wound fester".

Varres grinned wryly, for the last concoction he had
prepared for his sore would have been better used as a
liniment, his foot pounded and had an angry colour of
which he knew Phrenobalus would not approve, but he
dared not ask to see the surgeon.

"I shall come back when you have finished, and mark

155

you, I want to see an empty dish".

"You *must* eat. We have a long way to go".

The food made him feel sick so, with his friend out of the waggon, the boy made haste to clear his plate, into a linen cloth, which he tucked under his blanket securely at his feet. The warm soggy cushion strangely eased his sore.

When Rotus returned, his chores done and his men bedded, he was surprised to hear the lad ask, "May I have another dish of puls? The last has done me good". Thus Varres discovered the use of a hot meal poultice, and the physicician eventually healed himself.

By the time his foot was again worth standing on, the cohorts had halted at Lugdunum where they were joined by other cohorts under their own Senior Centurion, and had heard their familiar Rhodanus now called the River Arar. When at last it could sustain him on a full day's march they had crossed hills to the valley of the Sequana, and thence to Lutetia, the fort on its banks. There, their only orders were that they remain to refresh themselves for a week, and that Primus Pilus Aulus Atticus take charge of the entire company as acting Legatus until they reach, and reform at Eboracum in Britain.

Much of the week was spent, naturally enough, at the public baths, which were a feature of every sizeable Romanized town in any province.

Here as they bathed and oiled and scraped removing some of the layers of Gaulish grime accumulated on the way, Varres was pleased to observe that the striation of his friend's circus wound was less obvious than it had been, while Rotus was openly admiring of the strong, muscular hirsute youth who had been his young charge of a mere eight months ago. Eight months, was it only eight?

As he looked at Varres as he swam naked among other men, the Briton pondered that so much might occur, it seemed at random, in so short a time. Was it all without purpose, or for some very great purpose?

As the lad stood poised to dive again a fair, slim boy with

156

painted eyelids and reddened pouting lips, approached with a whispered comment, or question, and touched the lithe young form. Varres scowled once as uncomprehending, then with a beatific smile grasped the painted one firmly and tossed him into the water, where he landed face down on the porpoise form of a pot-bellied gasping old lecher.

"Let him paw or be pawed on by that one" Varres laughed after his sprint over damp slippery tiles. "Ech, such a one sickens me. Come Rotus, let us go back to where *men* belong, and see to-morrow's orders".

There were no orders, but an issue of clothing, which raised loud and ribald laughter. Aulus let a few jokes laugh themselves out, for well he knew that the boredom of the last weeks of marching had to explode itself somehow, preferably in laughter, then he clamped down on further ribaldry.

"These are brahai, leather leggings, to be laced against your legs with the thongs provided. They will withstand the coolness of the place we are going to".

"But centurion—sir—this is spring, soon coming on to summer. These things will tickle my knees". The clown caught his legate's look in time and refrained from further comment.

"You do not *have* to wear them. We merely provide these in case you need them". Aulus' tone was terse and final. His men wrapped their leggings in their packs and held their peace.

On the coast a fleet of galleys waited. The sight made Rotus flinch, for the memory of Gallus was still strong yet he felt somehow comforted that there were no slaves on these ships: the legionaries were to take turns themselves in rowing. Ah well, this was another new experience, and the sooner he got down to it the better.

Shifts at the rowlocks were short, for this was a job to which the men were not accustomed, but there was work to do besides propulsion. Baggage carts and the hospital waggon had also to be transported, and though their wheels

157

were off and the bodywork was lashed firmly to the poop, the list and swell of the boat set them at constant risk, so men not occupied at the oars kept watchful eyes and restraining hands on their all too readily moveables.

Yet no harm came to anything, or anyone. Indeed Varres, was vaguely disappointed that only a few of the men were seasick.

"Seasick? From Gesoriacum to Dubris, this short voyage? Now, if it had been from Noviomagus to Caletes, as when I went over last time. . . . ."

As they disembarked, Rotus assumed the slightly pompous tone of a seasoned traveller that he knew would irk the young man, and was rewarded with a spirited,

"Just wait till I get you a sick parade. . . ."

"I have no intention of being on sick parade now that. . . ."

"Now that you are home?"

"Home? I am far, far from home, yet, my lad. I *was* about to say 'Now that I am a centurion'. Here, help me with this wagon—it is your responsibility after all".

Rotus worked furiously at wheel and axle for his feelings were strangely mixed now that he had actually set foot in Britain. All that he had clear in his mind was that somehow he must find out how it was with Rufina. In the meantime his men needed his attention.

First the fort at Dubris, then the town of Durovernum, where they spent the second night, made his men feel much at home. Not only were they welcomed by the resident cohorts, but the very appearance of both town and fort was exactly as their counterparts in Italy.

Ten years ago the towns had not been like this, had they? or had he then been so soaked in his own misery that Rotus had neither seen nor cared?

Londinium, their next main stop, was a miracle of trade and organisation, on the bank of a broad beautiful river. On sight of it, a legionary gasped, "I had heard that the wild woman Boudicca had left the place in ruins. Surely it has risen fast from its own ashes?"

Later, however, as they marched from one town to the next, from fort to fort, on straight paved roads, even Varres to whom most things Roman were unquestionably good, began to weary of the sameness.

"I had wished to see strange places, new scenes, in this Britain, but it is still the same as home: colannades and stucco, tiles roofs and marbled fronts, little boys in tunics playing with knuckle-bones, and slaves escorting their mistresses to market. Wherever we halt next there will be public baths, or a theatre, or both, and all the streets will run straight and true from the forum to the centre. I am beginning to think that we Romans have little imagination".

If town and ports held the tedium of similarity, at least the scenery made them aware that they were no longer in Italy. From Londinium on its bright river, to Vermulanium on the great road Watling Street, soft, fertile land rolled on either side, thence a fold of hills led them across a track, the ancient Icknield Way, to the new Ermine Street and the north. On their left, wooded hills might ease the eye, tired of surveying immense stretches of flat land on their right; and so, eventually they reached Lindum.

Varres spent more time in the hospital waggon, dispensing potions, applying liniments and unguents and dosing with his inevitable laserpitium, for the very tedium of constant marching began to take its toll.

"I might wish for a brief uprising somewhere along the way", Phrenobalus saw fit to mention to Aulus, "for the men are bored and therefore sickly. Are there no rising Boudiccae or Carataci who might enliven our days for a spell"?

But all was orderly, organised, Romanised, and most tediously correct.

Even the numerous rivers, fords and bridges to be crossed before they reached Eboracum gave little relief to their boredom, for the rivers were sluggish, the bridges Roman.

Yet they did, at last, reach Eboracum.

TWENTY-FOUR

Unwilling to present a weary rabble to his colleagues, Aulus Atticus rested his cohorts on a wooded hill within sight of the large fort, and fed them extra rations of both grain and wine.

"With luck, Phrenobalus, we shall eat meat this evening, on the hospitality of our comrades down there. Our last meat meal was at Lindum, and that was stringy old mutton. My men need a change of diet".

The surgeon nodded. Fresh meat, some vegetables — especially his beloved cabbage — would perk the men's vitality, and a change of company would do their spirits good.

"Did not your orders say we shall re-form here, Aulus? Provided the changes are not too drastic, that will be a good thing".

Aulus attacked the cleaning of his phalerae with energy. He was not conceited, but to-day he felt he ought to let his medals be seen to advantage. This — he blew gustily on the metal plaque that usually hung nearest his shoulder — this he had gained in the east, that in Germany, and the third? — Actually he had forgotten.

"Not too drastic re-formation, as you say friend. I have a mind to take my cohorts to Agricola myself".

"Agreed, Atticus, but there are one or two friendships in

the ranks that are verging on the unhealthy. This, I know, is for the men themselves, yet my concern is for the health aspect. . . ."

"Your Varres is not implicated? I am aware he is young, and I may say handsome, and his Briton is a deal older but. . . ."

"You know the man is a Briton?" The surgeon for once was surprised.

"Of course; and that your assistant is under age though he does not look so. I know all I need to know of my men . . . now, though I did not, when these two were recruited.

"By the way, this last phalera", he gave it an extra burnish, "I gained under Cerialis back in 71. It might have been an oakleaf crown if Tribune Varres had not died on my hands".

Aulus grinned sideways at his surgeon.

"Oh, close your mouth, Phrenobalus; you are gaping like a landed mullet. I did say "Tribune Varres"—the father of your young medicus, the only people's tribune I found to be a real *man*. Abroticus, the tribune's slave, was really the one who deserved the award, but who could present a civil crown to a boy with no civil rights? Let me tell you the story one day when we have time. . . .

"Meanwhile, to the men: they must be smart as we enter Eboracum. Let me see if I can identify these friendships you complain of, as we make the rounds".

There was no need to exhort the men to smartness. Helmets, shields and swords were burnished; the silver plated standards of each cohort were being buffed with loving care, for the bearers took the greatest pride in their insignia, and indeed they stroked their leopard-skin headgear until one would swear the dead animal purred. Centurions with newly brushed helmet plumes and dazzling metalwork, were encouraging, urging, bullying their own sections each to outdo the next, till the hum of activity and friendly rivalry droned through the trees as a summer hive. Aulus grinned at his own trite simile, then scowled to see two effeminate sprigs lazing while their willing love slaves worked for them.

"Two queen bees in one hive". Aulus was no longer pleased with the likeness. I shall dispense with both."

To the century of Rotus the Briton he gave a special word of encouragement, and to young Varres the highest compliment he could.

"Your father was an excellent soldier — for a civilian".

The boy stared his question at his centurion, but Rotus merely laughed.

"Not much goes past our Primus, youngling. Remember and be warned".

Their entry into Eboracum had the air of a triumph, and the meal that followed was almost a banquet. Yet there was an uneasy undertone to civilities exchanged. As the second tables of the feast were brought in, laden with sweetmeats and fruit, the chief surgeon left the senior officer's company to whisper to Varres.

"How go your supplies of lasperpitium? There will be stomach pains in abundance to-morrow with all this rich stuff on top of our Spartan diet".

Varres, still gratified by Aulus' knowledge of his father, was proud to announce that he had a good supply already pounded.

"Good lad. We'll make a doctor of you yet".

"I'd rather have him soldier in my century, sir," Rotus smiled across the laden table, "then he could both fight and deal with my indigestion".

As the doctor turned laughing to go back to his own couch, a large lout of the resident legion, far gone already in wine, leered over Varres to the centurion.

"Your own personal property, is he, the young beauty? What would it be if *I* bought his services?

Varres flushed, and Rotus turned away, preferring to ignore the man, but he would not be passed over. The thick voice rose, insisting, "I said, 'How much must *I* pay for his services?'"

Rotus' fist took him on the chin, Varres' palm on the side of his head. The lusty one swore, twisted the boy's arm behind his back, but not before Varres grabbed a handful of honey-cheese sweets and ground them into the leering face. In moments there was battle, free for all, fists flailed, sweetmeats flew, a face was rubbed in a dish of jellied fruit. Rotus pounded the drunk in front, Varres eeled out of his grasp and pounded from the back, the two "queen bees" of Aulus' hive clung together on a table while their slaves fought two others for their possession. Insults flew, the mildest to the effect that "polished popinjays" were never good soldiers. Tables, couches, cushions overturned or took to the air, and everywhere was flying food. For a gleeful moment Varres wished his cousin Crassus was present—he had been a dead shot with digestible missiles—then he was knocked to the floor by an airborne wine jar.

The legate of the legion roared.

Varres recovered in a guardroom along with Rotus and half of his century, and a number more besides.

In the morning the new cohorts were withdrawn discreetly south-west to Calcaria, a fort then temporarily empty.

"There will be no-one there on whom to vent their undisciplined furies", the Legate's voice had been cold, remote, "unless your men care to brawl among themselves".

Aulus Atticus led his men out in grim hauteur. Inwardly he was furious. The surgeon told him what had happened, had told the Legate too, but the commander of the fort would see no insult in his legionary's words to Varres.

In Calcaria, Aulus made his feelings known in no uncertain terms and his men returned to their billets well aware that they had let him down, had bitterly disappointed their leader, and sure that they would remain in this miserable hole of a fort for months to come.

Each of the culprits was interviewed separately; Rotus as junior officer was last. Tall and straight, his long legs planted firmly, his sensitive fingers rigidly stilled, brown

163

hair short-cropped and helmetless, he took all that was said without dropping his eyes from his leader's face, and with no words but "I'm sorry sir; I should have restrained my fist".

Aulus talked long, pressing home his points effectively without repeating himself once. First — at length — there was discipline; then responsibility for discipline — at greater length; then a centurion's responsibility for discipline, at even greater length if that were possible; and finally, very, very briefly: one who could not discipline himself could not discipline others. Thus was Rotus demoted to the ranks; and having taken from him his vine-stick, Aulus suddenly unbent.

"Mark you, Tribune Varres would have approved of your defence of his son, as do I, but discipline must be *seen* to be upheld. . . . Anyway, it may be easier for you this way, now that you are nearly home. Doubtless you will leave us if and when we reach Agricola?"

Rotus saluted smartly and turned to go before the impact of the words struck him; then he hesitated, looked at his officer and put into words all that had confused his thinking ever since he landed in Dubris these weeks ago. Aulus listened sympathetically.

". . . At least, sir, you may be assured that if I find that my people need me, and I go, I shall not take up arms against my comrades. Even," he allowed himself a grin, "against that lecherous lout who thought to use young Varres".

The Chief Centurion nodded. "I have your word".

His century fumed and swore at his demotion and the injustice of their superiors in general. Varres wished to plead his case personally with the friend of his late father, but Rotus would have none of this.

"It is *quite* just; all he said about discipline was true: I ought not to have started that fight. The men of Eboracum were jealous, perhaps of the welcome we got, perhaps only of our display, and we were bored and ready for any diversion. But *I* should have not have started it."

"Even for me?"

"Well, let's say, for you I should have stopped it sooner
. . . or challenged him to a sword fight, just the two". His
eyes gleamed in laughter. "Why did I not think of that at
the time? I could have made him dance".

To Varres alone he related the rest of the Chief
Centurion's discourse, and his own reply, ending:

"He is right, as usual, you know: this will make things
easier when I do want to leave for home. I did not remember
him as your father's third centurion, but it seems he
remembered me. He is a truly just and tolerant man".

They did remain in Calcaria for months. In fact, the
remained there until the spring of 81 brought Decianus
Catus back from the frontier to Eboracum in a furious
temper to deal with some financial discrepancies between
supplies and costs. Yet another winter in the miserable
outposts of this ungrateful empire, on rations that seemed to
halve themselves in transit from the garrison fort did
nothing to sweeten his acid nature, and when he discovered
that not only were the cohorts of this fort living in luxury,
but that the Governor's long awaited reinforcements were
virtually immured a few miles away, then his fury knew no
bounds. As finance officer he dealt effectively with the
legion—he stopped their pay and halved their supplies.

Aulus would have enjoyed the legate's discomfiture and
the pungent comments of his own men, had he been at
hand, but they all had been despatched forthwith to the
frontier held by Agricola.

Their route north lay beside a range of hills that marched
endlessly along on their left. In the winter just past, when
they had been bored and humilated, forgotten in Calcaria,
these hills had lowered upon them in sullen gloom, or
hidden themselves in mists that shrouded Hades. They had
been hateful mountains. Yet now, in the joy of release, in
the fresh company of four centuries newly up from Lindum,
the cohorts of Aulus saw these same hills as cheerful

guardians of their well-intentioned way. Only Rotus looked about him with anything of trouble in his eyes.

These were not his hills: far from them yet, he knew; yet this paved road that they were on had the appearance of going on for ever. Would there now be roads through his own mountains, forging on inexorably like this? Towns were few, but there were forts, a vertitable chain of them, one now for each night's halt, and each had the same air of permanency as the road, each firmly, deeply entrenched and solidly Roman.

Gossip from the Lindum men — who quoted the Second Legion retired there for a rest — gossip pounced on by legionaries starved of news in Calcaria, was that Agricola had been raiding beyond the River Bodotria and that there was much rivalry between the men of his fleet and the men of his forts, to find out what they could of that barbarous country. There was much building going on too: a whole string of forts was arising between the Bodotria and Clota and at all sorts of places besides. Gossip had it further that Agricola would not be popular with the new Emperor if he wanted men for all stations constantly popping up. Domitian, jealous for his own popularity, would not countenance having a mere consul in favour of too many men.

However, Domitian was merely a name to them: Varres had not even known that Titus was dead. So far from Rome the city, who could feel much for its civic heads? Here, the man was Cnaeus Julius Agricola from Forum Julius in southern Gaul.

166

TWENTY-FIVE

Varres had his first sight of the notable Agricola sillhouetted grim and broad, against an evening sky. Beside him on the palisade of a fort, a tall, toga-ed gentleman stooped attentively to the general's pointing finger. Somewhere to the west something held them deep in discussion, seeming oblivious to Aulus' advancing cohorts; yet as the troop approached the ditch, Agricola turned sharply to call,

"Greetings, Aulus Atticus; and my thanks", and he was down in front of the commandant's quarters even before the cohorts reached there.

His greeting to Aulus was that of old comrades, quiet and sincere; to the men, his greeting warm, his instruction concise.

"As part of the IXth Legion you will occupy this fort under your Primus Pilus Aulus Atticus. There is much to do here for the good of this land and I shall expect it done. I shall dine among you at sundown".

The long-drawn summer evening passed busily as they settled in, before the sun finally began to sink over a soft wool swathe of distant hills and the general joined his new troops for supper. Below them, the blue estuary of Bodotria flared to their right, while an irregular line of forts like their own trailed to the western hills; and northwards beyond a tongue of firth and a sweep of plain, rolled fold upon fold of summer green.

From the Fort Caedigone lay a vista of such grandeur that could belong only to the Caledonia described by Rotus, and Varres felt sure that his companion must be eager to go home, but as he watched his friend at supper, Varres could see no hint of restlessness, of eagerness to be away; indeed the Caledon was totally absorbed in the conversation around him.

Agricola, with the officers, was brisk and friendly, yet leaving them in no doubt whatever of the consequencees of slacking or indiscipline; with the men, among whom he walked while the second tables were being brought in, he was brisk and formal, pleasant, but very much the supreme officer, a stickler for discipline.

The scholar Demetrius of Tarsus, who elected to have his meal with the lesser ranks, was charming and interesting, and it was on his words that Rotus hung. It seemed that Demetrius was attached to Agricola's forces in order to map the coastline of this strange, fascinating, if somewhat chilly island—for island he was sure it was. If he could, he told them, he would persuade the general to let him sail from the beautiful estuary at their feet, right round the north to the forts in the west, on the firth that had been called the Clota. It was easy to talk to Demetrius, to question him, even argue. Varres chuckled to see Phrenobalus make some flimsy excuse to the officers and join in the lively interchange of ideas round Demetrius, and he was not surprised when, the meal over at last, the doctor and the schoolmaster wandered off together deep in satisfying discussion.

He himself and his friend strolled on the palisade before retiring, to watch the last flicker of day die beyond the hills. Deep night closed down on blue-black folds of mountains, warming, comfortable, piled cushions for a migrant soul. Rotus sighed.

"Somewhere there . . . is my own land. Where I do not know—yet a Tarsan, a stranger, can tell me things of my

168

home that I may never know. There is much my people need to learn. . . ."

Varres waited. Here was the restlessness he had sought earlier in the evening.

"I have hopes that one day, not far distant, I may not only bring to my own people the best of what is Roman, but also bring to Romans the best of what is my native living—and all, I pray, without bloodshed. Perhaps I hope for too much? Yet certainly I shall not bear arms against either of my loyalties, my home . . . or yours".

Silence deepened around them: night noises of the fort were stilled, and birds had long since ceased to call; protecting hills crept forward to embrace them. Each, alone in perplexing thoughts, found comfort in the quiet dark. At last Rotus spoke again.

"I have prayed to the gods of the crucified, to tell me what to do. It seems I must wait, as yet, friend. Do you pray also, for us both".

Varres slept at last, in the full knowledge that soon he would lose his life-long friend to some purpose beyond his comprehension and that neither he nor Rotus really wished it so.

The week that followed brought diverse duties. Varres was sent on an exercise with the fleet and Rotus went with the hunt.

When in his turn Rotus went with the fleet, Varres was sent with the hunting party, beyond the next two forts, not to find boar or black-cock, or to destroy wolves or bears, but to collect a soft moss for dressings, of which Phrenobalus had heard. The day was clear and warm, his task a fascinating one, and Varres was nothing loth to be left behind by his companions while he scrabbled in brown fibrous moor to find what he was sent for. The tiny creatures he disturbed scuttered hither and yonder under his invading hand, like people, he thought, before an advancing army.

Like that ant with its load, had Gallus' sister trailed away when her father and brothers were destroyed? Was Rotus' family in hiding like these creatures beneath a stone, as the legions of Rome mauled over their land? To find comfort for Roman pain, he was here disturbing whole tribes of tiny things from an ordered, contented existence; was it fair for Roman hordes to disorder human tribes that they might salve a nation's sores with military success? What did the Circus rabble know or care about conquests in this distant place? What had he himself cared except for military glory when he planned to soldier in the IXth?

By late afternoon he was back at the hospital busily picking over his haul of soft moss, removing sharp spikelets of grass and flicking away foolish lingering insects, when he was suddenly summoned to the office of his commander.

"Bring ointments for a spear thrust", the messenger ordered. "The surgeon says: 'linen and padding and his instruments'".

The centurion's office was full. Six of that morning's huntsmen, Demetrius, the Pilus himself and his surgeon almost filled the little room, yet in a tiny clearing before the table, aloof, in an aura of their own, were two women, a young and an older.

Aulus was annoyed. His harangue broke off as Varres entered, but the boy knew that the soldiers were badly at fault. When Aulus rapped dismissal at his six he was halted by a movement from the older woman. Slight, proud, commanding, she held up a thin hand and spoke three gentle words.

"She says," Demetrius translated, "she wishes no trouble for the men".

Aulus barked, "They shall be dealt with in due course. . . ."

The grey head lifted higher, the words came again, insistent. Demetrius nodded kindly and spoke his reply. At a loss, Aulus barked once more, this time to the doctor.

"Look to the wound. I shall see that my cohort heals what it has inflicted".

The girl stilled, trusting what she found in the surgeon's face sat quietly for Phrenobalus to examine her slender forearm. Her companion, after assuring herself that the surgeon meant only good, turned to Demetrius with a soft lilting flow of words, which miraculously he seemed to understand. Aulus waited, not in vain, for interpretation.

"The lady wishes no harm to the men, for they were doing their duty as they saw it. She apologises for intruding, for setting her daughter and herself at risk in a hunting area, and for troubling the good surgeons; but she feels a strong persuasion that among the Romans there is something that is of good for her people."

Varres lifted his head at the words and surprised a strange look in the patient's dark eyes; a glint, he might have sworn, of mischief, before it drowned in pain. As Phrenobalus probed and cleansed her wound her free hand reached involuntarily to grasp the surgeon's arm. At a nod from his master, Varres transferred her grip to his own hand where it tightened on his fingers, bracing her to bear what was to be done, and sending a shock of feeling through the boy. The girl tightened soft red lips on pain that now Varres would gladly have taken upon himself, but she sat firmly still, her only movement short sharp palpitation beneath the stuff of her dress. Once she lifted her head, taut, poised, at strain, and the clear line of throat roused in Varres a wave of tenderness he had known only once before, when Aurelia at Sorrentum had wept for his mother, with her hand on his breast. He longed to touch that throat, the curve under her chin, the tendrils of hair by her ears, but one hand was imprisoned; with the other he held tight the edges of her wound.

Bound now, and padded with moss against unwary contact, her forearm fell, grotesquely heavy, on the slender length of her limb, as she bore it, amused, for the woman to see. A soft laugh bubbled up as she spoke and Varres knew he had heard nothing before that so pleased him.

Demetrius seemed to understand the words for he

laughed also, and called to Phrebobalus, "The little lady thanks you for your services. She now had a ram with which to batter our fort".

"Tell her I should rather she be friend than foe", Aulus was first with the reply, which translated, was rewarded by a smile from the girl and a dignified nod from her companion.

Demetrius interpreted further. "The lady says that her daughter agrees with her that we here may have something that will be of great benefit to her people".

Aulus' gallantry excelled itself. "Will the ladies be our guests until that wound starts to heal? Will they dine with us here, in this company to-night?"

It seemed that they would be pleased. Varres for his part was delighted.

Aulus dealt with his hunters, leniently, because the older woman insisted through Demetrius that he should, but alone once again in his office, he turned less leniently upon himself.

"Fool", he snorted. "Fool, you are, Aulus Atticus. Best not let the stern Agricola know how great a fool you are".

Yet he bathed and dressed for the evening meal with as much pleasant anticipation as he might have done twenty years before.

"Fool", he was still muttering as he supervised the setting of his office as a dining room, and "Fool, old fool" as he turned to greet his guests. Demetrius and the surgeon caught the murmer, sought each other's eyes and laughed.

"We are three, then; and a young one also". Phrenobalus nodded towards the boy. Varres, bathed, aglow, kept his eyes on the curtained door through which the girl would come, his dark eyes on fire with pleasure.

The women came quietly, straight and proud and . . . queenly was the word he sought, yet Varres knew that to a Roman the word was wrong. "Nymph-like" described the girl, her young form caressed by her gown of soft woven greens like the mosses he had disturbed that afternoon, her

172

straight proud shoulders mantled by a ripple of unbraided hair. Again that wave of feeling coursed through him ending in the hated blush.

Only Demetrius saw, and was kind. In a careful imitation of the woman's lilting tongue he asked the mother whether her traditions allowed that men sup at women's tables, and added laughing,

"But it is late to ask you that, as the meal is about to be served".

The reply sounded courteous and he translated with all the grace he could summon.

"The lady says that her household always share a meal. Only on formal occasions, at banquets, do they separate, the men to one side of the fire and the women to the other."

"This is no formal meal, tell her, Demetrius", Aulus declared. "She shall be on my right, and the young one, on Varres' left".

The woman sat, calmly, on the low couch indicated, as Aulus prepared to recline Roman style on the one beside her; the girl, longer of leg, reached her couch, eventually, with a bump and at once began to laugh. Oblivious of her mother's eye she watched Aulus, rose with a struggle and endeavoured to recline also, but her gown entangled her ankles and the laugh bubbled up again. In sudden insight, which pleased him greatly, Varres knew that she had not long reached the dignity of a woman's heel-length gown, that she was not older than himself. With only a glance for permission, he fetched from the inner room his commander's folded cloak to serve as a cushion, and at length amid laughter the whole company squatted on their couches.

The meal was the most genuinely cheerful one he had had since he had left his mother's house. Demetrius did his best to interpret the conversation, and when it seemed that he had difficulty with a word or expression, the woman rephrased her comments or used her mobile little hands to illustrate the meaning. Her sensitive intelligence and unstudied dignity pleased the three men; Varres was delighted with his companion. When Demetrius was too occupied to translate for them, they mimed their own conversation, to the accompaniment of the girl's bubbling laughter, and the boy's deeper, throaty rumble.

In her laugh Varres heard Stephen's effervescent joy and wished for his friend Rotus to hear it too. Since the death of Gallus, his freedman had been sober in thought, even melancholy, though tranquil enough, unworried: these people might cheer his sombre spirit. Yet too, Varres was glad that neither Rotus nor young Stephen were at hand as rivals for the lively one's company. This evening, even with the four adults present, he had her, mostly, for himself. This evening there was no past, no future, this evening was unique, it was for them alone.

TWENTY-SIX

For two more days the strangers remained at the fort, and Varres was in Elysium.

Rotus came back and reported to Aulus, spent an hour in the billet he shared with the lad, took lingering leave with the words,

"Varres, friend, I must go; I have seen my people". And yet the boy scarcely noticed his departure except that it allowed him to return to his new companion.

He acquired a few words of the lilt that was her language, while she learned some of the correct sonority that was his. Daily he helped the surgeon to dress her wound and was pleased, and sad, to see it heal quickly, cleanly and wholesome. When her mother finally decreed that they must go, she went obediently in her usual laughing spirits, leaving the boy yet again bereft.

It was then that he knew Rotus had finally departed and was now doubly, painfully alone.

Summer suddenly faded; Autumn drew in and the bleak chill on his soul matched only the cold winds that blew around the fort, tossing leaves and waves in helpless abandon. The deep aloneness of lost friendships sagged upon his spirit and he forgot to laugh. Joy departed, leaving a vacuum where first had been normal happiness of youth, of being alive, of companionship, and finally, this last, the joy of finding love. A girl's laughter echoed in his heart in the dreeing sigh of breezes from the north.

Phrenobalus saw his eyes turn dull, his shoulders droop, his step lag, and forebore to prescribe a potion. Instead he spoke to Atticus.

"The lad is lovesick, and ill with loneliness. If he had his Briton with whom to talk of the charms of his young lady he might even enjoy being ill for love. But I am too old to be his confidant, and his other friends, even the men of his faith, have little forbearance for what they choose to call barbarians, so the lad and his love are shut within himself. A change of place might do him good, and perhaps some action."

Aulus hesitated, only a little.

"In the Spring there is to be a reconnaissance into these mountains. I have volunteered our division."

In March they had reached Agricola's newest fort.

TWENTY-SEVEN

Set proudly in a strath below hills that crowded over the feet of far-massed mountains, the camp glared down through the valley and back over battlemented shoulders to a broad plain between the inlets of Clota and Bodotria, a flat land peopled by dour busy folk engaged in search for iron for their tools. These Dumnonii for the most part accepted the presence of Rome's eagles with quiet, preoccupied dignity, as long as there was left for themselves a fair share of the product of their industry. From time to time, however, raiding parties from further, bolder hill tribes descended to steal cattle or wreak sharp damage on unwary cohorts. Hill tribesmen if caught were dealt summary justice, were flogged, chained and despatched to Rome on the long weary road to slavery. Varres' heart ached for these scattered groups of wretches and he tended their scarred backs with infinite care, yet it seemed to him inevitable that slavery should be the reward of their foolhardiness. In speech with each patient he hoped, and dreaded, to hear an echo of that language he had tried to learn, and with each painstaking word of gratitude was relieved, and sad to hear no trace.

Months wore on. This winter's changing views seemed less dramatic, less touching to the heart, more dreary than of last season, yet this surrounding country was even more splendidly beautiful than he had seen. Mountains

177

shouldered their mysterious way out of sight, veiled one day in mist, the next day touched to glorious fire by a passing finger of their great god Sul; then again they would settle snug in piled fleeces of gleaming snow to sleep until came soft breezes stirring, lifting, folding their covers to tuck them away.

While his comrades complained, chafing cold limbs in vain hope of achieving warmth such as they had known at home, Varres quietly, doggedly pursued his occupations, dreamed his dreams, puzzled over the purposes of life — and knew that this season was not less beautiful but merely that he felt it so.

One night he took the watch of a sentry suddenly struck with the shivering fever. The moon hung high in its star-gemmed tabernacle; hills huddled close against tingling frost, and tiny mists from his breath soared lost and aimless to the cloudless sky. Silver dust lay on all things, making them precious. In heavens awash with whitened light Varres saw again the extraordinary luminescence of the rock cave at Capraea, the silk of his mother's banquet gown.

Later, when he slept, he dreamed that he was a child again in his cot at Herculaneum, with his parents by his bed.

"Take good care of my standards, son, Guard well the Neptune of the Ninth".

His mother's smile was tender. "Take greater care of my love, my infant. Take the greatest care of love".

Next day three cohorts of the IXth with Varres as their temporary surgeon, were sent a day's march north to yet another fort newly completed. Men grumbled more than ever and brought wildly varied symptoms for Varres' attention, until he remembered his master's panacea, the threat of instant amputation. In his heart he sympathised with the men, for this fort at the mouth of a deep valley seemed to them all to be the very farthest outpost of the empire, and they were a small force indeed to hold it. The

178

weather was at its least prepossessing: light, chill drizzle
soaked them as they worked and there was here no hot water
to provide the comfort of baths. A swollen stream gushed past
their ditch and heavily wooded mountains to right and left
gloomed sullenly over their shoulders. Varres wished that
their move had been made at a better season; and yet, he
had little sympathy for malingerers: discipline must be seen
to be upheld. Diffidently he asked for extra nourishment to
be provided against his patients' ills and depressions and was
pleased that his Chief Centurion ordered a meal that was
almost a minor banquet.

Again reminded of his mother, Varres ate his 'little feast'
in a mood of deep nostalgia, while those around him
warmed and relaxed and began to feel that life, even on
such a shrouded lowering night, was bearable again.

The second watch was far spent when uproar arose. Varres
awoke from a dream of Vesuvius to know that the noise was
not of eruption. Metal clashed, men roared, a hideous bray
reverberated over the palisade, a dull thud echoed around
his hospital walls. A man yelled,

"The barbarians are here, at the very gates".

Men awoke, confused, to keep their fort against a surging
tide of strangers, flailing, gashing, cleaving to right and left
with long vicious, two-edged swords. Men fell, rose again
and rallied. A Roman trumpet sang "Advance". A long wild
Caledon war-horn boomed "Beware". Sling shot whistled
through the camp from nowhere, going all-where, and none
stayed to reckon quite where. For moments the moon
cleared to show the battle's tale and Varres saw the north
gate taken, held by cheering light-skinned warriors, some
hide-covered, helmeted and grand, some naked, some clad
in breeches like his own. With a cry as of wounded elephants
a pair, chariot mounted, roared through the gate, the driver
plying whip on all, as on his ponies, the warrior hewing,
hacking, bellowing, slicing to right and left. Varres saw his
Primus advance on them, saw next his plumed helmet aloft,

the head still firmly encased, saw the war-wheels splash over his body.

The moon hid it's face in shame.

Suddenly the clamour at the gates changed from elation to fury, changed again to dismay and fear. Two chariots, over eager, had locked in the very threshold; ponies screamed and kicked, drivers cursed, warriors roared, barbarians behind pressed on, Romans in front pressed back, men, slaughtered, screamed and sank. The war-horn brayed a different note and the press behind fell back, untwining the blockage of animals, wheels and corpses. Legionaries surged through the gate in pursuit, and, for the space of a sword cut and javelin thrust, it seemed that Rome would once more conquer; yet again on the command of that imperious carnyx the barbarians wheeled in attack and spread Roman centuries abroad before their walls. Hand to hand, the IXth were at advantage first with shorter, more wieldy swords.

Varres thought of his freedman; could he be in this mob, this horde of yelling fury, who took heads by way of captives?

No, Rotus had left his word. The slight advantage wavered. War chariots screamed upon them, crushing down; trumpets bellowed abuse each to the other, men's cries and horses' choroused; away and beyond echoed the dream of a legion's call. The IXth heard the dream and rallied. Step by painful step they pressed their vantage, recking little of direction except that it was away from their fort.

The young surgeon wielded his sword as deftly as his master might a scalpel and as ever braced himself not to sicken over the reek of blood. The weaving horde were his enemies, like it or not, and his duty was to fight for his Legion and for his Legion's honour. The standard of the IXth must not be smirched by him.

Over beyond the carnage a signifer's challenge rang "To the standard, men, to the standard. On, press on". Faint moonlight tinged its gleaming pole, touching badges with mystery, its ribbons with faery light. The cohort sign of Rome, for a breath, took the shape of the cross of Christ.

Varres glimpsed an enemy spear aimed in the same brief glint of light and raced forward to the standard. Leopard skin covering offered little protection against that wicked barb, but with his final breath the bearer sent again the call "*Nona Triumphalis*; hold fast the Neptune of the Ninth".

As he sank, the standard tilted, but did not reach the ground: caught in the hand of Varres it rose again proud and high.

"*Nona Triumphalis*; on press on".

Blood, confusion, brutality, the need of each for his own to survive, sank and surged around him roaring to limbo his own feeble challenge, to oblivion blowing the bicker of trumpet and carnyx both. A tidal wave of battle noise engulfed him, a monster of Mars bulled in his ears; yet faint in the rolling distance echoed that dream again of a legion's cry 'Vicesima venit, the XXth comes. Hold fast".

"The IXth will hold", Varres yelled to heedless clamour. "We of the IXth will triumph".

Forward of the boiling surge he bore his trophy to a hillock, bearded in scrub, washed by vague, clouded moonlight, untouched by the moil below. There he would plant his Neptune firmly for his comrades-in-arms to see.

"Look, the standard, Ninth. See Ninth, how it stands".

Nearer now, the Twentieth's greeting was no longer only a dream.

A sling shot hissed, spitting contempt upon his boldness, cleaving a sickle of spite to Rome's symbol. Clangour shattered into silence, the ensign fell, not to the ground but over Varres' fallen body.

Silver birches, bare now, frostily fingered the sky, a known face, smiling, swam and sank from view.

Pines, close-armed, protective, silenced even breath, a

fragment of laughter shattered and fell.

Darkness, warm and redolent, murmured near, a spring of hair brushed by.

Neptune rolled, wallowed and went down.

Dreams twisted into dream, visions came and fled. Daylight and dark were nowhere in a dusk of unfeeling gloom. A void encompassed, in which was neither lift nor fall; all things were one, and life was not of them. Breath itself gave no sign of its being, time was, in that it passed, unsensed, unhindered.

At last a glimmer broke the gloom, a thin silver glimmer, and a sheen of bronze. A voice, careful, in his own tongue, proffered the thought of food, a face serene, persuasive, bent close; the bronze sheen and the voice were one, before the darkness gloomed once more.

Later the voice persuaded again, persisted, sharpened.

"It is wise that you eat now".

With a supreme effort Varres made his attention hold, to let a savoury brew flow over his strictured throat and kept open heavy eyes until it was done.

The room, circular and low, was dark except where a fire glowed in the middle and a glint of outer light shone from a smoke hole in the roof. His couch, of deep warm furs, all but enveloped him, so that his attendant with the food bowl was but a face and a crown of hair, and gently careful hands.

He slept again, this time undreaming, and woke content.

The gentle face had gone. Near his couch stood two stalwarts, bearded, tattooed, forbidding. Varres moved his head to see them better and at once one, in open tunic and leather breeches, approached unsmiling to touch the boy's head with a broad workhorned hand. The other man, toying with something beyond view gave a grunt of disgust and Varres rose among the furs, only to be thrust back again by the big hand planted firmly on his chest. Yet the man's toy, the glimmer of silver, had taken sudden shape. It was his cohort's standard. The guard's grunt of disgust had been caused by the Neptune of the Ninth.

Dreams and visions faded. Reality hurled itself upon him: he was a prisoner of the barbarians and its standard was lost to his Legion. Shame burned through his frame in white heat so that he shivered. The nearer guard growled as he piled yet another fur on the couch and added fuel to the hearth.

It would not do, Varres let a rueful, fuddled thought obtrude, for a prisoner to die of fever before his punishment was due.

Tales of barbaric tortures, ritual sacrifice by the priests of these people, vicious exchange of a life for a life lost in battle, tales half-heeded during his days at the fort, drummed in his mind as he pondered on his situation. These tales he had disbelieved — when he had deigned to hear them through — because all his experience of the barbarians had been with his kindly freedman and later with these gentle queenly women in the office of Chief Centurion Aulus Atticus. Such cruelties could not be of their people, he knew; but of these men here beside him. . . ? Who might know.

The fact was he was a prisoner and must take what would come to him. It was his betrayal of his father's ensign that shamed him and made him sick.

The shivering passed. He threw off the fur rugs and stood up in the gloom, to signify that he was ready for what was to come, but his head swam, dizzying him out of his poor shred of dignity. Four hands pressed him back upon the couch, two voices growled unintelligibly till he ceased to struggle, then one uttered with infinite precision *"Ad principem — cras ibis* — tomorrow you'll go to the chief".

183

TWENTY-EIGHT

Varres slept little that night, scarce surprising, since he had slept so much during the last weeks, but neither did he rest.

He was alone, but not unguarded: beyond the door, soft sounds of lightly sleeping men kept him duly aware of captivity.

There was no fear in his wakefulness, for fear had had no place in his scheme of life since childhood. Fear was an indignity to any Roman boy after he had first met his match in a wrestling bout, or had his first fall from a fast horse. He who had seen beauty in the boiling of Vesuvius, who with Crassus risked the anger of the Emperor and felt only revulsion for the things of the Circus, who had heard much of a man called Jesus and his promise of clear, uncomplicated life after death, he, with all such things behind him, could scorn apprehension in the face of death.

No, his wakefulness was spawned not of fear but of regrets: bitter regret and shame to have brought his standard low, his father's beloved standard, low to the level of imprisonment and a taunting guard; regret that he had made as yet so little of his life; regret that his father's line would cease in him, his mother's gentle courage have no heirs; regret that he had accepted the friendship of such as Rotus, Stephen, Gallus little Aurelia at Sorrentum, the lively laughing girl of the spear-thrust and had given so little

184

in return.

Unhappy as it was for a lad of eighteen to realise that his life was at an end Varres faced the prospect with equanimity, since he saw there to be no alternative. Stories told that these barbarians took no captives, for slavery or any other purpose, but kept human heads as trophies, ornaments, even drinking flagons. Varres looked at his limbs and regretted their loss.

Stories told too, that Druid-priests roasted human victims in wicker baskets over sacrificial fires, and claimed to read omens from the lie of a slaughtered body, the fall of gouged entrails, the pointing finger of a severed hand. The young doctor thought of blood and reek and feared that these priest rulers lacked both heart and stomach.

A strange anatomical abnormality floated in Varres' imagination and he laughed aloud. Life had yet much to laugh about.

But were these practices more cruel than he had seen in the Circus? Was roasting of war prisoners more terrible than making human torches of Christians as Nero had done? Dare he, Varres, a Roman stripling, condemn in another country what he had had to accept at home?

Misty grey light above the roof-hole showed that somewhere the sun had risen to another day as the lad pondered vast problems of national faults and foibles and found no solution to satisfy him. It seemed that what the Crucified had taught, a care for fellow men, was what both this race and his own sorely needed, and found so far at lack in its rulers.

Daylight strengthened, to filter vaguely above the fire. An attendant came to offer a bowl of stew, another to pile dry earth clods on the embers of last night's warmth, and still none came to summon him to the chief. Nor did his heavy handed guards of yesterday return. Varres ate, paced the shadowed room, and mused once more upon his position. New-fed firelight played upon the silver plate of his standard which had been propped carefully against a dark earth wall, and as he studied its clean piercing line, the gleam of phalerae and bright shimmer of ribbons, it came to him that there was none of the dust of battle upon it, no sign of the moil it had been through; in fact, it shone with care but recently bestowed on it.

"For a plaything", Varres grunted, "or for sacrifice", and he bristled to think of rough hands toying with these ribbons.

"But Druids, priests, rulers, whatever you are, you will find my Neptune hard to burn. The king of seas will not be conquered by fires".

And again his line of thought diverged. Neptune's monster in the bay below Vesuvius had sunk before Jupiter's eruption, not vanquished but subdued. Rotus' chain of firefighters had failed to quench the galley fire before it had overcome the Gaul.

His own life in the last few years bobbed and obruded on his thinking and ever and again he came back to the hopes he had had of meeting once more the lovely girl with the bubbling laugh.

Aulus Atticus could have kept her prisoner. Why had he not? Where was Atticus now? Had he heard of the fall of his cohort standard? Did Phrenobalus know of his assistant's default? Was he angry? . . . disappointed?

The word came unbidden, "Glad"?

The hide curtain over the doorway lifted, slanting a beam of grey daylight over the earth floor on to his couch of furs, before a shape obscured the light, a heavy shape that moved cumbrously to the fire. Varres turned and was surprised to see the gentle face he had imagined in his delirium. The woman lifted her burnished head, smiled and was gone.

As day passed and no other came to interrupt his wayward thoughts, or lighten the darkness of his prison, Varres became more and more dispirited. His equanimity of the morning changed to nervous irritation, to depression and finally to anger, at himself, his guards, this chief whose

186

prisoner he was, and the gods, any gods, his God. His life, however futile, was not for living in a dark and airless cell; no man had the right to hold another in confinement by himself; the gods gave him life — how dare they take it from him so soon? He kicked at a turf on the fire, sending leering shadows over mud and wattle walls, and sparking this dark flame of rebellion. He turned to the door, to burst out, to seek the chief, to live his life; and was forced back by four strong hands.

Then the complete injustice of his thinking struck him with the weight of these same hands. His guards could be Briton, Roman, Gaul; he, Varres, was a prisoner of war, a token between races. He must take what was to come, and with what dignity he might.

The curtain at the doorway had drooped, sending a fine sliver of light across his room to rest on the further wall, just where his standard stood. Once again the Roman signum took the form of the cross of Christ. Varres looked long on this phenomenon, willing his mood of resentful submission to resignation, to calm acceptance; trailing dark ribbons of confused thinking from shadowed caverns of his mind to the clear beam of this cross on the wall; staring, finally, with open, empty mind upon the only light about him.

The fire had dropped to brown embers; the room grew chill, the sliver of daylight and silver reflection dimmed to a vague grey shape in total darkness, and still the young man stared, empty of all thought, waiting.

"Up. Out. To the chief".

His guards had come. Stumbling, he let himself be jostled from the dark of his room to deeper piled darkness of the outer world. A moonless sky lay velvet thick on hills jowled close to looming woods and black, squat, menacing structures.

They marched him — and his head cleared — through a maze of round buildings, windowless, penetrable only by one curtained door, all of them gloomy and sullen as the

187

silence of his guards. The conversation of these, in any tongue, it seemed was restricted to commands.

Suddenly he was inside a building, larger than the rest, lit by innumerable torches, and by a huge fire burning strongly in the middle of the floor. Blinded by sudden light Varres dizzied, his senses thickened by heat, smoke and the press of noisy, sweating, jostling people. For a moment he was back in the throng of the Circus, and his throat constricted.

What had this mob in mind for him?

A voice from beyond the firelight's glare demanded silence. The throng parted. Druids, Varres remembered, were priests, men of authority. They spoke, and men obeyed. The lad drew himself up and stood forward, alone. Captive or not, his was a Roman's dignity.

Again the voice boomed, "Advance, young man", and the words were in good Latin. Druids were men of learning, one heard tell.

"Advance. Beyond the fire. We would look upon you".

Straight and tall, Varres stalked between the throng and piercing heat, and was pleased to hear a murmur, that might have been of sympathy, from women whom he passed. In the dimness beyond, he barely discerned a trio aloof from the rest, one a straight, commanding little woman. Gold of torcs at neck and wrist of each reflected a sheen of copper hair. A dark beard jutted, moved.

"Nearer" came the voice again, and exploded in unintelligible sounds. The crowd bearing torches, surged forward shouting some form of acclaim. Their leader signalled silence.

"Nearer, youngling, nearer. Varres, welcome to my home".

The bearded one clasped his wrist, the small lady kissed his cheek; the red-head sat where she was, lumpy, smiling.

"Rotus . . .?"

"The same, friend. Varres, you gape like a landed mullet".

The crowd roared again as their chief laughed aloud.

188

"See, Aunghais, the guest chair. Mother, have the women bring in the feast, and Rhuandha . . . Varres, this is my Rufina". The red one smiled into the boy's confusion.

"You will understand shortly. Meantime sit by me till the feast comes — I mislike these days, to rise or stand over much".

Then Varres saw that she was with child and the joy behind her eyes was incredible. In the chief's eyes too, was untold delight; the Chief, his freedman, his erstwhile slave . . . Varres burned with shame at the thought.

"You will understand", the Red One repeated. "All is well now; that is what matters. Tell me, do you understand my Latin? We . . . I . . . have been learning. . . ."

Seated firmly on the guest chair, on the Chief's right, Varres was given a huge bowl of stewed meats, and urged, in two tongues, to eat to the very last. A guest cup too of beaten silver, filled with strong wine, was pressed again and again in his hands, till confusion and fumes made him long once more for sleep. Rufina smiled at him across her husband.

"Keep awake until the songmaker has sung. Husband, Abrachan, have the musician come now".

Thin reed music heralded the songmaker, a bright-faced player with a gift for mime, on whose words the feasting crowd hung with avid concentration. Wine cups rested, jaws ceased to work, tongues stilled and all eyes turned on the actor. Before he too was caught up in the story told by hands and mobile face — the words were unintelligible — Varres was relieved, for the sake of the man's energy, that the fire glowed now merely in embers. The actor rowed, swam, drove a carriage, cradled a child, was annoyed; watched a spectacle, sickened and sank; he was a soldier, doctor, sailor, fought a fearsome battle and died. The lilting words haunted, brought a memory, stirred restlessness, and wept.

Varres searched the crowded hall for what he wished to see.

Rotus, the chief, his freedman, touched his arm.

"The story is for you. I shall translate part at least though with much less effect, than Tormaid has given it.

"You Varres, the guest of this tribe are their hero. You have saved the life of their chief by a . . . a strange divising . . . you have ridden fast and far, in a far land, and have saved their chief a second time from untimely death. The Rodents of Rome. . . ."

"Stop, stop. This was not what he sang of, I am certain. He spoke of the island, the baby of Gaius and Valeria . . . little monster . . . Crassus and the arena, all these that only you could have told him. Now tell *me*. How did I get here? How did you get here? Why was I kept prisoner?"

"To-morrow, youngling. To-night we sleep. My Rhuadha — and our child — are wearied. We depart now, each to our own house. Ferghais and Aunghais will take you to yours".

TWENTY-NINE

Morning was fluttering pigeon's wings across the drowsing sky when Varres pushed aside the door curtain of what had been his prison. There were no guards. From each round house came gentle sounds of contented awakening to the business of the day; here a child tewchered to itself its own morning conversation; there a lower tone grumbled the night's sleep away, girned a thick head into compliance; yonder a dog and man growled mutual fealty before the hunt, and beyond, horses and cattle queried delay in loosing them for pasture.

Varres stretched and listened. Which house was that of Rotus — Abrachan . . . his freedman, no, his friend . . . the Chief — he had no notion, nor would he have approached it even if he did. It was enough to be alive, free, among friends, this perfect dawn.

Some fifteen houses lay streetless within a palisade as high as their walls. Beyond this, to his right a dark wood marched close-packed to the foot of hills piled far and high in mystery. To his left a river burbled somewhere out of sight telling its tale to a shrubby plain, straight combed here and there in tresses of ploughed land and pasture; and between hills and plain a moorland rolled in gentle swathes.

A hound loped to within a pace of him and halted, its questing eyes deep probing his, then it moved to his feet and

191

dropped, fixing him where he stood.

"Dhuanbeg has accepted you, has made you his property", Rotus called lightly from a doorway. "Come both of you and break your fast before we begin the day".

A soft two-note whistle pricked the dog's ears, but move he would not until Varres stroked his throat and spoke.

"Come beautiful one, come and eat".

The Chief held open the door curtain of his house that man and dog might enter, and in this small courtesy the Roman read a dignity he had never met before: there was welcome too, as he had known from Aretria, love as from the Briton at Sorrentum, goodwill as from the bailiff at Uncle Aemilius' farm, but simple dignity that was the Chieftain's own.

"My wife is resting. The child is restless and heavy.

"Cheese and oat bread with suffice, I hope, for I am little of a cook. My mother, and Servilia, and latterly Rufina saw to that".

"But you are a chief. Have you . . .?"

"No slaves? No. I am indeed chief of this my tribe and so I am head of the family, but I ask nothing of my people that I may not do myself. To-day I pasture the animals and herd the cattle that are on the hill. Yesterday I was away from home and tomorrow . . . I may be needed here. Others will take their turn then, others whose heads to-day are thicker than mine". He bent laughing, to feed the dog. "Dhuanbeg answers only on whistle. You must learn it".

There was an inner chamber in this building, where Rotus spent many moments before they left to care for the animals, and when he came out his face was alight.

"My wife sends her greetings, and hopes that your head is moderately clear".

Together the two drove cattle through a broad gate in the palisade out to the strips of pasture land, lean now before summer's growth had started.

"Next spring we must move to other pastures. These have served us well these two years since I came home, but should

192

now be rested till the grass grows green again".

As they moved round the outskirts of his village from plain to moor, Rotus explained his people's mode of life in a difficult but lovely land, using the best of its fertility then moving on, to leave the last patch fallow for a time.

"Perhaps if we had ploughs that dug deep enough we might keep the same ground fertile. My smith works hard — it may be that one day he will perfect his plough, as well as keep us in weapons and hunting spears".

He laughed again, a sound of deep contentment. "My first description of your Roman plough must have been a careless one indeed for the poor man's interpretation of what I meant was little stronger than a strigil, yet even so that was better than my neighbour's hoe".

Dun shaggy cattle moved almost unseen among bracken and tough grasses, carefully cropping what little they could find to form a cud before Dhuanbeg harried them onward. Varres practised his whistle under direction, and soon he and the dog were fairly expert in doing what Rotus wanted done, until more than a score of the shaggy beasts had been moved over the moor and nearer to the pasture. Then finally the three turned back down to the village.

Rotus looked on the huddle of houses and it might have been that he sighed . . . "Wattle and daub are not beautiful as Roman bricks and marble, but are nearer the needs of my people. One day when my plough digs deep and my land is fat and there is no need to move on, I shall build a shining home for my family.

"Large and imposing, like my dear Aunt Marcia's?"

"Indeed no; like your home in Herculaneum".

Each for a moment had his own thoughts, until the dog nosed out a black-cock, and the bird's frenzied escape brought them back to each other.

"Rotus, your mother came to Aulus' camp . . ."

"Where I glimpsed her as I returned from the fleet. I had heard at the Granary Camp on the Tava that two women had been enquiring there; you see, my mother seems to have what we call the Sight—the gift of seeing what has not yet happened, without the aid of omens and portents—so that she sensed my arrival as soon as we landed in Dubris and knew—so she says—when we finally reached the Bodotria. Then she set out to find me, to give my people a leader. My father died, you see, while we were "stayed in some dreich hill place in the south of Cartimandua's lands". The words are my mother's. The place could be Calcaria—remember?"

"So your people were leaderless because you had fought for me in a soldiers' brawl?"

"Not leaderless. The old one has fire in her tiny frame. She sent for Rufina and her twin brothers from their father's tribe, and promised my people a chief *and* an heir when she would complete the plan she had in mind; then she took my . . . a kinswoman . . . for company, and scoured the camps for me. Indeed, the old one has spirit."

"And the young one too, your kinswoman. Where is she now?"

"With my mother's people beyond these hills. She is young and must mature. It seems", Varres missed his look askance, "that she has been bent on a doubtful marriage. She may cool her ardour with her uncles".

Varres gloomed. He had not thought of the lively one going to another in marriage, nor of thinking of marriage at all. He had forgotten that she, like himself, would have grown older, became adult, fit for adult life.

"The dog is her's" Rotus went on. "He was the rogue of a litter, tiny and helpless, so she took him".

Dhuanbeg clumped over Varres' feet as they halted to draw breath, and the beast's weight felt warm and comforting.

"My wife's brothers, your guards, found you wounded in undergrowth, where they had expected to find a boar. They coveted the Neptune for themselves, and you, a Roman, for the tribe, so they left you in a pine copse until I came. Dhuanbeg and the girl came upon us there—the . . . the dog decided then that he liked you—and so by stages we got

194

you home".

Fragments of dream, or delirium, returned and the youth heard again a sparkling laugh of bubbling joy.

"The twins gave up their hut for you, and together with the women nursed you of your blow—indeed it was Aunghuis who discovered the lump on your head and Ferhuis who measured it". He laughed. "No-one really agreed that it was quite as large as his fist. Then they elected to try your spirit by acting out that foolish ritual in the feast-hall.

"These two have the imagination and spirit of the good Stephanus, but so far not much of his trust in Christ. Yet, I have wooed them a little from their faith in the Druids. Rufina and my mother helped me there. My Rhadha's copper hair and the old one's Fore-Sight are suspect to the priests, while the Learned Ones' hieromancy from human sacrifice is totally repugnant to the women. In the same way, you and old Aemilius and many more in Rome, loathed executions in the theatre. Much, it seems, is a matter of personal decision.

"Up Dhuan. Varres rouse your hound for we must go on. My carpenter has a waggon for me to inspect before it goes to the wheelwright, and to-day", his brown eyes softened to honey-amber, "I have orders for my coppersmith to make a fine snake bracelet for Rhuadha for when our child is born. Her brothers wished me to use the silver of your standard, but I would not have that."

Varres loped through the heather, matching the Chief's eager stride.

"The Neptune worries me. I have disgraced my father's Ninth by its loss from the Legion".

"But disgrace comes only if you lose it to an enemy. At least, that is what Tribune Varres taught me, and Aulus Atticus told me no different. My people are not your enemy, for I swore I should never fight against Rome's Legions even in my own land".

"Yet, if they invade. . . .?"

195

"I shall evade, I and my people. We are, after all, a wandering race. It is natural to find other pastures.

"The twins, my good-brothers, are careful scouts. I told you they remind me of Stephanus? We shall not be caught unaware by the Eagles.

"For you, the decision is yours to go with the Eagles, or to stay with the humble black-cock on my moors. Do not decide now. Think, get to know us, learn our ways and our tongue, pray to the God of Stephen and Paul. At least, wait until my heir is born".

So the matter of Varres' future rested throughout silver summer days of glowing contentment. Varres took his share in the community's life, worked with the smiths, helped wheelwright and carpenter, felled trees and dug turf for winter fires, herded cattle with Rotus' brothers, shore sheep with the twins who had been his guards and were now his friends. He watched the women treat wool with plants from the moor and weave softly coloured garments for their folk, garments the tinge of heather and hill, of morning mists and mountains, and he wished for a woman to weave for him. Only the absence of the girl he now knew to be Rotus' kindswoman vexed his tranquility, her absence and the knowledge that she had been thinking of marriage.

After a sweating morning at the forge where he had helped to fashion another deeper plough, he wandered off to bathe in the river, without Dhuanbeg at his heels for once.

Pellucid water danced to the charms of Sul as the Sun-god smiled his pleasure; pastures flourished in his benevolence and ploughed land donned a viridescent veil to take vows of fealty to him, the great Provider. Ancient hills drowsed comfortably in shawls of summer pines and the whole world rested, content.

Through a fine fringe of trees at the river's edge lay a tiny beach of white sand, where Varres thought to spend a dreaming afternoon with only his thoughts for company.

But Rotus and his wife were there first. He lay, drying in the sun after a swim, naked but for a brief loin-covering and the flow of his wife's brilliant mane as she lay cradled on his shoulder. Gently with her hair she dried the last faint drops from his skin and feathered her fingers over the scar white on his breast.

Varres stood unseen, transfixed by a lance of envy at their deep pervading joy, yet strongly wishing to be gone and not intrude. He saw the woman's body heave, her lips draw tight and thin; he saw the Chief lift his head to search her face, saw her smile in reassurance. Then he loosed his feet and went: this moment was for these two alone.

Yet the words they spoke, had he heard, were commonplace.

"Your Roman is gentle and kindly. There seems to be no blood-lust in him".

"Many Romans are gentle and kindly. But blood-lust may be in any man if need for it arise — as with the gladiator who gave me this. . . ."

He captured her hand and pressed in on his breast.

"It was his flesh at risk, or mine, and I had no less appetite than he, with the mob keening for one of us to fall. . . ."

She put halt to his tale with a kiss. "These days are gone, love" and winced as she settled back.

"We think forward, do we not, for our little one's sake?" A moment of pain stayed her tongue.

"The future is for the Roman too. To-day he asked once more for your sister. It is cruel to keep them apart".

"More cruel to bring them together if he wishes to go back to the Eagles. Life at a fort is hard for a woman, especially hard for one who is not Roman, and to the legions our Bright One would be but a wild barbarian. That is not what I want for my sister".

"If Varres decides to remain with us and he wishes for her, he shall have her — she certainly wishes for him as she was at pains to tell me while he was ill — but here too their life may be difficult. You know what the High-Thane thinks of Romans".

"Calgaich hates Romans as invaders of his land, as would you if you knew them only so. But if you bring your sister home, Varres may decide to remain with us. He, with you, has much to teach our people.

"Also, I wish your little sister to be as happy as I".

"You *are* happy, Red One? *We* are happy, beloved".

His hand cupped her face as he kissed her then smoothed gently down the rest on the curve that was their child.

"Then our sister will return when the infant comes".

"Which, my love, will be very soon. Take me home".

Varres did not see his freedman lift his wife and tenderly carry her to his home, nor knew the fight the Red One had to birth the child. Varres was alone with his decisions under a tree at a bend of the river.

Rightly, Rotus had left the decisions to the boy, whether to remain in this land as one of the people, or to return to the country and ways of his father, and Varres appreciated that the choice must be his own and only his. This was a land of beauty and kindness and there had been much in Rome to give him pain, but here too, if he knew it longer there could be cruel and evil ways. All his years Roman laws had been his rule of life. There were rules here too, under Rotus, practical, kindly guiding lines for ife, but elsewhere . . .? The Druids were the judges, Calagacus was Great-Thane, a ruthless, sword-flailing warrior who took heads as battle trophies. What rules did they impose, the greatest ones, what cruelties, what pains, perversions, lusts?

Tiny white petals fell on him from the tree above as he pursued his arguments, against remaining here, or returning to his legion; against resuming a life that had been mostly a habit of thought, or remaining a stranger, among a people strange albeit kindly; above all, against losing the right to be known as a citizen of Rome; and ruefully he remembered what little attention he had paid as

198

his grammaticus taught the art of discursive thought. His head, being Roman, was practical; his heart was the girl's and she was away.

As the afternoon drowsed on through conclusions inconclusive, and fine white petals misted the river's edge beside him, Varres found the tree a more rewarding study than his personal problems. A frond leaf dropped prematurely, bringing a cluster of embryo berries, delicate, perfect, full of promise. The leaf itself was pinnate, as the winged Camp of Agricola.

Was this an omen, that he should return to his General? Or did the berries, food here for the future, offer a portent too? Did the berries—or the future—harbour nourishment or poison?

Rotus could tell him about this tree.

THIRTY

Back at the village there was no-one to be seen. A wagon tilted one-wheeled before the blacked-out forge, tools lay unused and cattle were astray on the pasture. Not a child nor animal roamed within the palisade and though vague cooking smells filtered from most of the houses, no kindly voice called him to share the evening meal. At the Chief's house the door curtain, usually hung free for anyone to enter, was tightly pinned.

Through this strange hush Varres reached the round house he shared with his friends the twins, and found there too no cooking pot, no evening meal; no welcome either.

Aunghuis' greeting was a nod, Ferghuis ignored his arrival. By the wall stood the cohort standard back from the workshop where a smith had been studying its badges, and fixed to the figure of Neptune hung a soldier's purse for money. Varres looked his question at the brothers and was astonished to see behind the scowl of Ferghuis the glint of threatening tears. Aunghuis looked fiercely from him to the standard.

"You have to go".

Varres paused. His decision was being made for him.

"Did the Chief put my purse and standard here?"

"We did", Aunghuis growled. "We give you this chance to go back to your people and take that thing of ill-omen with you".

"But remember", his twin half-sobbed, half-snarled, "if our sister dies — or her child — we shall find you and take your life in exchange. This is the law of our gods".

So Rufina was in uneasy travail. The village lay hushed because their Chief's wife was ill, their hoped-for heir at risk. He, Varres, a military medicus, could do nothing whatever to help, and worse, her kinsmen blamed him or his standard for bringing bad luck to the birth. The inference was absurd and being young he sought to argue, but their anxiety was extreme, they too were young, not yet weaned from Druid-lore, and they dearly loved their sister. Varres took his cohort standard and quietly went away.

Far in the moor he hid its gleaming length deep in heather by a rock, and turned about in search of Rotus.

The river ran red in the last beams of sunset when he came upon his old friend under the very tree where he himself had pondered the afternoon away. Rotus looked up from his task and spoke simply as to a companion who had been with him since the dawn.

"I have made this, that it may help me to pray".

A raw wooden cross lay small and forlorn on his palm, and Varres could have wept for both man and bauble in their defencelessness. Instead he clenched his hands, willing himself with physical force, to say or do what might help his friend, and to say or do no more. Such intensity of feeling flooded through him that assuredly the other must hear the sound throb in his head, feel the force of his blood-beat.

"Please help me to help him. God help me, *please*".

Rotus lifted stricken eyes, pleading, helpless, tortured; no sound had come from either.

"God help him, please. Christ's God, please help". The throb echoed in his mind incoherent, insistent, beseeching.

"In the love of the Christ they crucified, Lord, help him bear his burden.

"Lord, help her to bear hers.

Help us, guide us, help us Lord."

201

With the drumbeat of his heart each plea welled soundless through his soul engulfing them together in what was neither his nor his. The young man, and the older, stood apart, alone, yet one, their life's purposes and forces concentred on the one who fought for life to give another; and when they had done, drained deep, they leaned exhausted on a Presence. Calmly, even numbly now, the boy continued to beseech.

At last, with shadows lengthened all in one, the tribe's Chief rose.

"We shall go home. It is over".

Carefully he planted his cross by the tree, propping its base in river stones.

"I had not remembered that this is a rowan tree, warranted to keep away evil spirits. Even the Druids would approve of my sanctuary".

From a gate a torch, two torches, flickered and rose, then wove uncertainly towards the moor. Other torches joined the first as Rotus saw, understood and ran. When Varres caught up, it was with a jubilant group of kinsmen bearing off their chief to a festival. Only Dhuan the dog saw the lad on the fringe of the crowd.

At the feast hall, Rotus broke away, and made for the door of his own place, where the straight little woman, his mother, came to draw him inside. The door curtain closed and was fastened.

On the moor, Dhuan dropped on his master's feet.

"So you would keep me here, beautiful one?" Varres bent to fondle the beast's silky ears and stroke his murmuring throat.

"I have no wish, assuredly, to foist myself upon Anghuis in the big hall — I too am a rogue of the litter — but I cannot leave without bidding Rotus and his family goodbye. . . . So, you are right: I shall remain where I am for present. Move over, friend, and let me lie.

With his head on the dog's warm flesh he slept soundly, for strength had gone out of him and he was spent.

"Abrachan, we've found him. He's here." The shout wakened them both and the dog started up, to growl until Rotus joined the searchers.

"Varres, Rufina has asked for you. When you were not in the feast hall, Aunghuis told me of his foolish threat and we have been looking for you since. Come home, show yourself and let my poor wife sleep".

In the Chief's home the inner room was dim and warm. The Red One lay exhausted on her bed of furs, but her face lit as she saw Varres and she moved to take his hand. The screwed-up scrap beside her whimpered at being disturbed, then lolled his tiny red-fuzzed poll to express a deeper anger.

"We won". The words were barely a whisper. "It was a battle, but we won. Rotus told me how you helped".

"I. . . ."

Shy, in the presence of a miracle, the boy blushed, and was not, this time, vexed to know it. With an effort he rallied lightly.

"Rotus talks too much".

A question in her eyes sought an answer.

"But Rotus was the name of . . . my companion . . . in hot and festering Rome. These days are gone. Here in this cool, calm land, Abrachan is the head of your family".

"Abrachan, yes". Her eyes held his, her voice still whispered. "Rome is no more for you either?" and she alone caught his answer.

"No more".

Her eyes, satisfied, were allowed now to droop.

"Abrachan, my heart, you have a promise to fulfil to-morrow. Go now to the feast hall and celebrate for your son. Strange . . . is it not strange? . . . that men do the feasting in this event . . . as if the battle had been theirs?"

She was asleep even as her husband kissed her.

The celebrations were not prolonged. The Cheif's kinsmen had a journey to make on the morrow and would need clear heads and a light step.

Even so, the twins, the messengers, their peace made with

Varres, were at last to leave the hall, hilarious in delight in their new status of uncle. Abrachan bade them goodnight with a friendly thump and to Varres said loudly aside,

"You will remain here and help me to civilise these rascals?"

Outside together, alone in deep enfolding dark, he repeated, "You will stay in my land to help me Christianise my people?"

THIRTY-ONE

The chief's sister came home.

Days sparkled by, each more lovely than the last. The Red One blossomed and her baby throve, as the Sun God poured his blessings on the valley and Coventina sprinkled her dews. Crops and beasts fattened; pastures grew lush; the river fed her fish in quiet pools.

Seonaidh was even more beautiful and lively than he had remembered, and if once her heart had been set on a questionable marriage, she gave no indication of that now, for her pleasure in Varres' company was as great as his in hers. Now they could talk to each other in two tongues, but what they spoke was no man's affair. They too blossomed in that brilliant summer, and Abrachan and his mother watched with pleasure; but it was the Red One, as usual, who took a practical hand in matters.

"Why do you not build a house, young Varres? There is room for another within the walls".

Then, at last, he spoke to Rotus, claimed the girl and began to build.

Her brothers and Abrach's appointed themselves to the working band, and enlisted the aid of their near-cousins, the sons of the smith, the carpenter and the wheelwright. Cheerfully the young people cut straight stakes for house walls and trolleyed them down through the wood to their appointed site, where Seonaidh and her girl-kin made meals on an open fire. Each evening became a festival, such was the merriment and joy they had each in the other's company. Varres knew at last the pleasure and fun, the laughter and teasing, of being with those of his own age, with a common interest. In spite of mistakes and bantering arguments the work began to look almost like a building as days ripened towards harvest time under Sul's benevolent glow, and young laughter rang in wood and hill.

Only the Chief's mother looked with foreboding at times on the work and sighed in the midst of merriiment.

"You see something, good-mother? something you do not like?" Again Rhuadha the practical, the sensitive, put another's thoughts into words.

"Fear not, little mother. It will be well. You must pray with me, to your son's god, and it will be well. You will see".

The last few house posts were to come down, when the Chief decreed one day's rest before the harvest would begin, so Varres went alone to the wood to bring in his trees.

It was cool among the trees, and quiet. The work done, he sat to savour the peace, and to ponder the change in his fortunes since the battle at the fort. In the village of his friends he was accepted as kin, a man fitted to be betrothed to the Chief's sister, the girl to whom he had lost his heart long before he had lost his legion. He counted himself fortunate indeed, and sat, content.

Dhuan led Ferghuis to him in the serenity of the wood, and as always, pinned him with his weight.

"I brought company", Ferghuis grinned cheerfully as ever, but the light of his laugh died before it reached his eyes.

"Abrach wants you to stay here awhile until . . . some visitors depart. Seonaidh sent these, and the dog. One will come for you when the chief sends", and leaving a wine jar and a round barley cake, he turned to go as silently as he had come.

"Ferghuis, wait. Do you wish to banish me, or is this a

game? Why does Abrach want me to remain here?"

"There is no game . . . Calgaich . . . Calgacus . . . has come".

"Calgacus, the great-Thane? Why?".

"He is recruiting men from all tribes to fight your . . . to fight the Eagles. Abrachan will not join them himself — you know of his vow to the Legate — but our people must decide for themselves. After the conference to-morrow you will come back to the village".

"And to-day?"

"It is not . . . convenient".

"You mean, it is not safe".

Ferghuis climbed a tall tree, beckoning Varres to follow to where from the crotch of a heavy branch they could see over the village to pastures and fields beyond. Calgaich's men, in hundreds, sprawled on grass and crop alike, whittling stakes, sharpening swords, cooking over wide spreading fires, Two were slaughtering a cow.

Ferghuis silenced his companion's cry of fury: "The crops. . . ."

"Whsssht. Settle yourself and be calm. They will soon go. As must I — I must not be missed."

Ferghuis went, leaving Varres furious and bewildered.

For that night he obeyed the Chief's orders, sleeping between a fallen trunk and the dog's warm flank, and for most of the forenoon too he rested patiently enough, until stabbed by sudden longing for a glimpse of Seonaidh again, he climbed back to his vantage point. Of Rotus, his family and kin there was no sign, no move was made in the village; but beyond the palisade, activity hummed an ominous tune rhythmic with menace and unrest. Men trampled the fine crops of yesterday, hacked and tore at winter turves to scorch pastureland with their fires of hunger; they puddled coarse bodies in the stream and pillaged the smith's store of iron to replenish their knives and swords. Varres sobbed aloud for his friend's vain task.

What sort of ruler was Calgaich to allow his men to

wanton thus? This was no way to gain recruits. What else did he seek to find?

Suddenly Varres knew. His standard, the Neptune of his cohort, stood in the midst of the ravaging horde.

Galgacus sought its bearer, a Roman of the Ninth. He was . . . had been . . . that Roman.

Dhuanbeg growled as his master set off through the wood, but followed, close at heel. In the hundred paces, near enough, of rough scrub between wood and village boundary, beast and man progressed as one, until at sight of the first of the barbaric horde the dog halted, an uneasy whimper deep in his throat.

"Stay. Lie beauty. Lie till your mistress comes".

None bothered him as he moved round the palisade towards the gate; few, indeed, looked his way. His wool tunic and light breeches were as the barbarians' own, or those of Ferghuis, and he was being accepted as one of the village.

Pleased, he moved to a cooking fire where half a carcase roasted on a spit. Had his tongue changed as his appearance?

"You dine well, good friends. Do you spare a bite for an unlucky hunter?"

The man he addressed grinned broadly. "Hunt? With all this to feed on? He brandished a short knife towards a number of Rotus' cattle penned now on a strip of pasture.

"We shall eat well indeed without hunting while we are here. See, take".

A slice of the carcase was pushed forward on dirk point to Varres' reluctant hands. The beast would feed the Chief's family for days; for this horde it would scarce make one meal. But there were things he must hear, feasting made men talk.

"That . . ." he pointed boorishly at the Neptune, "that thing . . . what is it?"

His host laughed loudly, slapping a greasy hand on his thigh.

"That *thing* is a Roman standard, a precious find, but its bearer will be more precious."

"Varres grunted. "Precious . . .?"

"Worth a good reward, when we find him. What Calgaich seeks his men will find. Eh fellow?"

Their assent was a roar.

"So. Calgaich will find".

"And woebetide the Roman then, and all his friends".

The words hissed from a stunted hairy fellow bare of chest and daubed in blue, a vicious runt of manhood dwarfed in the arm and shoulder-guards of the Great-Thane's armour-bearer.

"The priests will deal with them". His venom spate again, as he leered into Varres' face. "It will be beautiful to see".

A heavy egg-shaped amulet swung forward from his neck with every stab of words, and Varres noticed that the others eyed the charm with awe. He finished his meat, thanked his hosts and left.

Another group tore apart a sheep; a third fell about and wrestled on a strip of ripened oats. A searching party returned, malignant in frustration. The way to the village gate lay churned and torn.

In Rhuadha's home her baby wailed.

The walls of Seonaidh's marriage house gauped crudely to the setting sun as, on an impulse, he took himself within the circle of the wall, and stood lost in thought, in what was to have been his home. Long moments passed. His presence endangered this family, had ruined their crops, would decimate their cattle. Unless this army moved away soon, next winter Abrachan's family would starve.

As the sun sank, the village roused; men spilled from black houses, villagers and strangers, his friends, his bride's uncles, and men he had not seen since the night he himself had been judged and been accepted. More strangers entered the gate, with them officers of the rabble. The conference must be under way. No-one noticed Varres in the shadows of his wall, before the village stilled again.

Soon a rumble of discussion brought him to the feast hall, to peer unseen through the inner door curtain. Again the cauldron of abundance hung at the central hearth; again the champion's portion was set to the right of Abrachan the chief, the women handed wine cups, traversing with the sun. Again the hall was packed with family's kin, met for celebration, or a crisis.

A stranger near the door gulped, awe-struck.

"This Calgaich must be as great as we've heard said. See, he has his Priests with him. The Wise Ones never leave their groves but to attend the greatest. There must be some ado".

His companion muttered: "So, indeed. Some matter itches both the priests there. See the long one scowl".

Beside the warrior, with, but not of, the company were two white-robed personages, ascetic, even grim. As they leaned to converse with the High-Chief it was seen that they wore amulets on golden chains, egg-shaped gold talismen like that of the man behind, the little spitfire armour-bearer, weighted now with his Thane's great sword and little shield.

The stranger by the door was no longer struck with awe.

"That little chap is over-laden. If he drops that sword these moustaches will be trimmed untimely".

His companion snorted. "If I were an honoured guest, to share the quaich with those whiskers would put me off the feast".

Varres chuckled in spite of his troubled heart and he looked carefully through the firelight to where his friend dispensed the hospitality of his home. Abrachan showed no strain nor did his wife. If Seonaidh and her mother drooped it might have been with weariness for they came and went continuously with Rhuadha, among the men, replenishing dishes and cups as if their stores need never see a winter.

The little armour-bearer seemed impatient. Suddenly he thrust his shield into his masters back and whispered to his mat of hair. Abrachan's eyebrows moved at such disrespect, but the Great-Thane merely flicked winedrops from his huge moustache and turned to listen, grinning. Then he summoned the smaller priest, and the shielded one nodded smug satisfaction.

What followed was obviously a eulogy although Varres heard little and understood less, for Calgaich leaned back grinning sheepishly, his men beamed proudly, nodding agreement, and the little hairy one behind the shield drew his short frame to its tallest. Even Rotus and his family seemed to the watcher to relax a little and to smile. Soon the rhythmic pace of the epic summoned a steady beat of hands which drowned even deeper the sense of the words.

The two men near the door seemed quite carried away.

"Eh, but the Bard tells the good story; it is a great man that Calgaich".

Subtly the poem's rhythm changed. Unable to take the beat, the clapping died, so that Varres heard again.

"Calgacus the great one, the warrior king, has unfleshed the Eagles of Rome, has trampled their standards to dust".

The shield-bearer licked lascivious lips.

"They have fled their winged camp in our mountains, have fled to the forts of the south".

Had the Ninth really retreated behind Agricola's forts, or had they merely withdrawn to rest and reform? Varres dearly wanted to know, but here was no place to find out.

"But Calgaich the Great will flush them out, and what stray fledglings he finds will he snare and roast, in honour of our Sungod Sul".

The shield-bearer drooled. Rotus stiffened; his wife and sister clasped hands; the little mother's lips moved in urgency.

Again the mood of the eulogy changed, and approving handclaps resumed the beat. Rhuadha filled wine and urged her women kin to do the same: the semblance must be made of seeming unperturbed.

Soon again the shield-bearer was bored. Once more his chief responded to the nudging metal boss, and the bard was halted in mid-breath. The other, the tall one, stood forward. Carefully he balanced his weight evenly on spread feet, carefully composed his eyes to a glazed stare, his voice to a necromantic monotone that yet reached right round the hall; and he began.

"The omens foretell". he intoned, "a dread time for Caledonia, a time of long-drawn evil brought by marauding carrions of Rome. Hard-won crops and cattle will fall prey to predatory hands".

Varres thought of his friend's devastated pastures, oats ripe for the sickle yesterday and now trodden under dirt; he saw the bestial armiger's delighted leer; and he fumed within himself.

The monotone persisted. The tide of doom rolled on and as the prophet eased his weight from foot to foot, the pendant ball of his talisman rolled on his chest with hypnotic fascination. The eyes of his followerers slewed in time with its swing until they lulled their former enthusiasm into torpor. With a start Varres realised that this was the prophet's purpose. The two men near him swayed to the rhythm of the ball, and beyond the hearth a silence lay of entranced and dominated will. The shield of Chief Calgacus swung on his squire's arm and the little man's pendant bauble rolled too in complete accord. Even the Chief's trailing wine-dewed whiskers seemed pendulous to the beat. Only Rotus and his family steadfastly looked away from that dominant hypnotic gleam, gripping hands, their own or each other's against the influence around that swelled and rolled like a monster of the sea.

Varres felt the evil grow, sucking on the people's will, fed by pulsing oratory, until very soon it could be sated only by devouring them all. This evil must be halted, this waking sleep of dominated will must be roused and broken.

It was a short dash to the hut he had shared with the twins. At the bottom of a pinewood chest lay what was left of his uniform but it was not the leather skirt or breastplate that he needed now; he would not appear as a soldier. The under-tunic, soiled and crumpled, was yet sufficiently

Roman, if he had but a toga to go over it to show he was a man of peace. There was a length of stuff, dyed by the girls in one of their cheerful experiments, to the colour of morning mist, dyed and discarded as cheerless then, but saved against future use. This would suffice. . . .

Hastily he dressed and left the hut, willing his Seonaidh to understand what he was trying to do. His entrance must be impressive. Neglected on the charred pasture stood his standard—might its silver badges serve to obtrude on the effect of that beastly bauble of gold?

The door curtain dropped behind him.

Still the priest rumbled on, to a crowd hanging on his every word. Only the tight little knot of Abrach's near ones defied the grip of his oratory.

"All Romans are evil. They must all be destroyed, they and the ones they have subverted to their ways. We shall find each Roman and destroy him".

The armour-bearer, glazed of eye, droped upon his shield.

The standard swooped and struck a trestle. "Hear you all: I am the Roman".

Seonaidh cried out and was restrained by her brother. Calgacus rose; the shield-bearer focussed blearily, the poet halted in the midst of a ponderous rolling phrase. Slowly the crowd tore itself from its hypnotic stupor.

Varres roared again. "I, men, am the Roman, the one *he* says you must destroy. Do so, and be gone, and leave these good people in peace". His voice lowered. "Your enmity is for me, Calgaich the king, yet your men destroy the living of your kinsmen. Surely that is not Caledon justice or fair thinking?"

It became clear that he had the hall divided.

"Or is it that your men care nothing for your discipline, your leadership, against a common foe, but only for themselves? Do you *prefer* that they live the easy way like parasites on what has been grown by others?"

The high Chief's men rumbled fury. Calgaich stared. His

henchman nudged again and whispered spite into the whiskers but was sharply pushed aside.

"You have more to say, Roman?" The tone was icy.

Varres caught the gleam in Rotus' eyes: approval, warning, dismay, protection? He saw Seonaidh's face that yearned with love. Rhuadha's look was complete understanding.

"Only this, sir: I was Roman. Abrachan your chieftain there, was once my slave, and for that I am truly ashamed, shamed for the custom of my people. Now I would wish to live in your land as one of *your* people, but . . ." He drew himself taller and looked coolly from bard to prophet to High Chief, and beyond to the spitting venom behind.

"But — what I mislike among my Romans, greed, avarice, aversion of the masses to honest work, ovine willingness to live on others' thoughts, I find among your followeres also. Are you aware, Great One, that your men are sheep, led by a spiteful little shepherd?"

The rumble grew to a roar, though among Abrachan's men were nods and grins of agreement. Calgaich's swordpoint hit the floor as the bearer exploded in wrath, and his gold amulet jogged on his heaving chest. The priests conferred together, and with the Chief, who nodded and gained silence.

"The Roman has courage. Let us test his spirit further by the customs of our gods".

Seonaidh's cry was anguished.

"The gods will let us know whether he will go free, or die".

The girl sobbed in her mother's arms and Varres stirred to go to her but two stalwarts of the army held him back. Abrach talked with his wife, spoke rapidly to his own men, and held his friend's eyes with encouragement. Silence fell on Seonaidh's people, silence woven to each from the other and reaching out to Varres, to fold them all proteected even from the fury around. The girl ceased to weep, but held her mother's hands so tightly that the spear scar on her arm

214

burned white. He looked again at Rotus, now kneeling in obeisance.

"Let us drink again, King, to our understanding, you and I, and to the needs of our people".

Flattered, at the title, or the show of humility where none had been seen before, Calgaich willingly agreed, and even the priests were cajoled by Rhuadha to drink from the silver cups which she provided.

The fire on the pasture outside had been renewed. Flames leapt high and beautiful as they touched the sky to morning glow. Nearer, they spat as viciously as the warped little man with the shield. Varres thought, with a strange feeling of detachment, of the galley slaves at Massilia and of the gladiator Gaul, but Rotus was busy with thoughts of his own.

The king's squire turned his attentions upon the prophet-priest that his omens would be sure to foretell death.

"Death to every Roman. The young female should be with him".

Protest roared from Seonaidh's kin and friends, Varres' own shout being loudest, but she stood forth calmly and took his hand. Her tear rimmed eyes were frightened but steady and loving.

"I would not live withoutout you, love. We stay together".

The flames, now fed, beat higher, yet the time was not yet propitious for the priests, as it seemed. Nearby on a pulley swung a basket cage. Seonaidh turned her face to his shoulder.

"God of my brother's Jesus, be with us now", and hearing, Varres held her tight. Behind, the silence fell again, deepened and held, expectant. Or was it shawled in some unknown strange woven omniscience?

"Now. It is now".

The priests advanced to the edge of the fire, and the pulley contraption was rolled forward to the victims' side. Suddenly the priest lurched and pitched forward, his cowl and robe taking fire; Varres leapt, dragged and rolled the man on cool grass, and caught the second as he too fell, before even Abrach reached them. The first was badly burned but breathing, the other merely in a faint.

In the hush only the flames whispered.

"You see, Calgaich, Great-one", Rotus called, "your gods have spoken".

Abrachan quelled the crowd's loud confusion. "Your gods have set the Roman free. He is a doctor. If he cures your priest-people he must remain unmolested to live as he wills. That is agreed?"

The crowd roared and Calgacus nodded.

"My people will be his people. They too will be unmolested? I may keep my vow to the Legion?"

"You have the High-Chief's word".

"Then your priests will be taken to my home, that the doctor may cure them in peace. But first. . . ."

He tore the gold pendants from each priest's neck.

"Show your people that these egg-balls are not made of hissing snakes, that they do not contain the power of the mighty gods".

He tossed one to the smith. "Open it and let us see".

As he accompanied the litters taking the Druids away, Varres saw the shield-bearer's face, and pitied him. In the dust that fell from the broken ball lay his hold on his master's followers. No twisting snakes gave power to his sacred amulet, no venom writhed in his golden egg to empower his tongue upon its objects. The man drooped, his stunted stature shrivelled as he gave up his own talisman to his Chief.

Inside her home Rhuadha grinned impishly at Varres.

"Mutton grease for the burned one, you think? and cold water for the drunk?"

Under the second flagonful of river water the bard stirred and woke. Abrach and his sister stood aside in the doorway to let him pass and laughed to see him hold hands to his head against the noisy acclaim of the army.

"Our barley wine is potent, wife, but I admit to having had a transitory fear that it would not work".

216

Varres raised his head from Soenaidh's gleaming hair and folded her lithe form closer, as Rhuadha smiled back at her husband.

"Fears, Abrachan? Why? We were all praying hard to your god of love, and he surely answered our prayers".

She smiled around serenely, on the prophet last of all.

"But the opiate your mother gave me in childbed has other uses, as I thought".

THIRTY-TWO

Before first light they had gone, all to the last pair of breeches, taking their bandaged priest, the Roman standard and all the village cattle not safely penned inside, and leaving only charred grass and a few pitiful edges of standing grain.

By noon these last were cut, milled and stored, and few indeed were the girnels required for their storage. Of pulped root crops, what could be, was salvaged and the rest was burned.

"So . . ." Abrachan wiped his wet brow with a grimy arm as the women brought out milk and wine for the workers. "So. We start again. To-morrow we find a new home place."

"Aye, Abrach, to-morrow. We must plan for next year".

"They've soured the land for us now".

"Find us a valley with clean sweet water, and we'll join you, all of us".

"Hills too, and trees. We are hill folk".

"And new untried land".

"Calgaich means war on the Eagles. Go northward away from the forts".

Varres listened to this discussion and knew wherein lay his friend's power with his people. There were no commands, no orders from chief to servelings: each man voiced his own opinion and was heard with equal deliberation, heard others and discussed, until the sum of all their judgments, trimmed and adjusted for the good of all, became the rule that they would follow. In dispute, though, his word was law.

An old uncle, now rose to give advice.

"Leave the making of your new settlement until the year is young again and live in our villages for the winter. We have had a good year and there is much in our stores for us all".

Cousins, brothers-in-law, near and far kin of each individual family made each his separate offer, but the men of Abrachan's village politely refused them all. The wiry old wheelwright spoke up for everyone.

"We are grateful for your offers, but we wish to remain together. Since we must start again in a new place we shall, with stout hearts, and the stouter for your kindness, but we must make our fresh start *together*. We—and you—are all Abrachan's people, one tribal family; he is Chief of us all, to whom we swore our fealty in war—or against Calgaich's war—but we of this village are also a community: we are one for all, and Abrachan is our village leader. We start his new home as soon as we can—together".

The cheer that met these clumsy words raised a lump in Varres' throat, and he saw that Rhuadha was openly in tears.

"At least", the uncle pleaded, "give us a chance to prove our fealty in this way".

"Your fealty was proved when you supported my proposal to Calgaich that my clan do not take up arms".

"And again and even more surely" Rhuadha's voice was tight with tears, "when you prayed to your Chieftain's god. In accepting Him—and our new brother here—you have proved loyalty indeed. We could ask for nothing more".

"My wife is right, Uncle. Your loyalty needs no further proof. But you may help if you will, with hoes and hands, some seed grain, and the loan of a good breed-bull, when we find our new location".

"*You* find it Abrachan. It is your duty as our Chief".

The smith chuckled softly, easing full hearts and tight throats.

"You ought to know good land when you see it, you who are so expert on ploughs. Besides, you are the farthest travelled of us all".

"Except perhaps the young one, your good-brother. Take him too".

At the carpenter's sally, Varres smiled in pleasure. Their acceptance of him was complete. Yesterday they had suffered because of him, the Roman: to-day, there was no more Rome. To-morrow? They were willing that their future would be where he would help to choose.

But Seonaidh was showing her mettle.

"Men!" Deliberately she withheld her flagon from a cousin's outstretched beaker. "Men! Ever since I decided to marry this fellow"—her pointing arm arched in supreme disdain—you have contrived to send one or other of us away. I should have made the priest marry us yesterday by firelight if he had not . . . succumbed . . . too soon".

She beamed beatifcally upon her brothers, her uncles, her cousins, while still witholding the wine.

"Now, if we were to be married to-day, it would be my *duty* to accompany my husband to-morrow, would it not, Rhuadha?"

The two women exchanged looks that neither Abrach nor Varres could fail to see. As the laughter died, the aged uncle rose again.

"The truachan is right and she knows it, as most of womenkind do. Let us finish what is left of Calgaich's feast in a better cause, since we are all here together, then to-morrow they, with you and your lady, will seek new land, while your people up stakes and move your belongings, and we go find a hoe or two, some grain seed and a rickle of bullock bones as before requested.

"And, first, I suggest, we all wash".

So a family's decisions were met and made, between tears

220

and good-humoured banter.

In firelight, the young people were married, with the handfast of the Caledon way, the responses of the Roman style: "Where you are Gaius, I am Gaia" and with a blessing before the company remembered from the cata-combs at Rome and endowed by Rotus with a fervour of his own:

"May the love of our Christ go with you, together and apart".

And in the morning, as the uncle had said, all went their separate ways.

Two waggons, covered and cushioned for comfort, jogged over moors and hills. In one, the young pair, with the devoted Dhuanbeg between them, told each other again the story of their lives; in the other, a landless Chieftain watched his woman nurse their firstborn child.

The day was chill, pearl misted, a day at the end of summer that had a smell of winter near, a day when Caledon looked on his stores of grain and turf, his wood and full-fed cattle, and thanked the great Rhiannon for her blessings to him and his. It was a day to strengthen roofs and walls, to look on the silvered saffron of stubble fields and rejoice that Sul could rest, to renew his efforts for another year. On such a day, a village would look to its mountain as she veiled her head, grandmotherly, to pray for her children below. On this day these five urgently sought a mountain, a river and its plain to be theirs and for their people.

As they breasted yet another hill, the child became restless and the dog whimpered to be out and away, so they drew to the top and halted.

A river ran in a silver sickle on a broad, lush plain below. Beyond, a fold of mountain cushioned misted heavens in a smooth long rise and fall. Oak woods rose from the valley to join a crown of birch, while here and there bright rowans

221

glowed in heavily berried clusters. Even as they watched, the mist vanished and a wash of sun broke through to lustre the valley in bronze and gold, and russet the talking water on its way. The shoulders of the mountain shrugged her rough shawl of woven pines.

A sigh escaped Abrachan.

"Tu es is fluvius: you are the river. You are our hill".

Surprised to hear his own language again Varres looked up at his friend. Abroticus—Abrachan—stood on the crest of the hill with his arm round his wife and child, and the fingers of Sul the Sungod played on two brilliant copper heads.

He himself and his wife slipped quietly down to the river.

"When we found our own home place, Varres, when we have helped to make the Chief's new village—next year or the season after . . ." Soenaidh was dabbling in the sparkling water, her heart in her eyes as they rested on her husband . . . "I should like to settle in sight of the sea".

"The sea?" This wife of his was full of surprises.

"In our tongue, '*var ius*': by the sea. We should have little need to search for a place name, Varres".

Belatedly he understood, and signified his love.

Later, like children they played in the mud. Suddenly Varres caught up a handful of the russet clay of the bank and called,

"Rotus, Rhuadha, see this colour. You will have your brick building here, friend, as red as the bricks of Rome. I cannot promise you marble, but this . . ."

He held out wet grit as they came to him. "This will make your bricks".

Rhuadha stared at the churned river water, beside where she had laid her child.

"*Rhuad*: red water. Red head. Rotus, love, this is indeed our home".

For hours they climbed, walked, prodded the earth, dug a turf, studied pasture, measured the girth and strength of trees, followed the river to quiet breeding pools; and they slept, at last, content, to awake before the light.

When Abrachan and his family turned back to fetch his people to their home, the red water glowed its pleasure, and podgy pink fingers of an infant day curled over the breast of their hill.

GEOGRAPHICAL REFERENCES

Bodotria	Forth (River or Estuary)
Calcaria	Tadcaster
Caletes	Calais
Clota	Clyde (River or Estuary)
Credigone	Carriden
Dubris	Dover
Durovernum	Canterbury
Eboracum	York
Gesoriacum	Boulogne
Lindum	Lincoln
Londonium	London
Lugdunum	Lyon
Lutetia	Paris
Massilia	Marseilles
Pinnata Castra	Possibly Inchtuhil (Perthshire)
Sequana	River Seine
Tamesis	River Thames
Tanaus	River Tyne
Tauredum	Cape Wrath